BY DOMENICA RUTA

All the Mothers

Last Day

With or Without You

ALL
THE
MOTHERS

ALL
THE
MOTHERS

a novel

DOMENICA RUTA

RANDOM HOUSE
New York

Random House
An imprint and division of Penguin Random House LLC
1745 Broadway, New York, NY 10019
randomhousebooks.com
penguinrandomhouse.com

LIBRARY OF CONGRESS CATALOGING-IN-PUBLICATION DATA
Names: Ruta, Domenica, author.
Title: All the mothers: a novel / Domenica Ruta.
Description: First edition. | New York: Random House, 2025.
Identifiers: LCCN 2024048251 (print) | LCCN 2024048252 (ebook) |
ISBN 9780593734056 (hardcover; acid-free paper) |
ISBN 9780593734063 (ebook)
Subjects: LCGFT: Domestic fiction. | Novels.
Classification: LCC PS3618.U776 A78 2025 (print) |
LCC PS3618.U776 (ebook) | DDC 813/.6—dc23/eng/20241105
LC record available at https://lccn.loc.gov/2024048251
LC ebook record available at https://lccn.loc.gov/2024048252

Printed in the United States of America on acid-free paper

1st Printing

First Edition

BOOK TEAM: Production editor: Kelly Chian •
Managing editor: Rebecca Berlant • Production manager:
Katie Zilberman • Copy editor: Kathy Lord • Proofreaders:
Deborah Bader, Annette Szlachta-McGinn, Frieda Duggan

Book design by Alexis Flynn

The authorized representative in the EU for product safety and
compliance is Penguin Random House Ireland, Morrison
Chambers, 32 Nassau Street, Dublin D02 YH68, Ireland.
https://eu-contact.penguin.ie.

For my chosen family

ALL THE MOTHERS

Wearing nothing but ankle boots and a raggedy pair of panties, Sandy sits on the seat of a lidless toilet, holding the shield of a breast pump against her left boob, and searches social media for the other woman her baby's father has a kid with. She is seething, and worried this anger will somehow seep into the milk and poison her daughter, who will grow up to be a mean girl who peaks in high school, but not worried enough to stop herself and calm down. Milk collects in a plastic jar one measly drop at a time. Her right boob leaks in sympathy with its left-side sister, dribbling down the soft rolls of Sandy's stomach. The waste of those precious milliliters kills her, but only one hose of the breast pump is working right now and she keeps forgetting to buy a replacement. She keeps forgetting to wear front-opening clothes to work, which is why she is pumping half naked in the same bathroom her boss uses. Again. A hideous beige nursing bra hangs from a hook on the stall door. It is unlike anything she knew existed in her before life—with the heft and durability of camping equipment and coronas of milk stains highlighting how askew her nipples are. Next to it hangs the navy blue sack dress that seemed like such a great idea this morning. These days, no matter what choice she makes, it always seems to be wrong. She blames this on *the other woman*, a person her baby's father has never mentioned, not once in over a year.

This is not the life I dreamed of when I was a little girl, Sandy thinks.

She is hunting for this woman like an FBI agent in pursuit of a serial killer, thumbing through various accounts, tapping pictures, enlarging them, following tags in pursuit of other tags in pursuit of . . . what? What would she do if she found her?

Her nipple is sucked in and out by the pretend mouth of the flange. It doesn't hurt, which, no matter how many times she's done this, is surprising, considering the intensity of the machine. It's weirdly pleasant, actually. Not pleasurable, but . . . nice? *Is that gross? Am I gross?* Sandy wonders this for half a second. An ironic gift of single motherhood: she doesn't have time to feel shame.

On the floor, the breast pump squawks in a pattern that is starting to sound like words.

"Wacko-wacko-you're-a-wacko. Wacko-wacko-you're-a-wacko."

She hasn't slept more than ninety continuous minutes in months. Even when her baby sleeps a long-ish stretch, maybe two or three hours, Sandy's brain jolts her awake every few minutes, as if to alert her to the fact that she is alone in the deep dark forest. But she's not. She's alone in New York City. Alone with a baby.

Pump breaks at work have become her little treat. Three times a day she can microdose the paid time off that her job doesn't actually offer. It is the only time all week she gets to zone out. She used to watch reruns of her comfort show on her phone. In twenty-minute increments, three times a day, she could lose herself in small-town Texas, where an extremely hot high school football coach offers unconditional love to the also extremely hot adults-playing-teenagers on his team, a town where not even paraplegia and attempted rape are all that bad in the long run. If traveling to this world means hanging a humiliating PUMPING sign on the office bathroom door, it's worth it.

Now Sandy scours the internet instead, looking for *her*. She examines pictures of women with nose rings and tattoos who look like they've never given birth, their waists doll-sized, their eyes glimmering with adequate rest. Other women show their children off proudly, and Sandy scans their faces for any resemblance to her daughter.

She enlarges an image with her fingers, her once well-manicured nails now bitten down to the quick.

That's her! I found her!

Online stalking gives the same dopamine high and crash of a video game. The woman in this post is so unbelievably sexy. She has Bettie Page bangs and huge breasts, much bigger than Sandy's, which have failed to fill a B-cup even while lactating. She taps deeper into the world of this woman, clicking, enlarging, until: *no, that's not her kid, it's her niece.*

It goes like this the whole break. She's supposed to be modulating the speed of the breast pump to mimic the natural sucking rhythm of a real baby, but she ignores it, leaving the machine on full blast. Her eyes are so tired she can feel them discretely inside her lids as she strains to absorb every detail of these digital women. Her sockets are dry from lack of sleep, burning with the pressure of imminent tears.

Don't cry. Not at work. A jagged rock flames in her throat, in her nose. *Stay focused. She's here somewhere. Just find her.*

Everything is so swollen and cracked with hurt right now, and it's all this woman's fault. It has to be. Otherwise it's Sandy's fault, and then the hurt might never go away.

Finally, she sees it: a profile for @SOSanto. In the grid are pictures of graffiti murals and flowering trees and liberal political memes. Pretentious. Annoying. Sandy primes herself for a world of hate. No friends tagged, no people at all, until in the tenth row a short, curvy brunette holding the hand of a toddler with gleaming coppery hair. The woman is facing the ocean, her back to the camera. The child peeks over her shoulder, an oddly familiar smirk on her face, as though spying right back at Sandy, clocking her as the interloper she is. Even cast in shadow, the child's eyes are a startling blue. The same blue as Sandy's baby. In all her anger, Sandy had forgotten the other half of the other woman—the kid, her daughter's sibling. The hatred she can't let go of starts to melt away.

She dives deep. SOSanto doesn't post often, almost never posts pictures of herself, and this half glimpse of the child is the only one in the grid. There's not enough evidence to spin out a fantasy, as much as Sandy wants just that.

The pump break is almost over. Her right hand cramps from balancing her phone and scrolling. She switches the shield of the pump to the other side, her left boob loose with relief, her nipple raw and a little sore. With her left thumb now, she continues tapping each picture, methodically scanning the captions and comments for intel. One day she will have to explain to a surgeon how she gave herself carpal tunnel syndrome from internet-stalking on the toilet. She'll worry about it then. Right now she's so close.

She adjusts the placement of the breast shield, then, with her cramping hand, Sandy makes a major tactical error: she accidentally hits "follow."

"Oh god no."

Stupidly, instinctually, she un-follows, knowing it will all be in SOSanto's notifications regardless. She shuts off her phone. Which accomplishes . . . nothing. Beads of sweat prickle at her temples. There is no way to win this game now. She looks at the bottle hanging off her boob. It measures a dispiriting 1.75 milliliters of milk, including bubbles. So actually more like 1.5 milliliters.

"Wacko-wacko-you're-a-wacko . . ." whines the breast pump.

"No one asked you," Sandy fires back.

She snaps off the machine, turns her phone back on and rests it on top of the toilet paper dispenser, rubs greasy lanolin on her nipples, starts to get dressed. *What are the encouraging words I would like a friend to give me right now?* she asks herself with forced cheer. If only a real friend were there to help, someone with the steadiness of an emotional EMT. None of the women she considers friends would understand what she is going through. They'd proven that to her already. An imaginary BFF will have to do.

Take a deep breath. Whoever she is might not check her notifications. She might not even notice.

Her phone chirps. The DM chirp. Still inching the zipper up the back of her dress, Sandy jumps at the sound. She grabs her phone, hands shaking, and it slips from her greasy fingers like a wet bar of soap, sailing toward the toilet bowl.

She dives into the toilet, catching the phone a second before it hits the water, feeling every bit as heroic as a football player in small-town Texas.

A direct message from SOSanto is waiting for her:

"Hi. Are you his new girlfriend?"

Sandy's heart is beating in her hands, her stomach, her feet, everywhere except her chest. She feels dizzy.

"I'm honestly not sure anymore," she writes back. "But I am his co-parent. We have a daughter."

Sandy holds her phone in her hands, breathless. A second later she gets a response.

"Me, too."

A bad breakup pulls the rug out from under your feet. Sandy's breakups made her doubt the concept of gravity. If there were any such thing as fate, or horoscopes, an interventionist god, or all of the above, they were in complete agreement: Sandy Walsh was not learning her lesson.

First in an impressive line of disastrous choices was Drew, her high school boyfriend, who dumped her and came out as gay at the same time. On social media. On prom night.

Sandy found out in another bathroom stall, this time at her high school gymnasium. "So brave," Sandy posted in the comments. Tears streaked her drugstore self-tanner, making muddy splashes on the bodice of her gown. "So proud of you. ❤"

That was the funny breakup, the one she could rebrand as hilarious after a couple of drinks. Alex still felt like a bad dream.

Tall and broad-shouldered with curly black hair and teeth so white they looked fake, Alex was the graduate student TA in Sandy's Intro to the Western Canon survey, freshman year of college. Sandy and her friends would snap pictures of him in class and make horny memes that they texted one another during the boring lectures. The girls in that class, many of whom would become Sandy's ride-or-die squad, were so smitten with Alex they agreed to "share" him. He was unattainable and therefore safe, until a week after the finals were graded, when Alex asked Sandy to coffee.

Sandy fell under the intoxicating spell of being chosen, and in all the time they dated, she never quite got over it. Sandy had grown up in Minnesota, where even the hottest girls were bred with a good dose of humility. Maybe it came from swimming in all that cold clean lake water, or the surplus of pretty milk-fed girls in her suburban town, but Sandy never felt she was anything special. If forced to give her looks a rating, she considered herself one tiny notch above average. Her blond hair required touch-ups every four weeks no matter what shampoo she tried to protect the color. She had nice cheekbones and eyebrows that she could accentuate with makeup, but her nose was not the one she would have chosen if shopping in a catalog of facial features, and her boobs were proportionally small for someone her height (five foot ten) and body frame (*hardy*, her dad once said). The flattery of Alex choosing her felt like a fairy tale, an enchanted apple that could turn her into a princess if she played it right, a frog if she didn't.

Twenty-five precisely measured hours after Alex emailed, she replied, "Yeah, sure, I like to drink coffee" (she didn't). Immediately the doubts crept in. What would her friends think? Would they be mad at her? Would they ditch her and force her to start all over in a new friend group? Was she pretty enough for Alex? Like, sitting inches away directly across from him at a café, full-on looking at each other? Was she smart enough to hold his attention? Was he also secretly gay?

With zero skill and even less critical thought, Sandy did as the quasi-spiritual law-of-attraction memes of her generation had bidden her to do, and that was *just be positive*. "He could be the One," she said into the mirror, where she applied foundation in three different shades to better contour her plain and unworthy face. Illuminated by this positivity, Sandy chose the fairy tale: she was a commoner transformed by Alex's gaze into a princess.

Once their relationship was official, her friends quickly transitioned from jealous to supportive, further proof that these friends were like sisters, always rooting for her. The group chat exploded.

"OMG! You're dating a teacher!!!"

Not quite. Alex was a little bit older but not controversially so, twenty-four to her nineteen. And he was a decent guy, they all agreed, because he waited until the class was over before asking Sandy out. None of them questioned whether it was his integrity or a school policy that made him wait.

After his graduate program ended, Alex stayed on at the university to get his PhD. Another cause for Sandy to feel unworthy of such a prize—she had remained undeclared until the last possible minute, choosing English as her major, not because she loved literature so much but because she was a fast reader and good at editing. After finishing his PhD coursework, Alex agreed to move in with her only if she put on pause all discussion of further commitment, insisting he couldn't even *think* about settling down until he completed his thesis.

It was all worth it because Alex was *amazing*. He was successful but chill about it, nerd-smart but conventionally handsome, and he always bought expensive gifts for her birthday (that she would pick out). Sure, he had some qualities she didn't love. Every winter he got low-level depression, which showed up as irritability, pessimism, and a touch of self-pity. He would sulk a lot about how other PhD candidates were getting more attention than him, that he was being punished for being a straight white man, that the cards were stacked against him. This was pathetically untrue, but Sandy could have earned a PhD in explaining away her boyfriend's worst tendencies. With frightening speed, she was able to reframe such stupid white-guy angst like this: his passion for his thesis was so powerful that he couldn't help taking things personally; this thesis was his baby; in fact, his fierce devotion to the project was proof of what a good father he was going to be one day.

After ten years of dating, five of them living together, Sandy was twenty-nine and Alex was thirty-four, deep in the season of their lives when everyone was getting married. After the pandemic, wedding season resurged with abandon. A small forest had been razed to print all the invitations, thick with good cardstock and foil inlay, filling their mailbox week after week. That summer, they had RSVP'd yes to seven different weddings. The door of their fridge was covered with save-the-date magnets like a weird shrine to straight monogamy.

Sandy was sitting at the little table in their galley kitchen, searching online for a dress to wear to the next wedding on the calendar, when Alex thrust his phone in her face.

"Look at this," he laughed.

Sandy glanced up from her laptop to examine the picture Alex was showing her. It was a social-media post from one of his colleagues, a woman Sandy had met several times and found as boring as all the other professors, though she always did the work of *trying* to find things in common with these people at faculty parties. This particular woman had just adopted a new puppy and was gushing about it in a ten-picture carousel. It was a lot, Sandy agreed, but the puppy was cute and the woman was obviously very happy.

"Good for her."

"No, look at the dog's name," Alex insisted, still sneering.

The woman had named her puppy Emma.

"Cute," Sandy said absently.

"*Emma?* Are you kidding me? How pathetic is that? If I weren't so busy, I'd write a satirical trend piece about middle-aged women naming their pets after the human children they don't have."

"Fuck you, Alex."

Sandy slammed her laptop shut, rattling the dishware stacked precariously on the open shelves they'd installed just above the table. She got up from her chair and pushed past him without letting any part of her body graze his, no small feat in a kitchen that narrow.

"What's your problem?" Alex cried.

First of all, Alex was always talking about the satirical trend pieces he would write if he wasn't so busy, and Sandy was always fake-laughing in encouragement. She was sick of it. Second, this woman was not "middle-aged." She was thirty-three, a year *younger* than Alex. Third, maybe this woman had no desire to ever have children, maybe she was perfectly happy and fulfilled by her child-free life—this was not a radical concept—and a supposedly educated man shouldn't need that to be explained.

Instead of saying any of that, she burst into tears.

"When are you going to marry me?"

She had been trying for so long to repress it. After ingesting many cautionary tales online and in real life, she swore she would never ruin her life by asking for too much. Pressure-to-commit was the ultimate torpedo to male desire. She had seen friends sabotage perfectly happy relationships by harping on commitment, girls who pushed for sexual exclusivity before three months, girls who posted couple-y-looking pictures on social media before six months, girls who asked about moving in only to get dumped via text.

Sandy would rather die than be too much. That wasn't who she was. Sandy was happy! Self-sufficient and happy! These were her most lovable traits, the very reason Alex had chosen her among all the other more attractive girls in that class.

Alex walked into the living room and sat down on the couch. Sandy got up from their bed, where she was sobbing, and sat next to him. He poured a little more coffee from the French press into his mug and took a slow, deep breath.

That's when Alex—mild-mannered, handsome, horn-rimmed-glasses-wearing Alex, who cried at the end of *The Color Purple* and called his mother every Sunday afternoon—said something so harsh that Sandy literally blacked out. Her vision blurred, the edges of their living room darkening as though all the light had been siphoned into a void. For a brief moment everything was black. Alex disappeared. The world disappeared. Sandy lost contact with the couch, with her own body. Then she returned. There she was on the itchy, too-stiff mid-century-modern-style couch they had chosen and paid for together, sitting just eighteen inches away from the man who had said those words.

"I'm sorry. I think I blacked out. Can you say that again?"

Alex sighed, looked at his coffee, then into her eyes. "I know it sounds horrible, and I'm truly sorry about that, but the reality is, I don't have any reason to settle down before I'm forty, and though I love you, I don't think you should wait around for that to happen. In fact, I'm telling you not to."

"Fine," Sandy roared. "Then I'm leaving."

She threw all her clothes and shoes into suitcases, laundry bags, and then—low point—garbage bags. She ordered an SUV from Alex's car-service app to pick her up. On that ride from Brooklyn Heights to her friend Mary's place in the East Village, a calm settled into Sandy's heart. Not because she had finally stood up for herself but because she fully expected Alex to be so stunned by her packing and leaving, so distraught by her absence, that he would come to his senses and beg for her back.

She waited three days for him to do this. She spent those days getting facials, going to expensive boutique workout classes, sitting through a guided meditation at Dharma Punx, walking through Central Park without her phone, so sure this would all work out if she simply *let go and trusted the universe.*

"He'll come back," her friends echoed. "He's just scared of taking the next step. That's normal," they promised, not one of them in a relationship as long-term as Sandy's at this point.

On the fourth day, Alex finally texted to say that he had packed her few remaining belongings for her. In what he thought was a mature and thoughtful gesture, he'd calculated her contribution to their apartment furnishings and offered to reimburse her. He would let her keep her stuff in his storage unit until she had settled into a new, more permanent place.

"However long that takes," he said, "no hurry."

Ten years. Ten years including a pandemic lockdown that felt like another ten years. Ten birthdays, ten Thanksgiving-Christmas-New-Year's sprees, ten seasons of prestige-TV series devoured together, ten thousand hours of talking about nothing and everything—all of it was over in the quickest, tidiest way possible.

"You're too good for him!" was the best takeaway her friends had to offer. It was an insufficient balm over the burn of her heart, but it was better than her deepest fear, that she had never been good enough for him, and so in the interest of staying positive, she chose to believe it.

I t would be two years before Sandy was someone's girlfriend again. In those two years she dated three guys briefly, once ghosting soon after sleeping together, twice getting ghosted, but it was fine.

Something had altered inside her heart; a new valve had opened, one that automatically pumped out an analgesic after three days of breakup crying. At seventy-two hours and one minute of moping, social-media stalking, ice-cream eating, and tears, her heart sounded the alarm. *Nope*, it said, loud and clear, *you're done. I will not let you feel one more second of this.* A numbness would then take over that was all-encompassing, and in that numbness, Sandy would be granted access to her rational brain, where the truth resided: everything was fine.

Sure, another relationship didn't work out, another guy proved to be disappointing, but she was still cute, still had her job as an associate editor at one of the only surviving print magazines in the food industry, a job that afforded her the things that made her happy—cheap beauty treatments and expensive workouts on a regular basis and a minuscule but charming studio apartment near Columbus Circle where she could walk everywhere she wanted to go and never bump into Alex. She didn't love her job, but it sounded impressive to people who didn't know any better, and she was pretty good at it. She had lots of friends, half of whom were married or engaged, half who weren't, a ratio that felt fair, if such things were subject to fairness.

Everything was fine! And it would continue to be, because happiness was a choice, and she was making the right one.

It was exactly this energy that manifested Josh into her life, or so claimed the spiritual-not-religious faction of her friend group. "That's just how it is, how it always happens—the perfect guy walks in right when you're least expecting him," the more secular crew declared. Both theories were equally shaky, conjuring a tightrope walk between two terrifying realities: *not craving love so badly that you become desperately repellent* and *sustaining vibes pure enough to call in the One.* Either way, if Sandy didn't want to die alone, she had better get perfect control of her desires.

The night she met Josh, she was so chill about the prospect of love. A friend of a friend's new restaurant was opening, and Sandy promised to pop in for just one drink. Yes, she had gotten a full Brazilian wax during her lunch break in anticipation of that night's event, but she wasn't even *thinking* about getting into a new relationship. Okay, sure, she'd swiped through two different dating apps while waiting in line to be admitted by the host, but, like, casually, not aggressively, and besides, she had actually deleted her profile in two other dating apps. Once inside, she scanned the length of the bar just to see how strong the showing was at this new restaurant, not clocking the hottest guy, not taking inventory of who was looking back at her. It was Tuesday, the most random day of the week, certainly not the twist-of-fate backdrop for the night she'd find her happily-ever-after!

The restaurant was in SoHo and had the square footage of a gas-station bathroom with cathedral ceilings tiled in unfinished pressed tin. Slimy cubes of steak tartar plated with a cilantro foam were presented to guests as they entered, and within thirty minutes the entire supply of food was gone. The waitstaff was all gorgeous and waifish, affectless and incompetent, as though battling a serious opioid addiction. Sandy sidled up to the girlfriends she'd planned to meet and gave them her full attention.

That's when Josh walked up to her. With his bright open face and warm golden eyes, he looked right at her. That same little shiver, the feeling of being *chosen*, bubbled up again, warming her body from within.

At first Sandy tried to include her friends in the conversation with Josh. She was nothing if not a girl's girl. The acoustics of the restaurant required you to speak intimately into someone's ear or shout at the top of your lungs. After about ten minutes of Sandy screaming and Josh whispering into her neck, her friends disappeared in the flickering candlelit fray, leaving them alone.

Josh offered to buy Sandy a drink, and she panicked. A cool girl who was not dying to be in love but was still open to an inscrutable cosmic plan for love would probably order a scotch neat, low-maintenance, impressively masculine. But Sandy wanted something sweet. "Espresso martini," she finally said, daring Josh to walk away forever.

If he had any opinion he didn't show it, and when the bar proved to be too understaffed for the throng, he offered to split his Heineken with her instead. Passing the bottle back and forth, their hands touching a moment longer each time, Josh and Sandy revealed themselves with the giddiness of high school kids. He was the same age as Alex but completely different in almost every way. Josh was an editor in the filmmakers' union, making good money when he was working but solvent enough to take time off when there wasn't a project he felt passionate about. Like Sandy, he was able to live in an apartment without roommates, the gold standard of New Yorkers in their thirties. Minutes into their conversation, Josh pulled out his phone to show her pictures of his pit bull, Rupert Puppykins. When she didn't immediately laugh, he explained that the dog was named after an iconic Robert De Niro character, then launched into an animated lecture on Robert De Niro.

"A dog!" her friends swooned on the group chat. "That says *so* much about him."

Josh loved his job editing films and TV shows and yet wasn't trying to rise to the top of the film world. He talked a lot about writing screenplays, but he didn't beat himself up if he didn't finish them, which he never did. He had started six different comedy scripts that

Sandy didn't find at all funny. But humor was so subjective, and maybe the reason she didn't find his screenplays funny was that, like the dog's name, she didn't understand them?

His quirks were pretty alien to her, but his core values were admirable, and this, her squad assured her, was the most important thing of all. Josh loved the movies in a way that was pure and infused with gratitude. He loved his life the same way and wanted to open that life up to Sandy.

That's how everything was with Josh, natural and easy. Though sometimes Sandy didn't love how easy it was for him to connect with other people—like at the wrap parties he invited her to, where he would take off and forget that Sandy was there, and she would catch him sort of just-under-the-radar flirting with a woman in the makeup-and-hair crew. But insecurities were a self-fulfilling prophecy. As long as she projected confidence, there was nothing to be insecure about. Maybe he wasn't ditching her at a huge work party where she knew no one; maybe he was *trusting* her to hold her own in a crowd, to mingle and make friends independently of him? This was one of her best qualities as a girlfriend, after all. What mattered was not that he talked to other women. What mattered was that he always went home with her.

Nine months into dating Josh, Sandy got a call from her mom saying she was really sick. She flew home to Minnesota to see her and ended up staying for two weeks. Her mom, it turned out, was not just sick. She had stage-three ovarian cancer.

After a long day of scans, consultations, second opinions, and grocery shopping, in which Sandy got shrill about "eating the rainbow"—a concept her mother had a frustrating, illogical contempt for—Sandy collapsed onto her childhood bed. As part of their divorce settlement, her parents had sold their house under market value to get rid of it as quickly as possible and never spoke to each other again. Sandy's mother had attempted to re-create Sandy's old bedroom in her much smaller two-bedroom condo. It was like stepping into her childhood in a corset. The bed took up most of the room, her yellow floral bedspread blinding, a sad refuge for the few anemic stuffed animals that had survived the move. Her sunflower posters—she had three different ones—were tone-deaf in their cheer. Gone was her old stereo system, which once created a barrier of sound between Sandy and her fighting parents. Playing music from her phone did not have the same protective powers now.

"lol does everyone get clinically depressed visiting their hometown!?!!" she texted Josh. "Anyway, stage three is good news! We caught it in time to fight!"

She was stabbing him with all these exclamation points, begging him to see these daggers of punctuation for what they were: terror. Two hours passed with no response. She reread her texts, trying to assess how weird she'd sounded. The truth was that she'd been weird the whole trip. Her mom was not okay. She was miserable and angry about her diagnosis, and Sandy was depleted from cheerleading her to do basic self-care. While her dad had remarried right away after the divorce, her mom had been languishing, isolating more and more with each passing year.

"How's that new boy, the one with the dog?" her mother asked when Sandy, ignored by Josh, had joined her in the living room.

"Ugh, he's not *new,* Mom."

Her mother was sick. Her mother had cancer. Apparently not even those stark facts could halt her juvenile regression. Exasperation infected Sandy like a vestigial strain of mono. She'd been dating Josh for nine months, but to her mother, anyone other than Alex was new.

"It's getting late. Why don't you lie down in bed, Mom? You can watch this on the TV in your room."

"I'm just as comfortable on the couch."

This could not possibly be true, but it had been a reality for well over a decade. At some point in high school, Sandy's mom started sleeping on the living room couch. She'd said it was because of her father's snoring, but anyone could see through the lie. Her parents' marriage was in shambles. For a brief period after the divorce, Sandy's mom lived in their old house alone, and she still slept on the couch. She could have gotten up and had a whole queen-sized bed all to herself, but most mornings she woke up in the living room. And now in her condo battling cancer, she hid under the blankets on that same couch.

Sandy sat next to her, glued to her phone like a teenager, ignoring the shapewear and rhinestone bracelets being peddled on the Home Shopping Network. She was pretending to read an article about alkaline diets and cancer prevention, but really she was refreshing Josh's social media to see what he was doing while he ignored her latest texts.

Her mother was a bloodhound for her daughter's desperation. "Be careful, sweetie," she said. "This new one might seem fine, but eventually they turn on you. Men suck."

This had been her mother's constant refrain since the divorce, a simple sentence that never failed to enrage.

Sandy took a deep breath. "Yeah, some do, but not all of them. And when your attitude sucks, you attract more suckiness."

"Oh, so it's my fault that men my age want to date women your age?" Her mom took a hit from her weed vape. Sandy had begged her to try edibles instead. They were safer, Sandy had lectured. Why stress out her lungs, a key place her cancer could spread? But her mom was afraid of the calories in those tiny gummy bears, because, of course, in the face of a life-threatening illness, nothing was worse than a little weight gain.

Her mom leaned back against the cushions. She looked at the ceiling and exhaled a white ribbon of vapor. "I just don't want you to make the same mistake I did, Sandra."

Don't take the bait, Sandy told herself. *Don't do it. Don't do it. Don't do it.*

"I waited too long to get married," her mother went on. "All the good men were taken. Then I got pregnant and had to marry your dad. Look how that turned out."

"Mom!" Sandy snapped. "You were only *thirty*!" Though Sandy was grateful for her existence, there *had* been other options. Abortion was legal when Sandy's mother got pregnant. She had not been forced into anything.

"If a man over thirty-five is still single, something is wrong with him."

"It's not like that in New York."

"Men are the same everywhere."

"Mom, please, try a little harder to be positive. You're funny. Men like that."

"Men like funny when it's thirty years younger than me. Men like funny when it's forty pounds thinner than me. Just wait. You'll see."

She had the same poor attitude about everything these days, especially her cancer, making Sandy cling harder to her terror-stricken faith—the happy mind's ability to stop maniacally replicating cell mutations with the power of positive thinking.

"Studies show that people who practice gratitude have better outcomes."

"At least I'll lose a few pounds from my hysterectomy," she laughed.

No, Mom. That's not the point. Sandy fought back tears. *You're fine just the way you are. You deserve to be happy just the way you are. You deserve love just the way you are. You deserve to* live *just the way you are. Please just try harder. Please try.*

She wanted to curl up in her mother's lap and never leave. She wanted to run away and never come back. If she held in her tears a second longer, she would puke right there all over her poor sick mother. Just when she thought she couldn't take it anymore, her phone chimed with a new text. It was Josh.

"Sorry. Late night in the editing bay. U sound good. Gnight."

When Sandy returned to New York, Josh was so busy with work that he sometimes slept in his editing suite, going home for only an hour in the morning to walk the dog, then heading right back to work.

One morning, after blowing her off yet again the night before, he offered to bring coffee and a bagel to her apartment.

Sandy had her period and had been up all night, crying. She was still in her pajamas when he arrived—not her silk booty shorts and a camisole, not her cheeky underwear and a sheer T-shirt. That morning she was in flannel pants printed with a variety of colorful donuts and a long boxy T-shirt.

Josh sat on the edge of her bed, saying nothing. He looked tired. "You seem so stressed," Sandy said. What she wanted to say was *I love you*—what she wanted more was to hear him say those same words to her—but she ducked away at the last second.

"Don't worry about me." Josh smiled his big soft smile and squeezed her shoulder. "You have enough on your plate."

A splinter of pain branched from her stomach into her chest and then her heart. She'd never felt weird telling Josh how she felt before. He was so comfortable with emotions, so easy to talk to.

"I'm sorry," Sandy texted later. She added a selfie to remind him of the normal, not-clingy woman she actually was, hopefully erasing the image of the sad, disheveled person in donut pajamas he'd seen that morning. "I think it's my mom. I'm just scared, and it's making me needy and weird."

"You have nothing to be sorry for," Josh texted back. "If you want, you can sleep at my place tonight. I won't be there, but at least you'll have Rupert. He'll keep you warm."

A month later Sandy's mom died. It wasn't the cancer but a blood clot in her leg that traveled to her heart and killed her.

I told her to get up and go for walks. I told her it wasn't healthy to lie on that couch all day and night, buying crap she can't afford from the Home Shopping Network. She gave herself that blood clot. She gave up. My mom could have saved herself, but she just didn't want to try.

It was the most shameful series of thoughts that had ever sprung inside her head. So painful it burned her scalp and made her sweaty. She wanted to tell Josh, to unburden herself from the weight of it, but she was afraid he would hate her. He was so compassionate and generous and kind. If he knew this about her, he would never look at her the same way again.

Sandy flew out to Minneapolis, and without being asked, Josh flew out the day after. He took four days off work to help her get through the funeral. Sandy's heart was so broken sometimes she would touch her chest and be shocked to find it was not wet from blood. It was a pain so profound she forgot what life had ever felt like before.

Then she would look at Josh and remember. There he was, chatting with her dad and stepmom in his easy, openhearted way. Her whole world had been hit by a tidal wave, but she still had this love to buoy her.

"Josh is amazing," Sandy's stepmom said to her, squeezing her arm.

"We're rooting for this one, kiddo," her dad agreed.

Ten days after Sandy came home to New York, Josh broke up with her.

"I'm sorry," he said. "I should have done this a while ago, but your mom was sick. Then after she died, I felt I ought to be there for you."

"Wow." Sandy observed the knives clinging to the magnet strip above her stove, certain a judge would at least consider her side in a court of law. "Thanks?"

"I know. I'm sorry. The timing of this is awful. But what would be worse—now or later?"

"Now was clearly best for *you.*"

"It's better for you, too. It's better for both of us."

"*Us,*" Sandy pronounced, "is not a word you get to say."

After Josh left her apartment that night, her mother's voice crept into her head, bitter and biting, snarky and sad, hissing in her chemo-ravaged rasp, *At least you don't have to throw your stuff in trash bags like last time.*

To soldier through those long, dark nights post-Alex, Sandy's heart had pumped a numbing agent into her bloodstream. This time anger, crackling and hot, stepped in as her own personal bodyguard. It was a glorious fire, burning away any trace of pain, any feeling at all. The light of this rage was so bright it bleached out the world. She hated Josh. She hated Alex. She hated relationships. She hated marriage more. She hated all her married friends' boring, basic husbands. She hated her dad for doing the most basic thing of all—leaving his wife in middle age and getting to have a whole second act with a younger woman while her mom died alone.

It was amazing how hot this rage burned. Sandy walked the frigid streets of New York with her coat wide open. There's a fine line between self-punishment and self-protection, and riding that line was an extreme diet app that Sandy installed for forty bucks a month. She ate poached skinless chicken breasts and sipped bone broth pretty much exclusively. She did so many barre and spin and HIIT classes that her muscles became hard as stone. It was an armor she was wearing, leaden and impenetrable. She hated her teachers and their loud, aggressive encouragement and their tiny headset microphones crackling too close to their mouths. She hated the other women in the classes, all of them punishing their poor bodies like she was. She hated herself. She lost seven pounds in a month. Her face was gaunt, and her jeans slipped off her hips without unzipping. Everyone kept telling her how great she looked.

One night Sandy decided to add some logs to her rage fire. She had finished work early, come home and got straight into her pajamas, the donut ones that had driven Josh away. She dug out the matching top to complete the look. It was only six in the evening, but the sky was black as midnight. She boiled some skim milk with cardamom and a splash of vanilla extract. That was her prescribed dessert for the day. With her steaming mug, she got into bed and stalked all of Josh's social-media accounts.

If you go creeping for trouble on social media, don't be shocked when you find exactly what you're looking for. The latest picture Josh had posted was of him and a tiny doe-eyed brunette. Josh's arm was wrapped around the girl's shoulders, her child-sized shoulders. The pretty little elf had to stand on her tiptoes just to kiss his shoulder. They were in some scenic desert swirling with variegated sand. A huge saguaro cactus stood behind them, its thick arms reaching out and up as though taunting, *Come on, you dumb bitch, what did you expect?*

The girl, Sandy learned, was twenty-four, a makeup artist who had worked on Josh's last movie. She was so pretty it was almost a relief. *I never could have competed with that.*

Then, with a little sleuthing, Sandy realized that the girl had been posting pictures of Josh since just before Sandy's mother died. All those late nights sleeping in the editing bay redefined.

Sandy picked up her phone to text her mother. "You're right," she started to type, then remembered—

Grief came swinging at her like a lunatic with a knife. Sandy's rage kicked it away, a cold-blooded assassin, disposing of the body without a drop of spilled blood.

It was time for a searching and fearless inventory of assholes.

Every guy she'd ever slept with would be found, investigated, and analyzed in her pajama-clad rage. Thorough contact tracing, timelines cross-listed and fleshed out, until the most complete biographies of these guys were laid bare and she could hate them with authority. She was alone in bed with her computer and there was no

one to tell her this was not a good idea, not that she would have listened. Sandy ordered a pizza and two pints of ice cream. She was
ready.

First she looked up her high school boyfriend. He was living his
best life, working as a hospitality consultant, whatever that was, at a
yoga retreat center in Tulum. He posted several times a day, pictures
of brightly blooming hibiscus flowers and avocado toast with paper-
thin slices of radish and his own glistening thirst traps disguised as
wellness inspiration—shirtless Dhanurasana and decontextualized
quotes from the Buddha.

Whatever. Next!

She creeped on the guys she'd dated briefly in the two years before Josh. All three of them were the same: shallow but not horrible,
cute but not heartbreakingly so. One of them had recently done a
polar-bear challenge, jumping into the frigid ocean to raise money
for diabetes. His stomach was paunchier and hairier than Sandy remembered, and that pleased her. Another guy was dating someone so
boring, Sandy gave up stalking after a single scroll through this new
girlfriend's profile.

Paint-your-own-pottery dates? You can have each other. Moving on.

The third guy hadn't posted anything in months, so who knew
what that really meant. Before she could do some deeper research on
him, her pizza and ice cream arrived. Sandy brought all the food
right into her bed.

"Okay," she said out loud, taking a deep breath. "I'm ready."

For the first time in years, she unblocked Alex. And what did she
find? Fireworks and a can of gasoline: Alex was married; Alex had a
baby.

Just that morning he'd posted a picture of his dark-haired son
sitting in one of those weird foam chairs that seemed to mold around
the baby's legs and hold them in place. Further back in the feed, Alex
stood next to his new wife in front of City Hall, a spray of flower
petals at their feet. Their wedding. They wore matching fedoras.

"Fedoras?" Sandy screamed into her empty pint of ice cream.

The bride had on a gold-and-black velvet dress that showed off
the sharp blades of her collarbone, her slim and chiseled biceps. Alex

wore a black velvet suit with a gold handkerchief in his pocket and a gold tie. On anyone else Sandy would think this look was exceptionally cute. On Alex and his bride, it was nauseating.

"Fedoras!" Sandy screamed again.

This had to be the wife's design. The Alex she knew lived in plaid shirts and wore the same pair of hiking boots until they got holes in them, at which point he replaced them with an identical pair. Alex, whose idea of dressing up was a plain navy blue sweater worn over one of his plaid shirts. Alex, who would return any hip clothes Sandy had bought him, even a wallet, and exchange them for more of what he already owned. Alex, who now was thirty-seven, still three full years away from his no-marriage-until-forty rule.

It's the tiny fractures in life that are the most dangerous. They make you limp just a little and think, *It's not that bad.* You walk with a slightly weird gait, get stiff after sitting down for too long, but it's fine. Pop an ibuprofen, have a glass of wine, forget it.

That's the dangerous part: you actually believe everything is fine.

Because it hurts only when it rains, or when the weather turns cold, or when you run too fast or too hard after something you think is important. And even then, it doesn't hurt much. A soreness, really, a dull ache, nothing you can't live with. So you keep going on the way you were, compensating in all these subtle, invisible ways you don't realize—favoring one foot just a tad, stiffening your neck to take the pressure off your hips—moving through the world a bit off-balance, unknowingly setting yourself up for another slip, another fracture, until the sum total of all these little sprains and twists, the slow incremental damage, leaves you crippled.

It's better to be broken clean, no matter how much it hurts. Sitting in her apartment, with one empty ice cream pint and one half-empty pint melting into a sticky puddle in her sheets, an open box of pizza she was too sick to eat, the voice of her dead mother saying, *See?*, the grief of missing her mother, missing even her cynicism, her laptop a gaping mouth ready to swallow her soul in its blinding light, among all these guys and their polar-bear challenges and dogs and girlfriends and wives and babies, Sandy finally broke.

And though the pain was stabbing and crude, it was the moment when everything changed. If it hadn't been for that dark night of the soul in her donut pajamas, she would have never given Justin Murray the time of day. Justin, the best mistake she ever made.

Justin was in a band called Pilot Error. Sandy listened to one of his songs almost to the end before yanking out her earbuds and massaging her temples. Justin called it *nü metal*. Because it wasn't a genre she knew anything about, Sandy tried to leave the door open for the music to be good in a way she just couldn't appreciate. Like those Rothko paintings that looked like plain stripes before an art history professor explained what they meant, where they fit in history, and then they were no longer stripes. Until after the final exam, when she forgot everything she'd learned, and they went back to being stripes again.

The point is, she tried really hard to keep an open mind about Justin's band. He sang in a low voice that sounded irritated and off-key. But maybe that was intentional? Either they were trying to sound awful for some artistic reason or they had no idea how much they actually sucked.

Sandy wrestled with this for a day or two—could she date a guy whose career she didn't respect? Could she fake liking his music for . . . years? This last thought was haunting. She had flashbacks to Alex and his dissertation and all the years she could never get back listening to him mansplain the same half-baked literary theories again and again.

Justin had light-brown hair and small ice-blue eyes, and while not devastatingly handsome, there was a pleasant symmetry to his face that she found herself returning to after swiping through all the other guys on the app. He was two years younger and two inches shorter than her, which wasn't ideal, but the whole concept of *ideal* was something she no longer trusted.

Most guys on the app seemed content to swap insufferably cool and laid-back texts for weeks, waiting for Sandy to prove herself worthy of a real-life date. Or they blasted her with dick pics. Some did both. A week after Sandy matched with Justin, a mega-superhero action movie came out and he messaged her, "let's eat popcorn and watch stuff blow up on the hugest screen we can find." This was the most perfect date in the world, given everything she'd been through.

That first night at the theater, Justin was late. He refused to give her an ETA, insisting only that he was "almost there." Sandy waited in the lobby, obsessively checking her phone, getting a lot of compassionate glances, looks that implied she was yet another woman who'd been stood up by a guy on an app.

Justin finally showed as the movie was starting. They had to ask about twenty people to stand up so they could inch awkwardly to their assigned seats. He smelled like too much soap, a strong industrial kind, and he was wearing a dirty Carhartt jacket and plain gray T-shirt with stains.

Why did I even bother? Sandy rolled her eyes in the dark. *I'm not that lonely. Sure, I cried for an hour after watching a YouTube tutorial on how to put on a duvet cover when you live alone, but that was 90 percent hormonal. I had all the hair on my vulva ripped out with hot wax, and he's dressed like he's grabbing beers with the guys.*

She had resolved to leave as soon as the movie was over and was brainstorming the lie that would get her out of there, when Justin reached into the inside pocket of his jacket and pulled out a large tinfoil-wrapped roll. He handed it to Sandy.

"What's this?" she whispered.

"Open it," he said.

"Is it something weird? Please don't be a weirdo. I can't walk through that row of people again."

"Nah," Justin said with a casual confidence that immediately put Sandy at ease. "I don't blame you for asking, but it's cool. I promise."

Sandy unwrapped the foil and found a dozen homemade chocolate chip cookies.

"Oh my god," she said, "they're still warm."

"I put them on the heating vent in my truck to get them toasty."

The word *toasty* rolled out of his mouth in a whisper close to her
ear and wriggled inside her fluttering heart.

Justin never apologized for being late, but he bought the first
round of drinks at the bar after the movie, and after that first drink,
Sandy no longer cared. He talked a lot about his band, the tour he
was planning, mostly small venues down south, maybe a gig outside
Chicago. It was the second time he was going on tour with this band,
he said. They were leaving just as soon as it got too cold to wash windows.

"Wash what?" Sandy asked.

"Some guys go out all year-round, but it's not worth it for me. It's
freezing, and everyone's always calling in sick. So my company is
seasonal."

"Company?"

"I have my own window-washing company. I got a crew of five
guys working under me. It's on my profile. You go on so many dates
you can't keep track?"

"Sorry! No! Not at all. I just— Sorry. I remembered about your
band. I must have forgotten . . ."

"Yeah, girls love that I'm in a band. But the band can't exist without grown-up money from a grown-up business. I'm an entrepre-
neur." He said this last word with same little flourish he brought to
toasty, and Sandy was charmed once again. She felt embarrassed and
contrite for not remembering his company, so much so that she never
stopped to think about what Justin knew about her, what details
from her profile he had remembered or thought to ask her about,
which so far were none. She bought the second round of drinks.

The bar got crowded and loud, and both of them decided to
change location. Sandy offered her apartment, as she had a bunch of
bottles of good wine a vendor had given her. Justin seemed enthusiastic, and Sandy was at the intersection of buzzed and flattered.

She was just drunk enough to sleep with him on the first date but not drunk enough to ask for what she wanted, so the sex was fine but not great. *Either this is a one-and-done thing or we have room for improvement,* she told herself in the shower the next morning. She was glad he had not slept over and gladder that he texted that afternoon to check in. A quick "hi" followed by a reference to some joke about the name of the wine they had, a joke that was a lot funnier when they were drunk. They made plans to see each other again in two weeks.

On their second date, he took Sandy out to eat at a no-frills Italian restaurant in Bay Ridge. The walls were scabby and decorated with ancient, ill-hung maps of Italy and old photos of rocky beaches, prints sun-bleached long ago into a palette of maroon water and pink cliffs. The menus were printed on grease-stained paper, bound in thin leather covers with gold string. The whole place had the aura of the *real* New York, an Anthony Bourdain–like chimera that was always eluding transplants like Sandy. She ordered the pork chop and broccolini.

"You sure?" Justin said. "The pasta here is homemade."

Sandy was terrified of a carb bloat, terrified of revealing herself as *that girl* on the second date, so she gulped some wine and nodded yes, she was sure.

"You gotta have a bite of this," he insisted, after their meals were served. He twirled linguini around his fork, reached across the table, and fed her. Sandy almost wept.

"That is the best pasta I've ever tasted in my life," she said.

"I know," Justin replied.

"No, you don't understand—I work at a food magazine. We have all this deconstructed avant-garde bullshit all the time. This? This tastes like an unconditionally loving grandma made it just for us."

"Stick with me, kid. I know some places." His smile crinkled his small blue eyes, giving his face the look of a baby, a teenager, and an old man all at once.

Seating was tight, so when the family at the next table got up to leave, Sandy and Justin had to scoot their chairs to make room. There were two parents, a bit older than Sandy and Justin, and a baby in a wooden restaurant high chair. The parents shifted dishes around and searched under the table to collect all the baby accessories they'd brought, the sippy cup and teething rings and small vehicles. They didn't notice when the baby dropped his toy garbage truck, which hung off the seat of the high chair, out of his reach. Frustrated and ignored, the baby began to cry.

Justin freed the toy from where it was lodged. "My dude, is that a garbage truck?" he asked him.

This surprised the little boy, distracting him from his tears.

"Aw, this is so legit. Look at that." Justin turned the truck over in his hands. It had the seal of the New York City Sanitation Department on it. Justin opened and shut all the moving parts. "It has real doors and everything." Quick as a flash, he hid the truck behind his back. "Oh no, where's your truck?"

The baby's eyes enlarged. He looked down, then up at his parents, who by now had noticed what was happening.

"Wait a minute," Justin said, producing the toy. "Is *this* your truck?"

The boy babbled a happy song. He reached his dirty fingers out to Justin, who placed the truck in his hands. "Thank you," the dad mouthed to Justin. He scooped his child out of the high chair. "Wave bye-bye to your friend, Miles," he instructed, and the boy waved. The mom collected their coats and bags, then leaned over and whispered in Sandy's ear, "Your boyfriend is good with babies."

After dinner they walked to a dive bar, where Justin showed Sandy his favorite Bukowski poem. He was in the process of chopping up the lines and using them as lyrics for a new song. "No one will get it," he said, "they usually don't, but that's the thing about music—you don't have to get it as long as you feel it."

"Yeah, that's really true."

"I know this sounds insane, but I believe Pilot Error is headed for big things. It's not an if, it's a when, you know what I mean?" His deep voice was full of certainty, free from both hope and fear. As he talked, his hand played with hers under the table, gently, like he was strumming soft notes with her fingers. His eyes were a troubling shade of blue, full of mischief and heartbreak and everything in between. But right here in this bar, he made her feel like she was the only person in the room. "I would love to be able to buy my mother a brand-new car. To do that with music money."

Sandy made him promise to send one of his songs. The next day, he did.

"What did you think?" he texted.

"So amazing!" she lied. She prayed he wouldn't quiz her on the lyrics, which she could barely make out. The only words she was sure of were *you* and *girl* and *bones*. "Is it a Bukowski poem?"

"No. It's something I wrote," Justin texted. Three gray dots floated up and down on her phone like tiny buoys on a white sea. Sandy waited. A feeling of elation pulled her up and out of herself. She could never have guessed what he was going to say next or the effect it would have on the rest of her life.

"I wrote it for you."

For Sandy, and for many women she knew, there was an ever-shifting amount of attention she needed from a partner, something hard to define let alone explain. How to differentiate between days like Wednesday and moods like Tuesday, a post-work need for silence versus a post-brunch inclination to gossip about brunch friends? It wasn't fair to expect a mind reader, but finding someone who responded to her catlike needs with his own compatible catlike habits was the goal, and Justin did that perfectly.

He always made plans two weeks in advance, and this consideration made Sandy feel important. He was busy juggling his band and his work schedules, so if they went some time without seeing each other, she was okay. After three months, at the urging of her friends, Sandy brought up the subject of sexual exclusivity.

"Yeah, that's cool," Justin responded. "I like you so much." He laughed, then took her hand and offered her a bite of the blueberry muffin he was eating. It was an oily prepackaged one he'd bought from a vendor inside the subway station. Sandy took a tiny ceremonial bite. She kissed him goodbye—he was busy all weekend, so she wouldn't see him again for a while—then dashed off to meet her friends.

"So, it seems like he's all in?" She floated this idea to Madison and Mary as they stood at the crowded reception desk of their spin class.

"Um, of course he is, dumbass!" Mary punched her in the arm a little too hard.

"You're so hot you're basically a model," Madison droned while texting someone who wasn't responding to her.

They were waiting for the class that had just finished to wipe down the bikes and file out. It was a tiny boutique studio in Chelsea where famous actresses worked out on occasion. It was impossible to book a class less than a month in advance, but like a miracle all three of them had been able to get in off the waitlist that morning. Sandy gulped down a glass of complimentary lemon-and-mint-infused ice water the studio provided. This citrusy water always gave her terrible heartburn, but the setup was so pretty—the antique glass jug with a brass spigot like something out of *The Great Gatsby*, real glass cups, not those paper cones that got all soggy, a vase of fresh irises—it seemed a shame not to drink one.

"He's literally perfect for you," Mary said sternly.

Sandy felt acid rising in her throat. She refilled her cup. "Yeah, he is."

Except.

For too long Sandy had a habit of ignoring red flags in favor of a cultish adherence to "making it work." But if she didn't want to get her heart sliced to sashimi again, she had to be honest: while Justin clearly liked Sandy, he wasn't all that interested in her.

Exhibit A: Sandy went on a meditation retreat with some friends, a lovely weekend at a lodge in the Catskills, and when she returned, Justin was not the least bit curious about it. Definitely odd, as there was a lot to be curious about. The lodge had all these strict rules about silence and locking cell phones away in a safe and not making eye contact with other guests. She'd joked about getting killed in a ritual sacrifice. "If I disappear," she'd said to Justin, "promise you'll make a podcast about me." But when she got back, he didn't ask a single question about her weekend in the woods.

Not that it was such a profound experience. Sandy had no big revelations about herself or the world, except that there was an ocean of pain still whirling inside her regarding her mother's death, an ocean she was afraid would drown her, one that she continued to avoid.

"The food was vegan but actually pretty good. It was so quiet I slept like a baby," she said to Justin. They ordered Thai as usual, delivered to her apartment because it was rainy and they didn't feel like going out, not when sex was the whole point of the night.

"They never make the green curry spicy enough," Justin said, as though she hadn't said anything, as though he hadn't said this exact thing the last time they hung out and ordered Thai food.

Exhibit B: Justin was not very curious about her job. Or her friends. Or her family. Or her day. Whenever she talked about those things, he got a glazed look in his eyes, asked no questions, and then changed the subject. When he texted, which he did at least once a day now, he never asked about what she'd been up to, not a casual "how was your day?" let alone questions about her past or her goals for the future.

"I can't tell if he doesn't care about me or he's just a really happy puppy dog or an accidental Zen monk who only lives in the present moment or what," Sandy said in the group chat of her closest friends.

"Don't overthink it," they all urged, followed by a barrage of memes illustrating this laid-back philosophy with pictures of perfect faceless women doing balancing yoga poses in the sunset.

It wasn't so much that Sandy wanted to talk about big things, like her mother's death; she just wanted him to be a little more curious about it, considering both how recent and how huge this event was in her life. Though, to be fair, he had his own issues in that department.

"My dad died when I was seventeen, so I get it," he had said to her the first time she mentioned her mother.

But what, exactly, did he *get*? There were so many complex layers to Sandy's pain: sadness that her mother was gone, guilt that she had not done enough for her, relief that she had not been forced to do more for her, guilt at her relief, anger at her mom for giving up so quickly, shame for judging how her mom handled her illness, rage at her dad for leaving her mom, desperation that her dad was the only family she had left, displaced anger at the unfairness of it all, and then missing her mother so much there were days still when it physically hurt to think of her. Did Justin understand all of that? Some of that? Her grief felt awfully specific, and what he'd offered her was vague.

Sandy presented this evidence to her friends at dinner one humid September night. Her extended squad attempted to assemble once a month, a tricky enterprise as there were twelve of them including Sandy. That month it was Mary's turn to choose the restaurant, and she picked a farm-to-table place in Brooklyn where they could eat cheeseburgers but feel good about it because the chef had been personal friends with the cow. Sandy resented having to take the train all the way to Brooklyn for a cheeseburger, but it was the tax she paid to keep in good standing with her ride-or-die girls. Besides, she really wanted to crowdsource their advice.

"Something's just *off* about him," she said as she picked at the crispy edges of her fingerling potatoes.

"He *likes* you!" Mary assured her.

"He definitely likes you *so much*!" Becca chimed in.

"Don't sabotage a good thing because you've been hurt in the past," Hannah said. "That was *then*, this is *now*."

"I don't know," Sandy said.

"What about Exhibit D?"

"Yeah, girl, we haven't gotten the D report."

"Bitch, tell us about his D!"

"It's kind of . . ."

Sandy left them all waiting a minute to build the tension.

"Gigantic."

The squad could not have been prouder of Sandy if she had won a prime-time Emmy. Sex in late-stage capitalism was like an incurable STI you learned to live with; one of its symptoms made certain women invert a man's anatomy as a measure of their own worth. If bagging a man was essential—emotionally it was, and with rent prices, sort of economically, too—and if competition for good-quality men was steep, which it was, especially in New York City, then locking down a boyfriend with a big dick meant blessed are you among women. Something was obviously special about Sandy to attract this, and wasn't that everything?

Except . . .

While Justin was surprisingly well-endowed for a man of his height and build, he was also really lazy in bed. Sandy didn't have the heart to articulate this out loud to anyone, lest she appear ungrateful or cruel. And her squad, while graphic when it came to discussing a suitor's size, was pretty quiet in all other areas of sex. Being able to share this sole sexual detail allowed these women to believe that they were uninhibited, sex-positive heroines of the post-post-sexual revolution. They congratulated themselves on the raw intimacy of their friend group. The reality was another thing altogether: a woman wide awake at 3 A.M., lonely and full of shame, googling on the bathroom floor in the dark, "he can only come if he's choking me—normal?"

Sandy's embarrassing observation about Justin was nothing new. It was common for guys of Justin's endowment to rest on that single, albeit huge, laurel, like really good-looking people who never developed a sense of humor and rich people who didn't know how to fold laundry. Justin was so relaxed about sex. Wasn't that what she liked about him? So different from Alex, who was controlling and edgy in bed, always tying her up with bristly packing twine, the knots so tight they cut off circulation; he would fold her in half and drip hot candle wax on her naked body, acts she had pretended to like for years because she was afraid of appearing as the middle-class scoop of vanilla that she was. And because she loved him. She definitely didn't want that kind of sex ever again. She should be grateful for boring Justin.

"Like, any bigger and it would *hurt*," she told her friends.

"Yeah, girl! Get it!"

"He's literally *perfect*!"

In their little world, she'd achieved EGOT status.

But after that cold winter night when she learned about Alex and his wife and baby, Sandy couldn't stomach the easy answers anymore.

Saying so was an act of betrayal to her circle of friends, where unquestioned loyalty was an unspoken commandment. Like her boyfriends', her friends' flaws were things Sandy could brighten up with a cute shift in perspective. Mary could be extremely self-centered, but that was part of what made her "a total girl boss!" Hannah said things that were hurtful and judgmental, but it was because everyone knew "lol Hannah has no filter!" Lily was a frightening combination of privileged and ignorant, but "she's seriously the sweetest person you'll ever meet!"

As they got older, settling into more and more compromised versions of their dream lives, it was getting harder to swallow the things her friends said, especially about relationships. Sometimes she just wanted to scream, *Hannah, your fiancé is so controlling you've replaced your entire wardrobe to please him! Mary, your husband is so selfish he refuses to have his sperm tested while you torture yourself with internet conspiracy theories about infertility! Lily, your boyfriend is not only a douche tech bro, he's a boring douche tech bro. You all deserve better!* But challenging one another was not something they did.

Dessert was served, two slices of red velvet cake that the twelve of them shared, diving fork-first into the plates like a flock of vultures at a deer carcass. The squad had all come to the consensus that Sandy was crazy, Justin was perfect for her, and there was nothing to worry about. The conversation shifted to a discussion about whether or not they were too old for glitter. Like, how old can you be and still get away with a sequins skirt, body glitter, a sparkly hair clip? There was an article about this that they'd passed around in a text thread, "30 Things to Get Rid of in Your Thirties," and glitter was in the top ten.

"What kind of glitter are we talking about?" Berkeley argued. "There's a huge difference between glitter eye shadow and a layer of glitter on a pair of one-season flip-flops."

The issue was hotly debated. Their waitress brought another round of drinks and cleared the cake plates and forks, licked so spotless they could have passed for clean.

"Microplastics from glitter are choking marine life all over the globe," the waitress said.

The squad fell silent. Everyone looked at their phones. At last Lily broke the silence. "Hey, remember, this night is about positive vibes only!" They clinked glasses and began talking again. Sandy felt herself drifting far out to sea.

Among the squad there was an entanglement of text threads devoted to whoever was in a new relationship. By October, Lanie was the one having early-relationship doubts, and all the attention once paid to Sandy and Justin was now showered on Lanie and Brayden. For the first time, Sandy started opting out of these conversations. She hadn't met Lanie's new boyfriend and didn't want to do that thing they always did, perpetuating the narrative that any relationship was a good one so *hold on for dear life*. She was also feeling needy, still wanting support and advice about Justin, but didn't want to be the one pulling focus.

"OMG he is soooooo hot!!" they all agreed when Lanie texted a picture of Brayden, who was completely average-looking in every way.

"Good for you!" they said.

"You deserve this!" they said.

"Don't forget, you're amazing! You deserve nothing but amazing things!"

They'd said the same thing to Madison when she was nervous about exchanging keys with her new boyfriend, telling her how lucky she was to have a boyfriend who wanted to take the next step. Then that boyfriend ended up illegally renting out her apartment while she was out of town.

They'd said it to Peyton, who later found out her boyfriend had a long-distance fiancée.

In response to this betrayal, someone in the group chat sent a meme of Marilyn Monroe, proclaiming, "If he can't handle you at your worst, he doesn't deserve you at your best." How did this apply to Peyton's situation *at all*, Sandy had wondered, as several other members of the squad hopped on to say, "I was just going to say the same thing" and "omg facts."

"We have almost nothing in common—nothing real, anyway," Sandy finally confessed at Quin's baby shower.

The married women all rolled their eyes.

"Who cares?" Aniston chirped. "I have nothing in common with my husband. We watch two different shows on two different tablets with earbuds in bed. It's perfect."

But shouldn't they share *something* besides sex and food? None of his passions—vintage guitars, tattoos, tax breaks for small-business owners—were of any interest to her. And her passions . . . Did she have any? Getting a boyfriend, getting married, having kids, getting to have what everyone else seemed to have, this had become so all-consuming, so terrifying (*what if it never happens for me?*), there was no space for anything else.

"I just have this feeling that any second now he's going to dump me."

Justin didn't dump her, but he didn't invite her to Thanksgiving with his family, either. Sandy had waited for it to come up in conversation, and when it didn't, she asked him casually what his plans were.

"Just Mom and some other relatives," he said. "Are you gonna finish that?" His fork hovered over a small plate of garlic shrimp they were sharing as an appetizer. Sandy shook her head no and pulled out her phone. The text her dad had sent two days before finally had an answer. "Yeah, I'd love to come home for Thanksgiving."

She could have invited Justin to come with her to Minnesota. Why hadn't she offered? Was it retaliation for his not inviting her first? Was she afraid he'd interpret it as too much too soon? She wondered about this on her layover in Chicago, watching the live soap opera of people flying toward or away from their families for the holiday. As if in tableaux, two couples sat in the bank of chairs across from her. One couple was fighting, hissing at each other, then escaping into the alternate realities inside their phones. The other couple was sharing a cup of frozen yogurt. When the attendant at the gate announced that their flight would be delayed three hours, the fighting couple groaned and started bickering again, while the other couple began to laugh.

"You'd better go get another one of these," the woman in the happy couple said, handing her partner the empty yogurt container. The man got up, took a few steps away, then paused and jogged back to her. Had he forgotten his wallet, the woman wanted to know. He shook his head and kissed her.

That's all. Just a kiss. A stupid nothing kiss in a stupid nothing moment that meant everything.

That's when it hit Sandy: she didn't love Justin. She would never love Justin, not like that. The big thing she was afraid of happening— that he would dump her—was a shadow truth. She was the one who wanted to dump him. Finally, she had her answer. All she needed now was to do it.

Sandy's dad didn't believe in setting the thermostat above 67 degrees, so she spent her brief stay padding around his house in itchy wool socks and double sweatshirts. They ate Thanksgiving dinner at the nursing home where her stepmother's parents lived. Sandy thought for certain that they would follow up this bland instant-mashed-potato fare with something nicer, but after a long, late lunch of geriatric dorm food, Sandy and her parents drove home, where there wasn't so much as a store-bought pecan pie to nibble.

When Sandy got back to New York, the Wi-Fi in her apartment wasn't working. No big deal—she could make the necessary calls to the cable company from work on Monday and it would all be solved within a few days.

After an hour in her apartment with no internet, the loneliness was strangling. She thought of her mother sleeping on the couch in the last decade before she died, then, without a pause or a breath or a thought, she invited Justin to sleep over.

Sandy had the ability to make herself happy. She didn't need Justin, or anyone else, to complete her. That became her perverse justification for not breaking up with him. What he couldn't provide—emotional depth, curiosity about the world or her—she could fulfill on her own, and what he could provide—solid companionship, someone to sit next to at the movies, to split a bottle of wine with, to eat dinner with—she could learn to be grateful for.

Gratitude. That was the key. Everyone said it, all the time. She had a dozen half-filled gratitude journals she'd received at bridal showers. If you wanted to be happy, truly happy, you had to be grateful for what you had, not focused on what you didn't have.

"You're right," Sandy said to her girlfriends at dinner a few weeks later. It was Whitney's turn to choose, which meant a sushi bar. "I'm not going to sabotage this with all my critical thinking. I'm going to let myself be happy. Justin is a good guy. I'm going to make things work."

The squad erupted into applause in the middle of the restaurant.

The next morning Sandy woke up vomiting. She'd had only one tiny thimble of sake the night before. On the second day her nausea was worse, meaning food poisoning or possibly a stomach bug. She texted all her friends who'd been out with her, and everyone was fine. That's when her mother's voice came into her head.

There's only one reason you're puking . . .

No.

Sandy ran to the nearest drugstore, retching into every public trash can on the way. She bought a pregnancy test and went into a bagel shop bathroom to take it. The box promised results within five minutes, but immediately after she peed on the stick, first one then a second pink line materialized. The test was almost glib in its certainty—the box said five minutes, not five seconds! So she took the second test that came with the package. The same result and just as fast: she was pregnant.

Arguments *for* . . .

So many of her married friends, women her age or a bit older, were struggling to get pregnant. This thing they had been terrified of happening in their teens and twenties had become the thing they were terrified couldn't happen at all in their thirties. Of her married friends (it was well over half the squad by now), only Berkeley had gotten pregnant quickly the old-fashioned way. All the others were *trying* to varying degrees, and all that trying, these friends reported, was at best annoying. Becca had confessed that reproductive sex had become just another chore to fight about.

"I've tried every over-the-counter ovulation test there is, and I can never get an accurate reading. Either I'm incapable of ovulating or these tests are a scam. So now we do it every day for ten days in a row every month, just to cover the whole span of possible ovulation," she told Sandy. "I am now repulsed by the sight of my husband's dick."

Many more friends had given up on the old-fashioned way and were enduring the physically painful, not to mention expensive, rigors of medical assistance. They were stabbing themselves with hormone injections, having minor and major surgeries, spending tens of thousands of dollars, only a small portion of which was covered by insurance. Peyton had been ahead of the game and frozen her eggs while she was in grad school. She'd evangelized about it to all of them, and Sandy had considered it, until she found out how expensive it was. Now married and in her late thirties, Peyton sang a different tune:

"We spent fifty thousand dollars of our own money, not including what insurance kicked in, trying to get just one of those eggs to fertilize and implant. None of them did. I froze them for nothing. Now we'll probably spend the same amount of money on an adoption lawyer. And who knows how long that will take."

It was disappointing enough when nothing happened month after month, but the miscarriages were far worse. The losses were becoming so common that some of her friends had taken to conspiracy theories. Madison heard somewhere that even one year on the birth-control pill could poison you forever, while Mary became suspicious of anything the doctors told her to do. She started doing her own research.

"I never got a flu shot in my whole life, and now that we all had to get vaccinated I can't stay pregnant for more than eight weeks?"

Saddest of all were the friends who blamed themselves.

"It's because I got so fat."

"I was so obsessed with losing weight and now my hormones are imbalanced."

"I shouldn't have waited so long. Do you think it's too late?"

Sandy felt guilty for doing this thing by accident that her closest girlfriends had spent months, some of them years, trying to make happen. It felt like throwing away food when people around you were starving.

And, if she was being honest, she was scared she would end up in the same bind herself. If she dumped Justin that minute and had an abortion, if she started dating someone new the very next day, met him in line at Walgreens while buying post-abortion maxi pads, if that guy was *perfect,* her happily-ever-after, the ideal man, committed to her and on the same page about marriage and children, realistically it would be another four years before they could start the baby-making process. The rules on this were clear: first comes dating—one year, minimum; then cohabitation—another year; then *talk* of marriage, then waiting for the proposal, trying to be chill about waiting for the proposal, finally getting the proposal, planning the wedding, securing a venue, getting married, getting a bigger apartment, *then* the baby. That was in the most expedient timeline. It was like betting on a shooting star crossing through the arc of a rainbow. If all these things happened in exactly this order with no delays, Sandy would be thirty-seven, maybe thirty-eight, by the time she could start trying to get pregnant. Not old. Not impossible. But with so many friends that age already struggling ... it was the most depressing math problem she had ever done in her life.

Arguments *against* ...

She didn't love Justin. She liked him, mostly. He was fine. She could do a lot worse. But were these reasons to start a family with someone?

She could not imagine him living in her studio apartment, with his guitars and clothes all over her floor. She'd been inside his apartment in the basement of his mother's Bay Ridge house only once, briefly, and it made her retch to think of living there.

Then there was his mother, Tara. Sandy had met her twice in the six months they dated. The first time was in the driveway of his house, where they had swung by to get him some clean clothes for a night at her apartment. Tara pulled up as they were preparing to leave, so they lingered in the driveway to say hello. Tara got out of her car, glanced at Sandy, and said nothing. She launched into a conversation about the furnace, when the guy was showing up to look at it, and what she should do if Justin couldn't be home when that happened. Then she and Justin talked about some woman they both hated. They seemed to be in their own world while Sandy hovered outside it, waiting to be acknowledged.

"Before I forget," Tara said, her voice suddenly softened, almost kittenish, "I got some penuche fudge." She jogged back to the car to fetch three large white boxes from a candy shop in New Jersey.

"Jesus, Ma, did you buy the whole inventory?" Justin laughed.

"I know how much you guys love it, and it's always sold out."

Here was Sandy's chance. "Mmm, sounds yummy," she said.

Never in her life had she used the word the *yummy* before. She felt like a foreign exchange student, aping the local customs. When Tara failed to open the box and offer her a sample of this mystical fudge, she extended her arm to shake hands. Tara responded with a limp dishrag of a grip, her smile pinched.

On the drive back to Manhattan, Sandy asked Justin who *you guys* were, as it clearly did not include her.

"What?" Justin turned up the radio.

"She said, 'you guys.' Plural."

"Plural?"

"More than one. More than you."

Justin ran his fingers all over his face. He stared straight through the windshield without turning his head a millimeter in Sandy's direction. "Oh, she meant the guys at work. My crew."

"Your mom's so sweet," Sandy said, trying to believe it.

"Yeah," Justin said, "she's the best."

Sandy remained cautiously optimistic. Sometime later, Justin invited her to a Mets game, not mentioning that his mother would be coming, too. When she arrived and saw Tara, Sandy wondered if it was a test. Sandy loved a challenge, and she was determined to ace this one. Instead of offering a handshake, this time Sandy moved in for a hug. Tara returned it with a one-arm pat on the back that felt as lifeless and dishraggy as her handshake.

Okay, not a hugger, Sandy noted. Not a problem, though. She had other ways to get this woman to like her. She would keep trying, keep smiling, show Tara what an easygoing and good-hearted person she was.

As soon as they got inside the stadium, she and Tara both realized they had to pee. Justin went to find their seats, leaving them alone together in line for the ladies' room. A second chance. She could comment on the weather or make a bold move and compliment Tara's shoes, which were horrendous. Why was this so hard? Boy-friends' moms usually loved Sandy. She knew when to be bubbly and when to be quiet. She was quick to help with chores. If only there were a sink of dirty dishes she could wash.

Before Sandy could come up with the first line for their banter, a stall opened up. Sandy was next in line but let Tara go ahead of her, a silent gesture she hoped would gain her some mileage. Another stall opened immediately and Sandy, self-conscious already, peed faster than she ever had in her life, washed her hands, then waited for Tara by the dryers. Women filed out in twos and threes. On the field, the national anthem was being sung. Sandy walked the length of the bathroom, looking beneath each stall door. No ugly purple sandals, not one pair of shoes anywhere. She stepped outside the bathroom and looked to see if Tara was waiting for her there. She wasn't. Maybe she was getting a pretzel. She waited a moment longer, then saw Justin walking toward her.

"What happened? Did you fall in?"

"What? No—I'm waiting for your mom."

"She's sitting in our seats. We were wondering what happened to you. Your stomach okay?" He patted her butt.

"I was waiting for your mom. I was in the stall for twenty seconds, tops."

She decided to drop it. Try again. She still had time to win this.

The rest of the day was tense in a way that Sandy couldn't really complain about. Nothing happened, but that was just it. Tara didn't ask Sandy one question about herself, was neither rude nor friendly when Sandy ventured to chat her up. Tara and Justin did the same thing at the baseball game that they'd done in their driveway, creating an impenetrable bubble of conversation around themselves, a boring and impenetrable bubble, talking about things that Sandy would have had to boldly interrupt (*Who are the Petrillos? Are they people you know or is that the name of a restaurant?*) if she wanted to be involved in the conversation.

So she did what many single American women in their thirties did at such times: she tried to like baseball. She cheered in the right places but not too loud. She booed in the right places but not too dramatically. She hoped to divine a win that would leave her boyfriend and his mother in a good mood, directing all the positive energy she had left in her heart to the players on the field. The Mets lost.

It was nothing. Too small to make a big deal about. But even her good-vibes-only chorus of friends agreed that things were weird.

"She didn't wait for you after the bathroom?" they said, aghast.

"No! And I swear, I was in there for *twenty seconds*."

"Maybe she was afraid you'd start talking about her son. Like you'd share girls' room gossip about her baby and she was avoiding it."

"Maybe. But there was no reason for her to think that. We didn't speak before we went into the stalls, so it was pretty safe for her to assume I wasn't going to launch into a discussion about how hung her son is while we washed our hands. Is it weird that I think it's weird that she didn't wait for me?"

"It's a little weird."

"Definitely low-key weird."

"If the roles had been reversed, I would have waited for her."

"Same."

"Ninety-nine percent of women would have waited."

Tara was in the 1 percent of women who would not.

If she decided to do it, to go for it, to have this baby, Tara would be the only grandmother her child knew.

Whether she had a baby now or later, she would have to do it without her mother. It was a sickening truth to hold. But what was also true was that this ball of cells inside her had little living pieces of her mother. She'd read once in a weird memoir for her book club that the fetus of a baby girl has all of her eggs already formed in her tiny ovaries before she's born, meaning that when Sandy was a fetus inside her mother, the egg that made this fetus was there, too, both of them inside her mom before they were born.

And so her decision was made, not by something big or important like love, or marriage, or even a clear desire for motherhood— just the tiny fact of an egg, an impossible memory of the time before she was born, and the love of two invisible people, someone who wasn't there anymore, and someone who wasn't there yet.

S andy's whole identity had been constructed around inexhaustible positivity, so it would be an abomination to say that her baby shower was bad. She got a nine-hundred-dollar stroller, after all. She got organic-linen swaddling blankets and a ridiculously expensive stretch-mark cream made of raw shea butter and swans' eggs and ballerina placentas, one that A-list celebrities swore by. She was surrounded by women who cared enough to give so generously. Some people never experience that in their whole lives, and Sandy was lucky to be the recipient of so much generosity.

Except.

Her friends had gone above and beyond in the gift department, that much was true, but she couldn't honestly tell if any of them were happy for her. One by one, as she told her squad that she was pregnant, this aura of pity, tinged with a subtle shade of disapproval, was cast over Sandy. Not one of her girlfriends squealed or jumped or emojied when she delivered the big news, as they did when one of their married friends got pregnant. When Sandy said, "I'm having a baby, due September first!" what she got in response was: "Seriously?"

Is seriously *the new slang for* congratulations? she wanted to reply.

"What are you going to do?"

The same thing all our other friends did? That women have done for, like, always—gestate a fetus for nine months, give birth, then raise a child, hopefully a cool one.

"What did Justin say?"

That was a valid question, but only if it came after *congratulations* or *how are you feeling?* Which it never did. When you're single and pregnant, *congratulations* is the last thing anyone says. It comes eventually, but only at the end of the conversation, and always with a little question mark scratched inside.

So what *did* Justin say?

"Whatever you want to do. I support you. I'm here for you. You don't have to do anything you don't want to do."

He emphasized this several times, until Sandy got confused. Did that mean she didn't have to have the baby? Or she didn't have to have an abortion? Because she wanted to have the baby. She'd made that clear.

"He's just overwhelmed," both her married and unmarried friends said.

"This is really hard for men, even under normal circumstances."

Normal?

Only about half of her friends identified as feminist, meaning they bought an overpriced T-shirt with *feminist* printed in petite gold letters across the chest, a shirt they wore to Pilates or yoga and nowhere else. But all of them agreed on the basics: unfettered access to birth control, the morning-after pill, and abortion; the right to a shame-free sex life on their own terms; a legal-justice system that did a better job of protecting women reporting rape and violence; and of course equal pay for equal work. The friends who refused to call themselves feminists, who "didn't like politics," still believed in all this stuff as fervently as the ones who wore the T-shirt; they were just afraid the label *feminist* would draw attention to their crow's feet or tummy fat. Either way, it was surprising how cold they all got once Sandy told them she was pregnant and not marrying or moving in with Justin. Her married friends were concerned that she was doing the baby a disservice by choosing to live alone in her studio apartment.

"Your baby deserves to have a father," they said.

My baby will have a father, Sandy wanted to argue back, *but that doesn't mean I have to live with him.*

"How hard can it be?" she joked instead. "Look at Reba . . ." Never mind that Reba was a sitcom character.

Her single friends were at a loss for what to say or do now that she couldn't go out drinking. The less she hung out with them, the less they talked in general.

The baby shower was the chance to course-correct. Now that everyone had had time to process and settle into the new reality, they should start to warm up a bit more. Sandy hoped it would be like the other baby showers she'd been to, where they just laughed and ate cheat-day pastries without thinking about all the hard stuff.

Tara had insisted on hosting the party at her house. Sandy would have preferred for one of her friends to host at a cute restaurant in the city, but it was the first kind gesture Tara had offered, and she was afraid to say no.

The midmorning affair was a mix of all Tara's friends, women in their fifties with extremely chiseled biceps and unsubtle lip filler, all of them bearing Tupperware bowls of mayonnaise-based salads, and Sandy's squad of thirty-somethings, armed with bottles of prosecco. They played awful games culled from a *Good Housekeeping* article in 1989. One of Tara's friends passed out a sheet of paper where all the women were supposed to guess how huge Sandy's waistline was in inches. Then there was something involving melted candy bars inside diapers.

After an hour of awkward mingling, each faction stationed themselves on opposite sides of the living room for the ceremonial opening of gifts. In a BarcaLounger that Tara had bedecked with pink and blue ribbons, the mother-to-be sat center stage, cringing all the way into the marrow of her bones. Her sole act of sad, covert revenge—she'd opted not to know the sex of the baby, preventing Tara from even more embarrassing art decoration.

All of that was bearable. The unbearable part was when Mary ran from the room and slammed the bathroom door so loudly that no one, not even the politest and most repressed among them, could pretend she hadn't done it on purpose. Sandy was grateful for a distraction, a reason to have an actual conversation with someone, something everyone seemed to avoid having with her. She excused

herself from the tacky, embarrassing throne Tara had put her in and
went to check on Mary.

She knocked on the bathroom door gently. "Mare, it's me. Can I
come in?"

Mary unlocked the door and pushed it open with her foot, almost
whacking Sandy in the face. Sandy entered and shut the door behind
her. Mary had buried her face in one of Tara's lace-trimmed hand
towels.

"What's wrong, honey?"

"Oh god, this hurts so much. It hurts so much. Brian and I keep
trying and trying and I still don't have a baby. We've been married
almost two years. Why is this happening? Why?"

"I'm not going to pretend I understand what you're going through
right now." Sandy rubbed Mary's back. "But I do understand how
insanely shitty life can get. How out of control it can feel. And,
sometimes, our friends group makes it worse. Not on purpose. We all
love each other so much. But it's like we're all so committed to this
storyline that our lives are perfect, or on the road to becoming perfect, that cheering each other on has become the only thing we know
how to do. So when life is shitty, there's this silence. It's excruciating.
And so lonely. But you're being so honest right now, Mare. So fucking real. I love you for that. And one day, your kids will be so glad you
are their mom."

Mary turned to Sandy, her eyes red and streaming black mascara
tears. She was blind with rage and a want so big it blocked out everything else. She blew her nose into Tara's hand towel and dropped it
on the floor.

"I'm sorry, but I did everything *right*. Your life is a joke and *you're
the one* who gets pregnant? How is that fair?"

She stormed out of the bathroom, grabbed her purse, and left
Tara's house. A few of Sandy's friends followed Mary out. The rest of
them left on more polite terms not long afterward. Sandy was alone
now with Tara and her friends. With no squad or family to protect
her, Sandy felt like a little girl in a fairy tale, about to be eaten by
a coven of witches. Not even her stepmother was there to protect
her. Sandy had invited her, but she was on a Caribbean cruise with

Sandy's dad, one they had booked a year in advance, so she'd sent a gift in the mail with her regrets.

Tara and her friends weren't interested enough in Sandy to eat her. Far more appealing were the prices of things they had recently bought or were planning to buy on Facebook Marketplace. Washable rugs, birdbaths, purses promising to be "like new." They clucked among themselves, an anxious flock of hens, perched on an eternal threshold of alarm. Sandy sat on the couch and listened to them, a plastic plate of beige food balanced on her lap. Potato salad and chicken salad and macaroni salad. All of it was giving her heartburn. She put the plate down for a minute to drink some water.

One of Tara's friends was doing a sweep of the living room, throwing all the stray plates and cups, the perfectly recyclable eight-ounce bottles of water, into a white trash bag.

"You going to finish that?" The woman pointed to Sandy's plate.

Sandy couldn't tell if it was a question or a command. "Thanks," she said, her default all day, the only word her brain was capable of manufacturing. *Thanks* began and ended every single sentence she uttered, even when it made no sense.

The woman shook her head, annoyed. "Are you done?"

"Thanks, oh, sorry, yes. I'm done. Thanks."

She took Sandy's plate and tossed it into the trash. "This one barely eats, too," she said to Tara.

"At least she eats meat," Tara replied.

"Thanks. Sorry—who is *this one*?" Sandy asked, and the woman, all of the women, exchanged looks. The pitch of their squawking got higher.

When Justin arrived to pick her up, Sandy ran out to the driveway and hugged him. He held her for a moment and stroked her hair. "You okay?"

"Yeah, just hormonal. It's all good."

She followed him into the house, where his arrival lit up the room. Justin, the only son of a widowed mother, commanded the celebrity and respect of a hero simply by showing up. After sampling each woman's contribution to the food spread, he began to load the presents into the back of his truck.

"Such a good boy."

"So handsome."

"Like his father, God rest his soul . . ."

The abundance of boxes and baskets and large items like the crib and stroller quickly filled up Justin's truck bed. He put the rest of the gifts into the passenger side of the cab.

"Mom, will you take Sandy in your car? My truck is full."

"To the city?!" Tara cried. "It's supposed to rain later."

"You can follow me. I'll drive slow. I won't lose you, I promise."

Tara sighed and got her purse. Sandy slunk behind her to the car. It was a long drive from Bay Ridge to the Upper West Side of Manhattan. Sandy thanked Tara for what felt like the hundredth time that day.

"Looks like the weather is actually pretty clear right now," she observed.

Tara said nothing. Sandy folded her hands over her huge belly and stared at them like a little girl who'd been scolded for talking out of turn. At a traffic light a mile past Justin and Tara's house, they passed a Mexican restaurant with an outdoor patio, where five of Sandy's friends sat talking and laughing. These friends had left her shower and continued partying without her. Was it an idea they had come up with in secret at the shower, while Sandy was sitting in that stupid chair, or had it been their plan all along? Was this the way it would be from now on?

In the passenger seat of Tara's car, Sandy began to cry. Tears trickled at first, then, despite tensing her muscles and holding her breath, they poured down her face. Her nostrils burned and her throat ached. She covered her mouth with her hand, as if to physically hold it all in.

Part of her wanted Tara to notice, to look over and see how much she was hurting, even if she could offer no consolation. She just didn't want to be alone with this feeling anymore.

Sandy took a slow, deep breath and then another. Maybe she wasn't being fair. Tara was a mother, after all, a woman who had raised a son alone at one point, a woman who most likely had experienced the complexity of female friendship in her lifetime. It was possible she would understand exactly what Sandy was going through. Maybe, Sandy thought, she should give Tara a chance. This was her baby's grandmother, after all. Maybe, if she opened up and told Tara how sad she was, this seemingly cold woman's response might surprise her. Maybe Tara's love language was something that took a little translating, and it was Sandy, not Tara, who was the jerk for not doing the extra emotional labor to find common ground. While it seemed unlikely that Tara would offer the exact brand of kindness Sandy wanted right now, she might have some tough-love wisdom that could help with the throbbing ache.

She looked at Tara, whose body leaned close to the steering wheel, as if the rain she was so afraid of falling could be warded off by her vigilance. Her hands gripped the wheel at ten and two, a wad of tissues balled in one of them. Tears were streaming down Tara's face, too. She was crying in perfect silence and had been for some time. Like Sandy, she made sure not so much as a whimper escaped.

It would be a while longer before Sandy would find out why Tara was crying that day, though Tara's interest in Sandy's tears would never be any different.

"Just did a twenty-four-hour spin class on a bike made of fire," Sandy posted to all her social-media accounts. Cone-headed, blotchy, and crying with all the drama of a daytime soap actress, her little Rosie had arrived.

All her single girlfriends came over in the first few weeks to hold the baby and take selfies, which they cropped and filtered and posted immediately with #babylove #sisterhood #auntie and "lol how long until Rosie's old enough to be the designated driver?" Then these friends disappeared into that same two-dimensional world, ghosts on the internet, who would send heart after digital heart but never appear in Sandy's real life again.

Her married-with-children friends had all moved to the suburbs and fell into two distinct camps: those who were hell-bent on getting Sandy married off to some single friend of their husband's; and those who were understandably too busy to respond to a text within a week's time. All of those in the first camp had their own "amazing guy" she just had to meet.

"If Chris Hemsworth begged to massage my shoulders and feed me tacos, I would say no. But thanks!"

These friends were well-meaning, but there was a covert message to their matchmaking, an implication that Sandy and Rosie were an incomplete story, a story that they, the loving and heroic friends, could write the happy ending to. Sandy was not a new mother with a perfect baby; she was a problem needing to be solved.

"What if my family is two people? Two people can be a family, can't they?"

"Oh, honey, you're amazing!" they all told her. "You don't know how amazing you are! You deserve it all!"

I know I'm amazing. I'm doing something you couldn't pull off for one weekend, let alone a lifetime. And I do have it all. I have Rosie.

These friends also had full-time nannies who sleep-trained their babies for them while they drank a glass of wine with their husbands, who made heaps of laundry and sinks full of dishes disappear without being asked. They had time to play matchmaker. The second camp of marrieds-with-children were not so resourced, desperately juggling work, kids, daycare, and backup daycare, plus husbands who were louder and needier than their babies. When they had a spare second and the bandwidth to remember that someone outside their house existed, they would text Sandy discouraging things like, "enjoy this time while it lasts!" and "cherish every second becaue it just gets harder and harder . . ."

Once upon a time, only a few weeks ago, these responses would have stung. Not anymore. Sandy had walked through fire. She'd made a baby appear between her legs, a whole baby. Hurtling into the world, Rosie ripped off all the protective layers of Sandy's heart, forcing her to see the people in her life as the vulnerable little babies they once were. She loved them all. She forgave them all. She was as happy with them as she was without them, as long as she had her Rosie.

Her dad and stepmom almost got Sandy into an emotional tailspin when they used their long-weekend visit to New York to take in not one but two Broadway shows rather than bonding with their only grandchild, offering to do a grocery shop, or babysitting—things typical new grandparents do.

"I'm no good with babies," her dad said, holding Rosie for the first time. He passed her off to Sandy's stepmom almost immediately. "I was the same with you. You can ask your mom if you don't believe me."

"Mom's dead," Sandy reminded him.

"Oh god, yeah. I'm sorry. Sometimes I forget that."

I don't, Sandy would have snapped at him in the past. She didn't need to now. Her dad was a child. Her stepmother was like a mother to him. That's what worked for them. *They're doing the best they can.*

It was a tranquility brewed out of oxytocin and coconut oil, tiny as a fingernail, infinite as the sky. She even sort of loved Justin. Several times a week he came over after work to help bathe Rosie. They knelt together on the tile floor of her bathroom, their thighs pressed close in that tiny space. Sandy sloshed a washcloth around the lukewarm water, stirring up islands of mild organic-soap bubbles that disappeared as soon as they arose. She squeezed a gentle stream of water up and down the length of Rosie's body while Justin held her.

"Her entire head fits into my hand!" he whispered, dazed with love.

Afterward they ate dinner together as a family. Always pizza, but at least Justin was chipping in. He was so good with Rosie— uncannily good, able to bind her in the tightest swaddles, to rock her in a football hold and relieve her worst gas pains. But he had yet to offer Sandy any money. She'd asked him to cough up some contribution to her hospital bill, and he said he was "working on it." Sometimes he brought food Tara had made, usually a casserole so greasy and disgusting she would throw it away after he'd left. He'd arrive with huge boxes of diapers that Tara had bought wholesale, even though Sandy had explained to him, at least six different times, that she had a diaper subscription service delivering precisely what she needed when she needed it, as she didn't have room in her small studio apartment for any extra boxes.

"Well, she gives them to me, and if I bring them back home she yells at me, and I can't have huge boxes of diapers in my truck. I'm trying to run a business."

Sandy rubbed virgin coconut oil into Rosie's legs, swirling her fingers in and around the fat rolls of her thighs, a massage technique the baby nurse at the hospital had taught her. Rosie's skin glowed. She smelled like a summer cocktail. The sparse blond hair on her scalp was a golden moss from the realm of fairies.

Only this matters.

Once every other week Tara came to visit, complaining about the drive the whole time; or, if traffic was good, she complained about parking; and if parking was easy, she said over and over again how small Sandy's place was, how cramped and claustrophobic she felt.

"Aren't you going to try to give her formula?" Tara asked as Sandy switched Rosie from one boob to the other. "It makes them sleep so much better."

"Why don't you feed her any formula?" Justin repeated the next night. "Mom says it's way healthier."

They're doing the best they can. We all are.

It was like this for six and a half weeks. Then, after all the visits from friends had subsided, a panic began to creep in. Whether at home with Rosie or at work, Sandy was left with days that felt held together by crepe paper followed by even longer nights, where sleep was the second priority after survival. Madness was approaching. She could feel it coming on like a flu. To fight it, Sandy made a plan: she would take Rosie to the story hour at their local branch of the library. They would go every day that Rosie wasn't at daycare. Once this routine was established, everything else would fall into place around it. Routines were something a good mom stuck to no matter what.

But that wasn't enough. Sandy was going to prove to the invisible audience in her head that not only did she have everything under control, she was a gorgeous MILF, too. The morning before Rosie's seven-week birthday, Sandy dressed her daughter in a white onesie with eyelet ruffles on the shoulders and a pink ruffled skirt. Sandy tightened her belly band and squeezed into a chambray wrap dress, pulled her hair up into an artfully messy bun, and put on a pair of knee-high leather boots with a low heel. She slung her diaper bag over her shoulder—the sleek black one that didn't look like a diaper bag—and left her apartment with her baby, proud of her ability to get out and go no matter how tired she was.

At the library there were two long rows of strollers parked outside the children's section. Sandy wrestled with Rosie's stroller for several minutes, at last getting it to fold down and wedge in among the others. Inside on a big colorful carpet sat a dedicated crew of mostly brown women and the mostly white babies they cared for, not a man in sight. Without a place to sit or even stand, Sandy waded through them gingerly, boots already committing murder on her low back, a sleeping Rosie making her shoulder ache. There was plenty of space behind the glass door where the story time would happen. All she had to do was survive the journey from here to there. She was opening the door when a librarian stopped her.

"Excuse me, do you have a ticket?"

"I thought this was free."

"It is, but space is limited. You need a ticket to get in."

"Okay," Sandy demurred. "Where do I get one?"

"You have to get here early to get a ticket," the librarian said in a hushed tone, as though protecting Sandy from humiliation.

"I am early," Sandy said. She checked her phone to be sure. Story time was not for another fifteen minutes.

"We got here forty-five minutes early," a nanny said, smirking from the crowded rug of babies. "And we got the last ticket of the day."

"What?! That's ridiculous."

"It must be your first time here," another nanny surmised. The other women chuckled and shook their heads.

Sandy reslung her diaper bag on the other shoulder and marched out. "I'll try again tomorrow," she said through gritted teeth. "I can do this."

Back home, she stood at the door to her apartment, waving her phone over the brass doorknob for a long time, waiting for a green light to beep her inside like it did at the subway turnstile. She tried again and again until she realized her insanity and found her keys. Once she shut the door behind her, the dam broke. The postpartum depression that she was certain she had eluded came flooding in, and she began to cry.

For weeks it was all she did.

"What are you doing?" she sobbed as Rosie awoke from a twenty-minute nap that, for both of their sakes, Sandy had been banking on lasting two hours. All the books and apps and influencers claimed that Rosie would sleep longer if Sandy wrapped her up like a tight little burrito, but there she was, wide-awake, her fat sausage arms broken free from the swaddle and flailing.

"What am *I* doing?" she said. Rosie's eyes tracked her as she paced the short distance from the bed to the apartment door. "I fucked this up so badly. I don't even know how it happened. I've never tried to do anything or be anything in my life. I mean, I *thought* I did. I had boyfriends. And friends. And apartments. A job. A job someone would call a career but, like, I don't know. I was just playing along. I was an idiot. And now I'm somebody's mother." She knelt by the bed and untangled Rosie from the Velcro swaddle. Her tiny feet were too much. Devastating. "I'm *your* mother."

Sandy's body morphed into a new state of matter: solid on the outside, liquid on the inside. A song from her middle school era that she never really liked now had the power to melt her into a puddle of tears. The thought that one day Rosie would grow up and go to school, that she'd wear shoes, walk down school hallways all by herself, had her doubled over in anguish. She soaked her shirts with milk and tears, apologizing constantly, to Rosie, to anyone, for nothing in particular.

"I'm sorry," she cried to Stelios, the man from the bodega downstairs, who delivered her bacon-egg-and-cheese sandwiches. These deliveries were her only tether to the reality she once knew, an indulgence she couldn't afford and couldn't give up, not yet.

"You are okay?" Stelios asked. He wore a white T-shirt with faded, well-laundered stains and smelled like coffee and cigarettes. His mustache and beard were thick and wiry, black brushed with silver. Sandy, the only child of only children, had begun to think of him as a pretend uncle, someone who both loved her and judged her life choices from a distance.

"Yeah. I'm fine. I'm sorry. It's just this thing my eyes do now," she told him, wiping her nose on her bare arm. Rosie slapped Sandy's chest with the tiny star of her hand. She grunted, rooting around for a boob. Frustrated, she settled for sucking on the milk-soaked tank top her mother was wearing.

The man dug into his pockets and produced a wad of white paper napkins. Sandy blew her nose. "My wife," he said, "she cry for three month with our first baby. Never stop crying. I think, that's it, she is breaking. Something inside breaking." He stabbed his forehead with his index finger to indicate the depth of his wife's mental anguish. "Four kids later, I know why the women have the babies. You are stronger than us. You are. Remember. God bless you and your baby." He kissed Rosie on the top of her head before leaving.

"We might not have everything we want right now," Sandy said to Rosie as she closed the door, "but we have this beautiful city to call home." And she cried until the two of them fell asleep again.

A million years ago, when Sandy was a little tween, there was an option on social-media profiles to define your relationship status as "it's complicated." Like everything on the internet, it was overused until it became a joke, but for some it was an earnest attempt to simplify a situation that was anything but.

Sandy had just gotten out of the shower and Justin, shirtless, lay in her bed, Rosie fast asleep in the crook of his arm. They were something very different from "dating," but what that was, well, it was complicated.

Justin dared not set Rosie down in her crib, and Sandy didn't blame him. After several failed attempts at sleep training, Rosie, and by extension Sandy, had become the ultimate failure of the baby-industrial complex: an infant who could sleep only when touching human skin, preferably her mother's, but Dad's would suffice. Rosie was miserable and needing to be held all the time when she was awake, too, as her first tooth cut through her gum. A little early at four months old but not abnormal, the internet assured. Scant solace for Sandy, who had to time when she used the bathroom around Rosie's erratic sleep schedule.

Justin was making an honest effort to come over a little more often. If he had a show he would come for an hour before. Nights with no shows he'd stay longer but not sleep over. He'd tried to sleep over a few times in the very beginning but claimed he couldn't do it anymore because "he had to work." Sandy also had to work. After six weeks of unpaid leave, the magazine let her come back to the office two days a week and work from home the rest of the time, which included weekends if she needed to catch up, which she always did. It was temporary and unstable and horrible, and for some reason Justin saw this flexibility as a vacation.

Sandy was too tired to argue about it. "Do you want to be right or do you want to be happy?" all of her married friends reminded her.

"I want to take a shower without holding her or hearing her scream for the ten minutes she's strapped in her bouncy seat," Sandy said. "I want to eat a meal, a whole meal, slowly, sitting down, and using both of my hands." She chose her battles.

Justin kissed Rosie's head as he stared at his phone. He was refreshing his social-media feed, Sandy could see from across the room. Blocks of color flew up his screen, his finger swiping, swiping, stopping a moment, then swiping again.

Sandy put on her glasses, fogged up from the steamy bathroom, and got dressed. She dropped her towel and bent down to pick up a pair of dirty sweatpants from the floor. Her stomach drooped several inches off her body and swung back and forth. One of her boobs, Rosie's favorite, had grown a whole cup size larger than the other. Who cared anymore what she looked like naked? Not Justin. He didn't look up once.

She loaded bottles into the dishwasher. Rosie was gaining weight at a fast clip. Sandy was proud of her big heavy girl. So solid and grounded, so unafraid of how much space she was taking up in the world. *She will be a hard girl to knock over,* Sandy thought happily.

As though sensing Sandy's return to the room, Rosie woke up and began to cry. "Hungry girl," Justin said, and Sandy smiled.

He handed Rosie over to her, then returned to his phone. Sitting close to Justin on her bed now, Sandy nursed Rosie until she fell asleep again and watched him scroll through the images on the screen. Pictures of women on beaches and standing on top of mountains, with friends and alone. Justin whizzed past them all, pausing occasionally on beautiful women baring lots of skin. Women in bikinis by turquoise pools or in skimpy lingerie lying in a tangle of sheets on an art-directed unmade bed. This was something she'd grown to accept as normal. Guys followed beautiful women they didn't know on social media. Every guy she'd ever dated had done it. It didn't mean anything. She didn't like it, but she knew not to take it personally. At least, she used to know that.

Maybe it was hormones. Maybe it was irrational. But for the first time in a long time, since she was that little tween just starting to live her life online, in the days of the "it's complicated" relationship status, Sandy was enraged that the man sitting next to her was looking at pictures of half-naked women.

Do you want to be right or do you want to be happy?

Neither!

"Who's that?"

Justin slipped his phone into his pocket. He got up off her bed and opened her fridge. "Hey, did you eat all the leftover pizza?" he whined in disappointment.

"Are you back on dating apps?"

"Come on, Sandy. Do you really want to do this?"

"Yup. I sure do," she growled.

"It's not like you're trying to do anything for me anymore. So now I have to become a monk until you let me loose or change your mind?" He had a point. Both their relationship and their sexual status were "complicated." Once they'd decided—or in Justin's case accepted—that they were having a baby, their relationship continued in the same limbo as it had before, with no movement toward breaking up or getting serious. For the first three months of her pregnancy she'd been too nauseous to think about sex. Then somewhere around month four, when the nausea had lifted, Sandy was insanely horny, and Justin seemed happy to oblige. At the end of her pregnancy, she was so huge and exhausted that the desire dried up again. If Justin had feelings about any of this, he didn't share them with her. And she didn't ask. He seemed to have an I'll-take-what-I-can-get attitude, and Sandy was grateful to be left alone when she wasn't in the mood.

But now? The doctor had okayed sex along with working out at her one and only follow-up visit six weeks after Rosie was born. "It's totally safe for you and your partner to be intimate again," he'd said.

"Are you fucking kidding me? My vagina literally ripped."

"You're all healed now. The stitches have dissolved."

"My memory of them hasn't."

Were there women who actually wanted to have sex six weeks after giving birth? This was not something any of her friends with kids had discussed.

Until that night, besieged by, if not jealousy, then at least resentment toward Justin and his pathetic online desires, she hadn't thought about sex with him as something she would do again.

Like the parameters of their relationship, sex was something that just seemed to exist in its own nebulous form, and they were both too busy or scared to look at it long enough to discern if it had any recognizable shape. The few times Justin slept over after Rosie was born, it was like siblings forced to share a bed while the grandparents were visiting. She was happy for any help he offered, and politically felt he should help more, but if she was being honest, she preferred it when he wasn't there. As hard it was to care for Rosie alone, Justin was an extra layer of annoyance, another baby to tend. Until that night, it had never occurred to her that he would leave her apartment and hook up with another woman.

"What do you expect me to do? We haven't had sex in months."

"I had a baby."

"You could have sex again six weeks after she was born."

"How do you know that?"

"It's what they always say."

"Justin, you didn't know that pee came out of an entirely separate hole from the vagina until I explained it to you. This makes no sense—"

"I'm not going through this again," he said. He put on his shirt, leaned over, and kissed Rosie goodbye. The door slammed behind him. Rosie woke up and wailed. It was forty-five minutes before Sandy could settle her down again.

Sandy got up the next morning with something new on her mind, a glowing ember from last night's fire. Justin said he wasn't going through this *again*. What did that mean?

She dropped Rosie off at daycare, a bare-walled facility on the ground floor of a dour office building that felt like a baby repository from a sci-fi movie. It was the only one she could afford, and the only place that didn't force her into a five-day-a-week contract.

Sandy was pushing a rock up a hill every day only to watch it roll back down. That month all of the writers and artists she was supervising were late on their deadlines and Thatcher blamed her. Every email from him was a new fire to be put out; every phone call strained her throat as she faked enthusiasm for the underpaid writer or photographer on the other end. But the task of finding a new job would just be another job added to the one she was already doing badly.

To survive as a niche print magazine in a digital world, Thatcher had stripped down the office to a bare-bones operation. The whole staff was doing work that in the past would have been distributed among twice as many people, with no increase in pay. They went to publication bimonthly instead of monthly and downsized their headquarters to a small loft in Midtown that had only one bathroom for the whole staff to share. Thatcher was constantly reminding them how lucky they were to have a physical HQ. "Most print magazines of our size have gone all-remote, never meeting in person. Can you imagine?" he huffed.

With not a single closet to spare, Sandy had to use the all-genders bathroom as her pumping room. After walking in on her pumping, Rob, the office manager slash HR director slash executive editor, made a laminated sign she could hang on the bathroom door handle. It was an illustration of a stork holding a pink teardrop-shaped bundle from its beak, with the words: A NEW MOMMY IS MAKING FOOD RIGHT NOW. DO NOT ENTER FOR TWENTY MINUTES. THANKS!

Sandy grabbed the sign and was heading to the bathroom when Rob stopped her.

"Oh, sorry, Sandy, are you going in . . . now?"

"Well," Sandy said, holding aloft her little dairy machine, "yes, I am."

"I'm wondering if I could sneak ahead of you real quick? Honestly don't think I can wait another half hour." He rubbed his stomach. "Indian food, am I right?"

It was amazing how expertly he had nailed two levels of gross— one gastrointestinal, one racist—all at once.

"Sure, Rob, go ahead."

Sandy sat back down at the co-working table that had become her desk. A co-working table she shared with an unpaid intern. "Oh my god," Sandy said to the intern, "I am sitting here waiting for my boss to take a shit. This is my actual life."

The intern smiled. She had luminous skin and wide, clear eyes. A single speck of glitter flashed on her temple, probably left over from last night dancing at a club, like vibrant young people do.

"I used to be an intern here," she offered the girl.

"I'm just fulfilling credits for graduation. This was way easier than writing a research paper," the girl replied.

"Cool." Sandy whipped out her phone and checked Justin's social media again. She had never played the jealousy game with him. But what had he meant by "not going through this *again*"?

That night Justin came by for an hour before his show. He brought pizza as usual, which Sandy was sick of, but he seemed contrite. Rosie was awake and alert and smiled a big drooly smile as Justin scooped her into his arms. He offered the second knuckle of his right pinky finger for her suck on.

"I got your favorite knuckle right here, kid. Don't worry," he said. "She's so funny," he told Sandy. "If I offer her another finger, I swear to god she rolls her eyes at me like I'm an idiot."

"She's smart," Sandy agreed.

"One day she's going to grow up and not remember she used to do this." He kissed her forehead. "I'm going to get a tattoo *R* on this knuckle so we always remember."

Moments like these were so confusing. Justin could be so wonderful sometimes. Sandy didn't know if she felt guilty for not working things out or guilty for not wanting to try. It was hard to discern any feeling besides hunger and exhaustion. She pulled a slice of pizza from the box and dabbed it with a paper towel.

"Hey, it's really hot. You should let it cool off," Justin warned.

Sandy took a big wolfish bite, scalded the roof of her mouth, felt filaments of burned tissue dangling inside, and kept eating.

"Listen," he said, "I'm going on tour Friday. I've been avoiding telling you because you're all hormonal and the timing is bad, I know, but this tour is different. It's a huge opportunity. Another band is asking me to front them. Their lead guitarist is in rehab. They're much bigger than Pilot Error. We're booking big venues. West Coast venues."

"L.A.?" She choked down a swig of cold milk directly from the carton.

"Spokane."

"Cool. Congratulations."

"Are you being sarcastic?"

"No." Sandy sat down. "I'm happy for you. I really am. I'm just so tired." She closed her eyes, massaged her temples. "Does this mean you can chip in for daycare right now?"

"My mom can watch Rosie for free," Justin said. He smiled at Rosie, who was pulling at the beard he had been growing for the last month, a clue that this tour had been in the works for a while.

"Your mom hates coming over here."

"I was thinking you could move into my place. Just for the month that I'm gone. It will save a lot of money on daycare. Mom's a lot more available if you go to her rather than expect her to come to you. And the walk to the N train is under fifteen minutes."

Even with that commute, this was objectively a good idea. The reality was that she needed to be in her office more than two days a week if she wanted to get her name on the masthead again. Plus, when she worked from home, Rosie limited much of what she could do. Justin pitched in for daycare when he could, but it was winter and his window-washing income was in hibernation, so Sandy ended up covering most of the daycare bill herself with what was left of her mother's life-insurance payout. Adding one more day a week to the childcare bill would tip the balance, meaning she would be paying more to work than she was actually earning from said work. She tried to explain all that to Justin. Again.

"I get it. All last year's profits from the window-washing business got eaten up by my investment in the band," he said. "And Rosie, too," he quickly revised. "But the merch, the promotion, the tours— that's all on me. If Mom made me pay rent, I don't know how I'd do it. That's why this is such a big opportunity for me. It's costing me nothing. All I have to do is show up and get paid."

"What are they paying you?"

"A thousand bucks, plus hotels, food, and beer."

"You're leaving town, leaving your daughter, for a month, for a thousand dollars?"

Justin stared at her, mouth agape, then shook his head sadly. "You really don't get it. I thought all this time you were the one who would finally get it. But I was wrong again." He looked down at his shoes. His voice became low and somber. "Are you going to move in with Mom or what? She wants to know so she can get things ready."

The right answer was yes. With a month of free daycare, Sandy could throw herself into work five days a week and try to earn back some of the respect she'd lost among the other editors. But then what would happen after that month? In no time she'd be back to where she was now. It didn't seem worth it, not when the price to pay was Tara and the N train.

"We're going to stay here."

Justin got up and put on his coat without looking at Sandy. He opened the door and stood there for a moment, unwilling to leave until he'd had the last word.

"Just remember," he said, "that *you* are the one making this difficult."

There was a lot about Sandy's life that wasn't ideal. Never had it been her fantasy to live with her daughter in a 380-square-foot studio apartment whose only window was too shady to keep plants alive. She definitely did not love how completely she'd given up on working out and socializing with friends and all the other self-care activities that she'd found so essential before becoming a mother. Sitting on a toilet to pump breast milk three times a day at work was not the girl-boss persona she'd pictured for herself when she was a college kid full of dreams. Worst of all: Sandy had become a woman who stalked her baby daddy's social media while he was on tour with his not-famous band.

It was a new low. She was actually glad she was no longer close to her girlfriends, because admitting this to them, to anyone, would be humiliating.

She should have been doubling down on work. Coming up with refreshing ideas for the magazine to attract a younger readership, ways to make print subscriptions worthwhile to Millennials and Gen Z. But every spare second she had was sucked up monitoring Justin's personal social-media feeds, cross-referencing his new band's feed as well as the profile of every club they played at on the day of the show. Her eyes were primed for pictures of . . . what? What did she expect to see? Justin locking lips with some hot girl? How would that change her situation at all? She didn't know. She just *had to* see what he was doing. It became an obsession.

Two weeks after Justin left on tour, Tara made her usual visit to Sandy's apartment. Normally Sandy would dash out the door to maximize every second of free babysitting she could get, but this time she stuck around. She was hoping to get Tara to talk a little, maybe reveal something she'd heard from Justin, information she could use to refine her sad social-media espionage.

What Tara lacked in cooking and social skills, she made up for as a laundress. She was talented when it came to stain removal, and her folding game was so tight and precise it made famous organizers on the internet look like slobs. Rosie had had a blowout in one of her expensive designer baby frocks, a gift from Sandy's single friends. She'd been hoping to get a decent resale on the dress after Rosie grew out of it. She was ready to throw the two-hundred-dollar garment in the trash when Justin offered to bring it to his mom. No way, Sandy had argued. By the time Tara got it into her machine, the stain would be set. Justin guaranteed his mom could work magic. *Magic* was the only word to describe it when the frilly white dress returned to her looking brand-new.

That Sunday she offered Tara a pastel-yellow onesie stained with beet puree. It was more than a chore—Sandy hoped that, once deep into her almost religious practice of stain removal, Tara would relax and become pliant, ready to spill.

"You got any white vinegar?" Tara said. She put on a pair of readers and examined the stain like a scientist.

"Would balsamic work?"

"Never mind," Tara groaned. She opened Sandy's freezer, cracked out an ice cube, and began rubbing it on the onesie with baking soda and dish soap.

"You're so good at this, Tara. Who taught you how to do that?"

"No one," Tara said. "I figured it out myself." Her body bent over the kitchen sink with intense focus. She scrubbed harder. "What are you still doing here? Don't you have class?"

"Class?" Sandy hadn't been to Pilates in over a year.

"Senior moment. I was thinking of Stephanie."

"Who's Stephanie?"

Tara's face was so different from her son's. Her cheekbones were sharp, her nose narrow and pointed. With his round cheeks and blue eyes, Justin clearly took after his late father. But what mother and son shared was an ability to freeze their faces to such stillness you wondered for a minute if they'd had a stroke. Tara stared at Sandy without seeing her. She said nothing. A pregnant pause if ever there was one. Sandy was not in the mood to wait for devastation to be born.

"Who's Stephanie?" she said again.

Tara started to cry. She blubbered to herself, "His father is rolling over in his grave right now. He's . . . thank god he's not alive to see this . . . It's a curse . . . This isn't the life we deserve. If his father were alive, he'd be . . . he'd be . . . *so disgusted with us.*"

"Tara, you need to tell me who Stephanie is."

After this cloudburst of tears, Tara collected herself quickly. It was unnerving to see someone pull the plug on their emotions so completely. She wiped her eyes with one of Rosie's burp cloths. "Justin has another child. The mother, Stephanie, is a nightmare. A witch. She'd make our lives hell if we let her. It's not my place to explain. It's for you and my son to discuss. I'm staying out of it."

"I never lied to you."

Not technically, no. Just a pattern of omissions, a story knit with holes. Like the way Justin never asked Sandy about her day—because he didn't want her to ask about his, or else he might slip and say something like *I had to pick up my kid from school.* Hiding the truth in plain sight, Justin trained her subtly over time to stop asking questions. If she wasn't so enraged, Sandy might actually be impressed; Justin did not come off as all that bright. He was no mastermind. But it turned out that even a basic dude of average intelligence can manipulate the woman he's sleeping with.

"You failed to tell me something very important. It's the same thing."

"No, because I never actually lied . . ."

The way he would disappear for a few days, texting enough to keep Sandy from feeling neglected but remaining vague about any details. About every other weekend he would be "busy" or "tired." Of course he was busy and tired—he was taking care of his kid. Though she didn't know that for sure. She'd ambushed him the moment he came home from his tour.

"I didn't tell you because it's none of your business."

"I think the fact that my kid has a sibling is absolutely my business."

"She's a baby. She doesn't even know what a sibling is."

They went back and forth. It was pointless and exhausting. Even if she could win the argument, what would be the victory? The fact remained that Justin was a liar, that he gave nothing more than the bare minimum to Rosie and her. Any admission of guilt on his part, even the sincerest *I'm sorry* from him, would not change that.

"Just tell me who this other woman is."

Sandy unzipped a fussing Rosie from a padded sleep suit. It was somewhere between a marshmallow Halloween costume and an astronaut suit and cost a hundred dollars. It promised to add an extra hour to a baby's sleep time, but so far it only made Rosie more pissed off. Justin paced the short distance between her kitchen table and the one window in her apartment.

"She's . . ." Justin faltered, looked at the floor. "She's a bitch, okay? I know I'll get canceled for saying that, but it's true. She's an evil bitch. Like, capable of ruining my life if I let her. If you don't believe me, you can ask Mom."

"I don't care what your mother has to say. I'm asking you. Who is Stephanie? Who is your kid? How often do you see them? What's your arrangement?"

"I see my kid all the time. But it's hard with that witch poisoning her against me. As soon as Ashley gets old enough to understand, I'm going to tell her the truth about her mother, and she'll probably want to come live with me. When she's older."

"Ashley. So you have a daughter. How old is she?"

"Seven. No—eight."

"Can I see a picture?"

Justin sat down next to her on the bed. Rosie lay in a sleek angular bouncer between their feet, sucking on her pacifier, a small plush llama attached to a rubber nub that she could grip and hold. She pulled the pacifier out dramatically, a little wet *pop* escaping her lips, then returned it to her mouth, vividly proud of her own abilities. Justin scrolled through the pictures on his phone. It took a while before he found one of Ashley, meaning he hadn't taken a picture of her recently or he didn't see her as often as he claimed. She was a beautiful eight-year-old with gleaming auburn hair cut in a chic pageboy style. She had the same icy-blue eyes as Justin and Rosie.

The rest of her face, her wide smile, her thick brows, pointed toward this witchy mother.

"Can I meet her? Can Rosie meet her sister?"

"Yeah, yeah. They will. In time they will."

"When?"

"You really need to relax. These hormones are making you psycho."

With that, they hopped back on the howling merry-go-round—Sandy pushing for information, clarity; Justin evading, accusing, playing the victim, until Sandy came to her senses. She told him, calmly, to leave. Nothing more was going to come out of this, and Sandy more than ever needed to preserve her energy for battles worth fighting. They were done for the day.

Sandy wrote Tara a long letter in her phone's Notes app the next morning, rewrote it several times throughout the day, then waited a night before texting it. In the message, she appealed to Tara as a mother. Wouldn't she want to know who her child's sibling was? Then she went on and on about her mother being dead, how hard that was, that she was so far away from her family, that Tara and Justin were her only family here and she really needed them to trust her, that she could handle this situation with the diplomacy they all wanted and needed.

The plan worked. Tara seemed to want nothing to do with this conversation, and so without a single extra word, ignoring everything else Sandy had said, she responded with:

"Ashley's mother is Stephanie Santorella. She lives in Staten Island. Stay away from her. She's trouble."

Stephanie became Sandy's vocation while her actual career fell apart. Thatcher offered a promotion to Jess, the other associate editor and the only woman on staff besides Sandy and the intern. Jess had started at the magazine a year after Sandy, so the message was clear: Sandy's trajectory was stagnating. After work all the editors were going out to eat at the hot new Syrian–Korean fusion place. It was both a celebration for Jess and a chance to connect with the head chef there, whom they wanted to interview for a cover story. Rob made it clear that Sandy should come.

"This is part of the job," he said. "Thatcher notices who goes to these things and who doesn't."

"I can't," Sandy said.

"You say that a lot these days," Rob answered.

He was right. She was no longer available for the late-night restaurant-industry parties that had made up so much of her working life before Rosie. Sandy felt hopeless, and so she stalked Stephanie Santorella. It was a problem with a clear solution. She would find this woman and confront her. That was something she could control while everything else was unraveling.

Sandy took longer and longer pump breaks, sitting on the toilet while she patiently reviewed every single one of Justin's two thousand followers, until she found the one she was looking for.

When Steph was pregnant, she dreamed of a child who would run home from school breathless with gossip about who said something funny, who cried at recess, and why. At bedtime they would make up long stories together and lie in bed late into the morning recounting the previous night's dreams. Every feeling would be a treasure they examined together. No subject would be off-limits. After so many years of painful silence, feeling like an alien in her frozen, stunted family, Steph could create a new family, the one she'd always wanted. And then came Ashley.

Ashley is so unlike Steph that her whole existence feels like a cosmic lesson. She had been quiet and secretive since the womb, when she would roll away every time the technician ran her wand over Steph's stomach, refusing to provide a clear view in an ultrasound.

Slow to talk, she worried Steph, a new mom at eighteen, with her stubborn refusal to develop at anyone's pace but her own. Then, at age two years and one week, Ashley's first words were also her first sentence, the first of many impassive observations she would make of her world. Standing at a windowsill, watching tree branches thrash as if fighting, she said, "It's so windy."

If she had an opinion about that wind, she was keeping it to herself, like everything else.

There is nothing Steph can do to get her kid to talk when she doesn't want to. Even when Steph tells Ashley she has a baby sister, that they are going to meet her and the baby's mother, the kid remains poker-faced.

"Okay," she says.

"Come on, kiddo! You have a baby sister! That you didn't know about. At all. Before just now. And we are going to meet her!" Steph is incredulous. Apoplectic. All she wants is to hypothesize about what the baby will look like, what the mom will look like, what they will be like, sound like, act like.

"Okay," Ashley says again.

"How do you feel? Excited? Nervous? Curious? Confused?"

"I feel fine, I guess."

With cool determination, Ashley chops at the pixelated trees on her tablet's screen, smashing them with a retro 8-bit ax into perfect brown cubes of wood. Steph hates this game. A capitalist's wet dream, it trains kids to strip-mine in a world of unlimited natural resources. But it is the lesser of two evils, a hard-won compromise between mother and child. If she had her own way, Ashley would watch other people play video games on YouTube for hours, games about serial killers and kidnapped children and biohazard spills. Razing a digital forest is fine for now. Steph keeps her mouth shut. She tries.

"You seriously have no opinion? No questions?"

"Where are we meeting them?"

"At the noodle house you like. The one near the ferry."

Ashley says nothing. Steph seethes. She loves this kid. She loves this kid so much it makes her woozy to think about it for too long. She would take a bullet for this kid. That is the spiritual contract she made the moment Ashley was laid into her arms, sticky with blood and fluids, staring silently into her eyes for the first time. But it is a special form of torture to be shut down so coldly from the most amazing piece of gossip of their life.

Ashley looks up at her mother and studies her face. The two of them are like oddballs on the lam in some old movie, each a different brand of weirdo, forced to work together to survive. They love each other wildly, insanely, passionately. They just don't understand each other. This makes Steph feel like a failure and sometimes a little lonely.

"Let's meet them at that carousel," Ashley says. "The one that looks like an aquarium."

"The SeaGlass Carousel?"

"It's in Battery Park, near the noodle house."

"Yeah, it is," Steph says, a little stunned. But also not. That's her kid—stunning. "Good idea. It's the perfect place to meet." She runs her hands through Ashley's glossy coppery hair. "What did I do to deserve a kid as great as you?"

One Saturday morning in April, Sandy flings all the clothes stuffed in her closet onto her bed and tries on six different outfits. She sweats through shirt after shirt while trying to get herself and Rosie ready at the same time. There's only time to flat iron the top layer of her hair, which she hopes will stay put and hide the frizz underneath. Rosie has been developing an absurdly cute curl in the middle of her forehead. People remark on it all the time. But today of all days, the curl is falling flat. Sandy squeezes herself into a pair of pre-pregnancy jeans that are now anti-trend, the length and cut of jean styles perpetually in flux, marking her from a distance as a new category of woman: a mom, and not a cool one.

The second she exits her apartment building, a wave of humidity washes over them, carrying with it the stench of braised garbage from the trash barrels strewn around the sidewalk. If she stands perfectly still and doesn't breathe deeply, her jeans fit. Walking makes the waistline gouge her intestines; sitting will not be possible today. The best decision she can make is to bail. An easy lie would cover her. *Rosie got sick, sorry, can't make it.* Curiosity is the only thing pushing one foot in front of the other.

Sandy arrives at the Battery Park carousel neurotically early, and Steph is running late. She texts Sandy with updated ETAs and genuine apologies and drag-queen GIFs, hoping to appear sweet and funny, to distract them both from the chaos already in motion.

The sky is a smooth, colorless slab that wants to rain but can't. Sandy can feel her hair already betraying her. Why is it so important that this other woman find her pretty? Why is *pretty* the primary impression she wants to make? They're not sexual rivals. Justin isn't her boyfriend anymore. The impulse to best another woman, to win a contest with no prize, is hard to shake even now.

Desperate for air-conditioning, Sandy carries Rosie inside, where a young man with gluey side bangs informs her that she can't wait there for her friend—fire-hazard code, etc., etc.; she has to get on the carousel or leave. She hands over her debit card, feels the familiar pinch inside her chest whenever money leaves her wallet these days, and gets on the ride.

The carousel is a glass nautilus full of huge donut-shaped fish that spin and orbit one another. Each fish is illuminated from within by LED lights that shift between underwater shades of blue and green. Everything sparkles with the quality of water in the dim sunlight. Rosie's eyes ignite as they climb inside their dancing fish.

"What do you think, Roro?" Sandy asks her.

"Ohhhhhhhhhhhhhhh!" Rosie exclaims.

She holds Rosie on her lap and buckles them up. Xylophone music is piped in, a song Sandy recognizes but can't name. Rosie is unusually quiet, her eyes wide with amazement. They are enveloped by the sweet chimes of the song, until the melody becomes familiar and the words tumble out of Sandy's mouth.

Don't worry. About a thing. Cuz every little thing gonna be all right . . .

The sting behind her eyes, inside her nose, the pressure building in her throat—*no, not now!* Tears come on like a storm. Sandy stares up at the ceiling swirling with colored lights and tries to blink the tears to the corners of her eyes, where they might fall without smudging her mascara. She checks her face in the camera app of her phone. Just a normal person, a normal mom, having a nice normal Saturday with her daughter.

When the ride ends, Rosie screams with rage and the helplessness of someone who wants *more* but can't say it.

People constantly ask if Rosie is a "good baby." Sandy never knows how to answer the question. She is a baby, the one time in life when it should be assumed you are inherently good. Most of the time she is calm and happy, easy to make laugh with a tickle. Merely saying *tee–hee* sends her into a fit of deep belly giggles. But the second Rosie feels the tiniest pang of hunger, she throws her head back and wails, as if trying to tell the world how starving she is.

Her skin flushes a dark pink as she bawls, and people turn to stare. Sandy finds an empty bench in the park outside, where she unbuttons her shirt—she's forgotten to bring a cover-up—and nurses.

Rosie latches on for a few seconds, then spits out her boob and looks around. She babbles and coos at the blank sky, the scrawny gray saplings planted behind the bench, the birds cheeping in the branches. Then she nurses again. She pops on and off her mother's boob, too excited to eat.

According to the latest text, Steph is still about twenty minutes away. Sandy tries angling Rosie onto her other boob, hoping it will inspire her to concentrate. It would be ideal if Rosie was fed and happy by the time Steph and Ashley arrived. *I'm pretty and my body bounced back without effort and I'm wearing anti-trend jeans on purpose, this other mother will see. My baby is a good baby because I am a good mother, not the kind of woman who gets herself into this huge mess of a life.*

Rosie spits out her boob again and smiles at her mother. The ends of her blond hair are starting to curl. Her light-blue eyes focus on Sandy with a wordless intelligence. "You get it, don't you?" Sandy says to her daughter. "We're in this together, huh, Ro?" She *is* a good baby, whatever that means.

Then that good baby ejects a stream of puke directly into her mother's face. Hot and chunky, it gets in Sandy's hair, dripping down her neck, soaking through her shirt. Her white shirt. Such a rookie mistake. She rifles through her sleek black baby bag. There are two changes of clothes for Rosie but nothing for herself. Another failure.

Sandy wipes her face with her bare hand. She looks up. A woman and her child are standing in front of them.

"Oh, hi," Sandy says. "Are you—"

"Yeah," Steph says. She smiles.

She is tiny and strong, like a gymnast, with thick brown hair that was bleached and dyed pink several wash cycles ago and shaved in a left sidecut. She reminds Sandy of the girls in college who were so sexy and intimidating without trying, women who ate because something looked tasty, who made the first move. Whatever beauty contest Sandy had conjured in her mind is lost.

Steph had also wondered if this woman would be as pretty in real life as she presented herself in the fictional realm of social media, or if she was just a trick of filters and angles. No layer of puke is gross enough to hide the fact that Sandy is beautiful. *That motherfucker Justin does not deserve you,* she thinks.

"Babies have genius comic timing," Steph says instead, gesturing to the explosion.

"I'm sorry," Sandy says, fumbling to put her boobs back in her shirt.

Between Steph and Ashley is a Sherpa's haul of backpacks, shoulder bags, and totes. Steph and Ashley sit down on the bench and begin rummaging through all their stuff.

"I'm a mess," Sandy says.

"We got you," Steph answers. "Check that other bag, Ashley."

"Here." Ashley unearths a long light cardigan from one of the bags. She is short like her mother. Blue basketball shorts hang below her knees. She wears an oversized black hoodie with a picture of a chubby glowering teddy bear, gold chains hanging from his neck and brass knuckles on his paw.

"This will do the job," Steph says, handing the sweater to Sandy.

Sandy holds Rosie on her lap, then tries to change without being arrested for public exposure.

"You're not used to having help, are you?" Steph reaches to take Rosie from her arms, and having no other choice, Sandy lets her.

Steph presses her face into Rosie's neck. "Oh. My. God," she says.

"Look at the way her hair does this," Ashley says, tracing her finger around the spiral of Rosie's cowlick.

"Look at her cheeks. I think I might die."

Steph and Ashley catalog every single one of Rosie's features, as if no other baby on planet earth has ever been as cute. Several times Steph bites her own fist and Ashley presses her face against her sister's then pretends to die. They fall over her face with kisses.

"Mama, can I eat her foot?" Ashley says.

"Ask for forgiveness, not permission," Steph answers, putting Rosie's foot in her mouth.

Sandy balls up the dirty shirt and holds it in her hand.

"Here, put that in this." Without taking her eyes off Rosie, Steph pulls out an empty canvas tote from another of her bigger bags and hands it to Sandy. "Should we hug?" she says once Sandy is all cleaned up.

"I think we should definitely hug," Sandy replies.

The two women hold each other awkwardly on the bench, Rosie wedged between them, their backs angled in a way their skeletons cannot abide for long. Yet Sandy doesn't let go, and Steph makes no move to pull away from her. Sandy lets out a little sob.

"You've heard the saying, when the milk comes, so do the tears, right?"

"No. Oh my god. Story of my life these last seven months."

"Is that how old she is? She's so cute. And she looks so much like you! Justin's DNA loses again."

"She's got his eyes. Same as yours, Ashley."

Ashley sits next to Sandy on the bench and peers at the baby sitting in her lap. Her body leans into Sandy's with such trust. "I really like her ears," she says.

Steph met Justin at a punk club on the Lower East Side when she was still a high school kid from Staten Island. They were both in their militantly sober phase, part of a small faction of straight-edge kids who went to all the shows, trying, perhaps a bit too hard, to prove they were every bit as ferocious as the drug addicts in the scene. It was a phase they both grew out of, finding a healthy relationship to the occasional beer, letting go of the need to wage war for no reason, though not with each other.

"I thought I was hot shit, dating a guy in a band, a guy who could buy beer legally but didn't because he had principles." Steph rolls her eyes. "Now that I'm a mom, it's disgusting." Her voice lowers slightly, assuming it's enough to shield her child from what she says next. "What was he doing with me? I was a teenager. I'd murder anyone who tried that on Ashley."

Ashley looks up at her mother and also rolls her eyes, then returns to the long skeins of embroidery floss she's tying in elaborately patterned knots.

"It was basically trauma-bonding," Steph goes on, not bothering to whisper anymore. "My family is riddled with addiction, and his dad died of liver cirrhosis, and we were both desperately trying to control the chaos that made us super fucking sad."

"Mom, that's two curse words so far."

"Oh, so you are listening?" Steph opens the bag nearest her and pulls two dollars out of her wallet. Ashley snatches the money away. "She's extorting me a buck a swear. You better go to a state school, kid. I won't have any money left by the time you graduate high school. Where was I? Oh yeah, next thing I know I got knocked up."

Early in her pregnancy with Ashley, Steph moved in with Justin. A month later she moved out. "His mother and I don't exactly get along. She's Ashley's grandmother, so I respect her. But I definitely didn't need to live with her. I'm sure she'd agree if she was willing to, you know, *talk*."

"It's not just me?"

"God no. In all the years I have known this woman, she has only ever spoken to me about the weather and whatever preservative-laden food was on sale this week at the big-box store."

Sandy pantomimes every gesture of *yes, yes, me, too, same!*, nodding her head so enthusiastically it could snap off.

"You've had similar experiences with the Murrays?" Steph laughs.

"You have no idea," Sandy says. "Except, actually, you do. You know exactly what I've been through, I think."

"Did Tara throw your baby shower?"

"Yup."

"Did she play that gross game with the melted candy bars in the diapers, then measure your stomach in front of everyone and make them guess how fat you got?"

"Oh my god! Yes!"

"That woman is—" Steph looks at Ashley, who is in a flow state with her rainbow of strings. "She's . . . *interesting*." Her voice drops. "I have theories. We can discuss later."

The word *later* fills them both up like hot cocoa on a freezing cold day.

"But she's a genius for stain removal," Steph is quick to add.

"Legit talented," Sandy agrees.

Over the years she and Ashley had bounced around a lot, Steph goes on. She had apprenticed as a tattoo artist, painted sets for Broadway plays, worked in a shelter for runaway teenagers. Between each of these gigs were backbreaking stints in the restaurant industry. Now she is getting her PhD in psychology at Columbia.

"We're with my parents again in Staten Island. It's temporary. I have enough debt to make a homeowner wince, so I'm trying to chip away at that. My folks help a lot with Ashley, which is good because," her voice drops again to a bad whisper, "*you-know-who* has very limited availability."

The sun has burned off the low layer of clouds, revealing a hazy-blue sky. Sweat streams down Sandy's chest and back inside the cardigan Steph gave her. Why did she wear jeans? Why didn't they do this at home in their comfy weekend clothes with their feet up on the coffee table, just relaxing?

"Next time we hang out, we'll come to your house," Steph says, as though reading her mind. "Make life easier for you and Little Miss Pukey."

"Can we go on the carousel now?" Ashley asks.

Sandy explains that they've already ridden the carousel and apologizes for not waiting.

"I can't in good conscience spend more money on that thing."

"Don't worry. I got you," Steph says, whipping out a credit card.

Ashley and Steph cannot stop smiling and waving at Rosie, who flails her arms and shrieks in unbridled baby joy. Afterward they go to a noodle house on Wall Street with a half-off weekend special. The walls are covered floor to ceiling with graffiti, sigils, characters, and runes, some in English, some in Japanese, some a magical language mysterious to everyone except their authors. Steph gets out a Sharpie and writes her initials on the wall. As she's writing Ashley's, she asks Sandy, "What did you do about her name?"

Sandy looks uncertainly at the people behind the counter. They are young, possibly teenagers, blasting hip-hop from all over the world. They see the added graffiti and nod in approval. "I hyphenated. Walsh-Murray," she says, turning back to Steph. "I'm just Walsh."

Steph adds their initials next to hers and Ashley's then draws a heart around them all. They slurp huge bowls of ramen and talk and laugh until it is time to go. Ashley has a sleepover party back on Staten Island and they need to catch the ferry. Before they leave, Ashley presents Rosie with the bracelet she had been weaving earlier.

"She's been working on that all week," Steph says, astonished and proud. "I didn't know you were making that for your sister, honey."

"I have the same one." Ashley holds up her wrist to show a bracelet in the same chevroned pattern of blue and purple and green.

"It's beautiful," Sandy says. "I think if Rosie could talk, she'd tell you she loves it. Do you want to tie it on her?"

Ashley nods. Rosie squirms as Ashley struggles to hold her arm still to tie the bracelet ends together. Steph takes Rosie again so Sandy and Ashley can work together. She presses her nose into Rosie's head and inhales deeply. "Mmmmm, she still has the new-to-the-earth smell."

They finally get the bracelet around Rosie's chubby wrist. "There," Sandy says, and lets her hand find its way to Ashley's short, shiny hair. It feels like silk, the softest thing she's touched besides Rosie's skin.

"Thank you, Sandy," says Steph. "You've given us the greatest gift. I didn't want Ashley to be an only child, but I'm a one-and-done mom."

"She'll never have another baby after me," Ashley explains. "I ripped her hole to hole coming out."

Sandy spits out her water.

"Ashley!" Steph exclaims.

"What?" Ashley smiles. "You said we don't have to watch our mouth around family."

In any other world, they would never be friends. Sandy is aggressively basic. She watches reality TV without irony, only likes music you can dance to, the occasional Top 40 song you can cry to, and Taylor Swift. She does yoga for its ab-toning effects with no inkling of the myth of Hanuman, the spirituality of pranayama. Steph strongly suspects that Sandy had been in a sorority. Her nail color is always on trend. She deploys the cat-with-hearts-for-eyes emoji *a lot* for someone who has never owned a cat.

As a lifetime social-justice warrior, Steph has a major blind spot for straight white chicks. Who is she to assume that Sandy was in a sorority? *Are those even a thing anymore? Probably not.* Sandy is as complex as any other person on this planet, even with her laminated eyebrows and Brazilian waxes (she assumes).

And yet, the more she and Sandy keep talking, the more love keeps flooding in, engulfing her in a helpless devotion.

They have been talking two hours and their respective phones burn against their cheeks. It feels a little like high school, a little like falling in love. After Sandy gives Steph her whole life story in all its gory detail, Steph offers her own, the R-rated version she couldn't tell in front of Ashley.

"Justin was my first boyfriend. He was always cheating on me. I was always breaking up with him then taking him back. I was eighteen when Ashley was born, just graduated high school, super depressed. I didn't know what I was doing. I slept with him a couple times while I was pregnant, so I thought that meant we were still together, even though I had moved out of his mother's basement and back in with my parents. I thought the problem was Tara, and that once he 'lost' me he'd come to his senses and move out of his mom's place and we'd get our own apartment, where everything would be perfect. Again, I was eighteen."

"It's okay," Sandy tells her. "I was just as naïve at thirty-three."

"It's not triggering for you that I mentioned having sex with him, is it?" Steph asks. She had felt such intimacy so quickly with Sandy that she's lapsed into the carelessness she enjoys with people she's known forever.

Sandy laughs. "Not. At. All! Sex with Justin feels like one million years ago, like something a cavewoman ancestor of mine did."

"Okay, good! I feel the same way. Poor Justin."

"Poor boring-but-hung Justin."

"Do you want to hear the most ridiculous part?"

"Yes!"

Steph had been napping at home when she went into labor, two weeks before her due date. She called Justin, who didn't answer, and then pinged him over social media to get his attention, which worked.

"And he messages me, 'You're not in labor, it's just the calzone you had last night. I told you not to eat the whole thing.' Because, you know, he'd been pregnant and given birth so many times, he obviously knew what it felt like. So there I was, in my teenage bedroom with my posters of Patti Smith and Frida Kahlo, feeling like I'm going to shit a whole baby onto the floor any second. My parents weren't home—plus they're Catholic and kind of hated me for not getting married, so even though I'm living with them, in a lot of ways I'm on my own. The doctor finally called me back and I told her about my contractions and she said, 'Yeah, come in, you're in labor.' I tell Justin that now the doctor is saying I'm in labor. And do you know what he does?"

"I can't wait."

"Justin has me *call a car service*, because he doesn't want me to make a mess in his mom's car."

Sandy screams.

"So I call a car. Then he asks me to take the car all the way to Brooklyn to pick him up at work first so he doesn't have to worry about paying for parking at the hospital. I'm in too much pain to argue. I ride across the Verrazzano bridge trying not to have a baby in the back seat. Then, once I pick him up—I'm doubled over in pain, full-blown contractions electrocuting my uterus—he asks if we can stop at his house to pick up his fucking Xbox to take to the hospital with us. Because one of the guys he worked with said childbirth can take a long time and he might get bored."

"Oh. My. God!"

"And I said yes! I'm about to puke from pain but we go get his video games then cross the fucking Verrazzano again so I can have this baby."

Steph is laughing so hard, tears are falling down her face. It is the funniest story in her whole life. Now, finally, someone understands.

"It was the best thing that could have happened, honestly. Because by the time we got to the hospital, any trace of love or attachment, any notion that we might be okay *if only*, was completely gone. I was officially over him. It was the cleanest and most complete breakup I've ever had, at least in my heart. In my day-to-day life, all the co-parenting tangos, it's hard. But, yeah, that's when I ended things with him once and for all."

"I had to dump her," Justin says to Sandy later that night. "She's a bad seed."

He's come to see Rosie before going to another band's show. His beard is full and bushy now and it makes him look older but also more ridiculous. "Stay away from her," he says gravely. "I'm serious. There are dark spirits in this world. Not everyone can see them. But they walk among us all the time, and she's one of them."

Sandy hasn't told him about the carousel date, that she and Steph are in contact. Instead, she affects a curious, sympathetic attitude about his side of the story.

"She's bad news. Just bad. I'm going to apply for full custody of my daughter once she gets a little older. Then her mother will be the one paying me child support, not the other way around. But for now I have to play it all real careful. She's a dangerous woman."

"So *you* dumped *her*?" Sandy asks. "Just to be clear."

"Uh, yeah." His eyes narrow and dart away. "Yeah. I mean, I had to. She was going to sabotage my whole music career with her vindictive spells. When we first broke up it was like . . . she put a curse on me. I got bronchitis and then laryngitis, and for six months I couldn't sing. She made that shit happen with her mind."

"He's still on that *Steph, Mistress of the Dark* shit? Wow."

Sandy is in her bathroom, practically weeping with laughter, trying not to wake Rosie up. Steph paces the driveway at her parents' house, Ashley safely asleep inside.

"To be fair, I did go through a goth phase in high school. You know, like sixteen-year-olds do. I met Justin at the tail end of that phase. I'm sure I creeped the hell out of Tara. I guess she's never gotten over it. But yeah, apparently I am very powerful? Like I cast spells or something? I don't know. I can't keep track of their conspiracy theories. I wish it were true. If I had magical powers I'd reverse climate change, shake up the Supreme Court. I wouldn't waste them on Justin Murray's music career."

She looks at her parents' house squashed between their neighbors' identical houses, at all the broken homes full of broken people she can't fix. *If I had powers,* Steph thinks, *I wouldn't be living here.*

"I can't tell if his mother fed him this dark-arts stuff or if he came up with it on his own," she goes on. "I honestly never believed either of them was creative enough to conceive of something so bizarre."

"Tara said you were *trouble*," Sandy laughs.

"I think it's because I slept with a guy who used to be in his band. This was about seven years ago, after Ashley was born and Justin and I had broken up. I was still kind of in the same music scene as Justin, so I saw his crew from time to time. This one night I just wanted to get laid. And here was this guy, Logan, I'd known a long time. Neither of us wanted a relationship. It was a onetime thing. Simple as that. He quit the band after. It had nothing to do with me, though I did validate all the shit Logan hated about Justin and Pilot Error. I'm not good at keeping my mouth shut. Justin found out and *poof!* I've been riding a broomstick ever since."

What resulted, according to Steph, was the inverse of what Justin had detailed—he was so jealous of Steph's fling with his friend that he wanted to get revenge. He threatened to take her to court, to get full custody of Ashley. Justin had been taking his daughter only on the occasional weekends when he didn't have a show, so the visitation schedule was chaotic and unpredictable. He had offered Steph no money for anything, claiming she didn't need it because her parents took care of her.

"That was back when he was washing windows for this shithead in Greenpoint who paid him next to nothing, before his mom spent his dad's life-insurance policy buying him the truck and helping jump-start his own business. He didn't have much to give me back then. But I called his bluff," Steph says. "He's too ADHD to call a lawyer, make an appointment, all that. He sees Ashley as much as possible. He loves her, I know that, and she loves him. The upside to his immaturity is that he's a super fun dad. I'd never get in the way of their love. He's still a shit about keeping to a schedule—he cancels on her all the time—but I choose my battles. You have to with him."

The walls of Sandy's bathroom are dotted with stains—drips of product, splatters of essential oils, possible Rosie-poop. How did even the *walls* get filthy in this place? She takes the towel she uses as a bathmat and starts attacking each stain one by one.

"One day I'll have to ask him for money," Steph says. "I'm dreading it."

They hang up and Sandy gets on her knees to scrub. It's Justin's brand of craven idiocy to spin things exactly as he did. He probably believes his own lies. The more troubling thing is that Sandy has asked him for money, too, and he's given it to her—not much, but more than he'd ever given Steph. Sandy has had multiple opportunities to tell Steph this. It is something she ought to know. Even if Sandy had never met Ashley, she would feel guilty about her daughter receiving some kind of financial support while her big sister got nothing. But something stuck in Sandy's throat each time it came up, and she found herself staying quiet.

One morning Sandy wakes up and Rosie is one year old. She's the biggest she's ever been and still so small. She sleeps on her back, her right arm bent and resting on her forehead, like an actress in a silent film on the verge of fainting. "I've known you a whole year," Sandy whispers to her, only a little jealous of her sleeping in.

Tara buys a sheet cake with a photorealistic Disney princess screen-printed in edible ink, and they eat it awkwardly together at her house in Bay Ridge. According to Steph, Justin has not told her or Ashley about Rosie's existence. Sandy snoops for pictures of Ashley that she hadn't noticed at her baby shower. She finds four five-by-nine-inch framed school pictures of Ashley on the wall in the hallway leading to Tara's bedroom, but many more of Justin, as though he were still a child.

On Halloween, Sandy and Steph get together for a costume parade in Union Square. Ashley dresses as a ninja, which for some reason involves drawing a mustache and a thick black unibrow across her forehead with Magic Marker. Sandy dresses Rosie as a chicken. Ashley pushes her stroller in the parade and tells anyone who will listen, "This is my chicken."

That Thanksgiving, Sandy's dad and stepmom come to New York. Sandy sets the stage for her most pathetic rebellion—power-clashing Rosie's rainbow turtleneck onesie beneath a brown corduroy dress with rows of tiny pink horses galloping across it and a pair of tangerine tights. *Take that, you Midwestern rubes,* Sandy thinks, trying not to implode from dead-mom grief.

"Wow," her stepmom says as they arrive at the restaurant, "we certainly won't lose that baby in a crowd." Sandy's dad makes an obligatory goo-goo face at his granddaughter, then swivels back in his chair to spy the football game playing on the bar's TV.

After the second chardonnay, Sandy's stepmother expounds on a movie she'd watched on the plane, carping, "Girls these days think they can sleep with whoever they want, then they wonder why they're single and lonely at thirty. . . ." After dessert and another chardonnay: ". . . It's like my mother always said, why buy the cow if you can get the milk for free."

Both times Sandy looks at her dad. She searches his eyes for some recognition, some instinct to protect her or his granddaughter. Nothing.

Before she can process this, lights are strung up across the city for Christmas, and with it the pull to return to a home that no longer exists. It is not the easiest time of year for most people, but Sandy holds it together for Rosie, keeping things just friendly enough with Justin and Tara. She lets her friendship with Steph develop at a speed that feels safe and mature, resisting the urge to gallop into no-boundaries BFF-hood like she had with her old squad, women who are now ghosts of social media.

In December, the snowy streets of New York turn a shade of browning gray that makes the most cheerful Christmas-lights display look polluted. One dark afternoon, Sandy picks up Rosie at day-care and comes home to a depressing stack of envelopes in her mailbox. A notice says her building has been sold and the rent is going up an extra six hundred dollars per month in the new year. Next is her student-loan company saying the reprieve she'd applied for when Rosie was born is expiring, with monthly payments resuming in January. Then she opens an invitation from her friends Berkeley and Becca to Mary's baby shower. It is as thick as a wedding invitation, printed on cardstock with gold foil inside the envelope, a formal RSVP, and a save-the-date magnet of Mary showing off her baby bump. Sandy didn't know Mary had gotten pregnant. After

Mary stormed out of her baby shower, Sandy had texted her once to check in on her and never got a response.

Mary had been one of those fast friendships that got real deep real quick and always felt like it was based on a misunderstanding. She and Sandy met at a fraternity party in college. Mary got her period unexpectedly, making a big conspicuous stain on her white denim skirt. Out of pity, Sandy dumped a Solo cup of boxed merlot on her skirt as a literal red herring and escorted a very drunk Mary to a cab. Mary declared that Sandy's shoes that night—a pair of hot-pink high-heeled espadrilles—were *killer*. "Oh my god, I fuckin' love this girl," Mary slurred as they clopped through the crowd, stained and stumbling, drunk and giggly. "I knew you were cool the second I saw those shoes. I was like, this girl is my BFF." But they weren't Sandy's shoes. She'd borrowed them from her roommate. None of that mattered to Mary. Friendship was easy in college and seemed to stay that easy for a long time, until it wasn't anymore.

Now Mary is getting her moment in the motherhood sun, and while Sandy wants to be happy for her, a part of her is, there is so much resentment left over from her own baby shower. Besides, this is no ordinary shower. It's a full-blown girls' weekend at a disgustingly expensive spa in the Hamptons (but don't worry, the invite said, the spa had day rates if the full-weekend package was not an option). There are added fees to share the cost of Mary's prenatal massage treatments and facial and whatever else she wants, in addition to her regular registry of baby gifts.

"Whether you can make it or not," the invite proclaims, "please send a video of yourself sharing a funny story about Mary and any incriminating pictures from her wild party days for our PowerPoint on Saturday night."

"A PowerPoint?" Steph says, when Sandy texts her pictures of the invite. "Straight girls have gotten out of control."

"It's like a funny PowerPoint. An ironic one." Though, actually, it isn't. Her friends are nothing if not earnest in all things baby shower. She feels sad and jealous and resentful and just plain shitty after reading the invite, but sharing it with Steph makes it so much better. "They were my sorority sisters."

I knew it! Steph thinks. "I shouldn't judge," she says. "All my girl-friends from high school are alcoholics and drug addicts. I didn't re-alize what a messed-up crew I ran with until I had a baby and was forced to grow up. Ten years later I'm doing my thing while they're all still getting high or drunk every day."

"That's so intense," Sandy says.

Steph changes the subject. "What are your plans for Christmas?" There is a long pause. "Sandy?"

"I'm sorry. I swear I'm not this much of a crybaby. . . ."

"It's okay, honey. It's a hard time of year. If you want to talk about it, I can listen. I don't have class for an hour."

Sandy unloads. Her dead mom, her distant dad, her judgmental stepmom, her involuntary friend purge, her job, the rent hike, stu-dent loans, everything. Steph listens. She doesn't offer advice or try to change the way Sandy feels about things. She doesn't encourage her to be positive or point out ways she could be more grateful. She just listens. When she does speak, she says things like "Oh, honey, that's brutal," or "I'm here for all the gory details. Pop off." The un-burdening is like its own form of pleasure. Sweet emotional release.

"I was going to ask you this anyway, but now it's even more im-portant. Do you and Rosie want to spend Christmas in Staten Island with me? I have to warn you, my family kind of blows. My parents watch the Angry White Men news network all day long. At a deaf-ening volume. It's the worst. They've conveniently forgotten that their own grandparents were immigrants fleeing starvation and pov-erty and survived in this country only because of generous immigra-tion policies and social-welfare programs. They are absolutely terrified of everyone who doesn't believe exactly what they do, which includes me, their daughter. My sister doesn't talk to me. She's embarrassed to be related to me because I'm such a failure in her eyes. But my mom and my aunts are the best cooks in the world, and there is always way too much food. I know I'm not exactly selling it right now. You can wait until the last minute to decide—the invite is wide open. No pressure."

"What about Justin?"

"Who cares."

"I know, but seriously. I haven't told him about us yet."

"I'm happy to take the damage. He hates me anyway. I can say that I stalked you on social media, that I was the one who reached out to you, and that this is not about us but about his daughters getting to know each other."

"Do you think he'll be cool with that?"

"Probably not. He asked for Ashley to sleep over on Christmas Eve. He's blown her off so many weekends lately because of this new band he's in, and I think he feels guilty. So you and Rosie could sleep in Ashley's room if you want, and then when Justin drops Ashley off on Christmas morning, we'll have ourselves a dramatic reveal. He's scared of my dad, so he won't dare yell at us. It will look like a stunt, and it kind of is, but what's the alternative? Have a thoughtful, nuanced conversation with him? I've tried that a thousand times and never had any success. So we might as well do what we want and let him have his reaction, which is more about his insecurity than about us."

"Can I think about it?"

"Of course! And I mean it, no pressure. Something tells me we have a lifetime of holidays together in our future, so if this isn't the year, it's okay."

For the most part, Sandy had grown up among white people who were simply white. Maybe some long hyphenate of Swedish-Finnish-German-Scottish-Dutch. But all that really meant was Midwestern white. The Santorellas are an Italian American stereotype come to life.

"Just remember the first rule of Christmas," Steph says when she opens the front door of her parents' house. A cacophony of voices tumble out like it's a Midtown bar. "Everything that's bad is worse on Christmas."

"Okay," Sandy says. "What's the second rule?"

Sweat curls the shorter hair of Steph's overgrown sidecut in cute little commas. Her face is flushed, her dark eyes febrile. She takes Rosie into her arms and ushers Sandy inside. "I don't know. We never make it that far."

The men of the family are gathered in the living room, yelling over a TV on full volume. "The war on Christmas" is mentioned several times, both on and off the screen. The women sit around a large dining room table with coffee mugs, picking at the food—a golden-brown turkey, linguini and clam sauce, a trough-sized pan of baked ziti, scallops wrapped in bacon, shrimp cocktail, lobster fra diavolo, an enormous bowl of salad, several loaves of bread, every kind of cookie. They buzz in and out of the kitchen, lingering over the men periodically to replace empty plates and cups with full ones, then back to the dining room and kitchen. Children chase one another and yell, get yelled at to be quiet by the adults, and yell right back at them.

Steph's mother, Nancy, is barely five feet tall, a shorter, rounder version of Steph, her thick brown hair laced with white. She stirs a bubbling pot of fish stew on the stove.

"Ma, this is Rosie."

Nancy takes one look at Rosie and screams. "Are you kidding me with this face?!" She takes the baby from Steph and kisses Rosie aggressively on her mouth, cheeks, and neck.

"Poor Justin," Nancy says. "The genes are very weak in his family."

"She has his eyes," Sandy offers.

Nancy wrinkles her brow, shakes her head. "His stone, your setting. See?" She traces the outline of Rosie's then Sandy's eyes with her finger, and Sandy's muscles go slack. It had been . . . she couldn't say how long since someone touched her with such tenderness.

A pair of aunties descend on them. One grabs Rosie and slaughters her with more full-on mouth kisses. The other aunt puts a heaping bowl of stew into Sandy's hands.

"What are you doing?" Nancy snaps at her sister. "Give her some bread."

"Oh, thank you, it's okay. I'm fine with this."

The aunt tears off a hunk from a sesame-crusted loaf and drops it into Sandy's bowl. She pulls a chair out for Sandy in the breakfast nook and pushes her into it, yelling at her to relax. The moment Sandy has finished her stew, another woman puts down a plate of prosciutto and cantaloupe for her to eat. A slice of cheesecake soon follows. Rosie is passed around the house from woman to woman, all of them kissing her face and leaving smears of frosty-pink lipstick on her cheeks.

"You can try to say no to them, but they don't have the ability to hear it." Steph peels the ham off a slice of cantaloupe on Sandy's plate and plops the salted melon into her mouth.

"Aren't you ashamed to waste food like that?" An elderly uncle hobbles between Steph and Sandy and lifts the thin slice of prosciutto off the plate, tsking them before swallowing the meat in one gulp. "When we was kids, our mother woulda given us one of these if we tried this vegetarian snowflake crap with her." He raises his hand like he's going to strike someone, a ghost of his child self, on the head.

"Hey, Uncle June," Steph says. "How's Pete doing on the methadone program? Is he home on work release yet?" The old man grumbles and walks away. "You have no idea how glad I am you're here." She squeezes Sandy's hand.

"I feel like I should be worried about my daughter," Sandy says.

Steph cranes her neck to search for Rosie in the fray.

"Looks like my sister, Vickie, has her now. Bad news is Vickie is a judgmental bitch. Good news is all the Santorella women are baby whisperers. Rosie's too young to be indoctrinated by their bullshit, so for now she's actually in good hands. I have to deprogram Ashley every night before bed. Yesterday she referred to the cashier at our grocery store as 'an illegal.'"

After an hour the crowd starts to disband, prompting more voices booming their goodbyes. Steph's mom finally sits down with them at the small table in the kitchen. Her hair is sweaty and matted to her neck. Dark circles beneath her eyes confess a lifetime of nights like this, cooking, cleaning, serving. She looks more than tired. She looks sad. Sandy reverts to the sorority-girl playbook: when confronted with a woman in silent ineffable distress, compliment the hell out of her appearance.

"You have the thickest, most gorgeous hair I've ever seen, Mrs. Santorella. What products do you use?"

"Call me Nancy, hon. And I use whatever is on sale at the grocery store."

Nancy's face is still sour, so Sandy continues, "You're lucky. You have naturally beautiful hair."

Nancy munches on a pizzelle and points with her chin to her daughter.

"Stephanie has naturally beautiful hair, too, but she won't make the effort."

"Yep, getting my PhD at an Ivy League school, seeing clients at the most underfunded clinic in New York, raising a kid—just floating down Lazy River," Steph mutters.

"See how nice Sandy does her hair?" Nancy goes on. "You could be so pretty if you tried."

"Ma, please, why don't you go lie down, put your feet up—"

"I've become chemically dependent on keratin treatments," Sandy jumps in. She has unwittingly started a fight, and now it's her responsibility to fix it. "My kid might not go to college because of how much I have to spend so that people don't mistake me for a scarecrow."

"All's I'm saying, it wouldn't kill my daughter to take an interest in her appearance."

"I like my appearance the way it is." Steph rolls her eyes, looking exactly like Ashley.

"You want to scare men away? Fine! Die alone. See if I care." Nancy storms off.

"Wow," Sandy says. "That pivot was wild and fast."

"The Santorellas are a master class in displacing your inner pain," Steph says, watching the hallway where Nancy has disappeared into a bathroom. She listens for the sound of her mother crying, not knowing which is worse—to know her mother is crying alone, or to hear the silence of her holding it in, even in private. She turns slowly back to Sandy. "My brother died on December twenty-ninth. It'll be eleven years this week."

"Oh god. I'm so sorry."

"It's hardest on my mom. Her only coping strategy is to run herself ragged until she drops from exhaustion. Last Christmas she ended up in the emergency room. We thought she was having a heart attack. Turns out she just got dehydrated. From cooking."

"I saw her drink a little water, if that helps."

"It's okay." Steph looks up from her hands, where she has been ripping tiny threads of skin off her cuticles. "I mean, it's not okay at all. I miss my brother so much. We all do. But I'm lucky in that I can actually talk about him. So while it hurts to think about, especially this time of year, at least all my hurt is surrounded by light and air.

The rest of them swallow their pain until it festers and rots and comes out sideways. Usually as anger, often at me for talking about him. Or at me in general."

"Oh for Christ's sake—would they stop whining about global warming!" Steph's dad screams at his television. "It's colder than a nun's *mutande* outside! What warming?"

"Owning the libs is also a super fun way to escape the pain of your dead son," Steph says.

"How did he die, if you don't mind my asking?"

"Fentanyl. Another thing they won't talk about. As far as they're concerned, the heart of a perfectly healthy nineteen-year-old just stopped beating one night in the bathroom of a bar."

"Steph, that's devastating."

"It is devastating. Thanks for saying that. For using that exact word." She wipes away some tears. "I miss him a lot. I wish he could have met Ashley. I wish I could have helped him. I wish he were here."

"I get it now," Sandy says. "The first rule of Christmas. But you know, the opposite is true, too."

"How so?"

"Everything that's great is at peak greatness tonight. Rosie has never been cuter or more loved in her entire life than she is right now in your house. Like, I could cry how happy I am watching all these people freak out over how cute she is. I didn't know until I met you how badly I needed to see this reaction to my kid, and here it is, louder than ever. This food is the best food I've ever eaten. It would be good on any random day of the year, but these women clearly went all out because it's Christmas, and I can taste the difference. And you." She forks a few strawberries from Steph's half-eaten cheesecake and lets them sit in her mouth a moment, absorbing the sweetness. "You're a very cool chick, but I've never been more obsessed with you than I am tonight."

Steph smiles. Her dark eyes sparkle with tears. "How did you get like this?"

"Like what?"

"Like this radiant being made of light."

Sandy waves it off. "Story of my stupid life. Always looking for the bright side."

"No, it's not a generic be-positive meme. It's this off-the-charts empathy."

"You're super empathetic, too."

"Yeah, but I work at it. I have to trick my mind to stop fighting and accept things as they are, then hope that my heart follows. With you it's . . ."

She takes a deep breath.

"What?" Sandy asks.

"Natural."

The next morning goes exactly as Steph had predicted. Justin comes to the house with Ashley. Steph's dad is there to open the door, and though the old man is a good three inches shorter than Justin, he is physically intimidating, like a Roman statue. Justin shifts from foot to foot and does not make eye contact. When Steph and Sandy come downstairs to meet them, Justin's small eyes bulge.

"Merry Christmas," Steph says, tossing a dash of peppery mirth at Justin's discomfort.

"Yeah," he says.

"Rosie, can you say Merry Christmas to Daddy?" Sandy urges.

Rosie utters a slew of impassioned vowels that vaguely resemble *Merry Christmas,* then puts her fist in her mouth.

"Can I hold her?" Ashley asks Sandy. Sandy puts her into Ashley's arms. "Isn't she so cute, Daddy?"

"Cute as a button. Just like you."

Steph wants to ask Justin if he smells burning sulfur. *Do you feel a tingling on only one side of your body?* She's hoping he has a tiny little stroke, something he survives but that leaves him speechless for the rest of his life. "Want to come in? We have a full spread laid out."

Justin looks at Steph's dad, who has said nothing this whole time, his face a sculpture carved into the side of a building, something that has survived millennia of earthquakes and war and gives zero fucks.

"Daddy?" Ashley says.

"Um, I can't, sweetheart. I promised Grandma T that I would drive her to my aunt's house, then I have some work to do later."

"On Christmas?" Sandy asks.

"Yeah. No rest for Daddy."

"Well, feel free to come by later," Steph offers.

"Yep." Justin bends down to kiss Ashley and then Rosie, makes an awkward military-style salute to Steph's dad, then leaves without looking at the two mothers.

The rest of the day is a slightly softer version of the night before. Ashley opens her presents then food, food, and more food is laid out on the table. As soon as something is finished, Nancy puts out a tray of something else. The living room TV blares angrily. Steph's dad sits in the same spot on the couch all day, dozing off, then waking up to shout back at the TV, over and over again. Nancy continues to bring him food and drinks and clear away the plates he's finished.

Around dinnertime Vickie comes over again with her husband and their two kids, Montana and Mason. Without all the extended family to fill the room with noise, the tension of her arrival is starker. The second they walk in the door, there is a palpable shift in the house, like the air pressure before a storm.

Nancy hugs Vickie's husband, Joe, first, then her grandkids, and Vickie last. She thanks Joe for plowing their driveway in the last storm, apologizes proactively for the next snowstorm that is coming. There is a timbre of fear in her voice, an anxiety to please this son-in-law. Nancy will not allow herself to rest now that there are two men who might possibly need her.

"Ma, sit down. They can get their own beer," Steph tries, and when that doesn't work, she tricks Nancy into sitting down by asking for a better look at her brooch. It's a Christmas tree made of green and red rhinestones, a small but significant effort toward self-care on Nancy's part. "It really brings the whole outfit together."

Nancy quickly takes the brooch off and pins it on Steph's flannel shirt.

"Here, you have it. It will look better on you."

"Mom," Vickie cries, "you said I could I have that brooch when you die!"

"Relax, Vick," Steph says. "She probably got it free with the purchase of a foot scrub from the Avon catalog. You don't need to call a lawyer."

A powder keg explodes: after a brief but intense shouting match among the Santorella women, Nancy locks herself in her bedroom.

"I'm going to take a little nap," Steph says to Sandy. "I don't mean to ditch you, but I need to preserve my strength for the emotional marathon. If you want to take a nap, too, I promise Rosie will be safe. Like you saw, my family loves babies."

"Should Rosie and I go home?"

"If you want. I won't make you stay."

"Do you want me to stay?"

Steph bites her lip. Her eyes start to well up. "Yeah? You don't have to! It's just so much better with you here. I'm okay. I've been dealing with them my whole life. I got this."

"I'm staying," Sandy says firmly. "And I'm going to take that nap offer. I haven't slept in over a year."

Steph retreats to her bedroom and Sandy naps in Ashley's room. It doesn't seem like sleep. It's more like Sandy is a machine that someone has unplugged. She sinks into a deep nothing. No dreams, no tossing or turning, just a black void in which she doesn't move or think or feel anything. She wakes up feeling better than she has in years.

Out in the living room, Steph is on the floor with the kids, assembling a large multilevel dollhouse, the big present her parents had gotten for Ashley and Montana to share. Rosie is ripping scraps of wrapping paper and shouting in solidarity every time Steph's dad yells at the TV.

"Did he text you?" Steph whispers to Sandy.

"I honestly forgot that I have a phone," Sandy replies.

"This is what he sent me." Steph hands Sandy her phone.

"Your not going to get away with this you fucking witch" it says.

"Let me go find my phone. I lost it somewhere in the blankets."

Her message from Justin is milder but not without threat: "We need to talk."

"He needs a juice box and a nap," Steph says.

Sandy sits down next to her on the floor, and the two of them get to work assembling the dollhouse. There are tiny squares of imitation linoleum to adhere to the floors and different patterns of wallpaper printed on stickers that need to be cut around windows and doorways in the various rooms. The four children play alongside them.

"That's the mom's room," Ashley tells her cousins and sister, pointing to the room Steph has just finished with a pink floral wallpaper. "Her kids will sleep here," she says, placing a tiny crib in the room upstairs with the gabled ceiling.

"What about the daddy?" Montana asks.

"There is no daddy," Ashley says.

"But there has to be a daddy," her cousin replies.

"Not necessarily," Ashley replies. "Not if the mommy used a donor."

"Shhh!" Vickie covers Montana's ears with her hands. She looks at Nancy, who's standing over the whole scene with arms crossed. "Does she actually teach her daughter sick stuff like that?"

"Of course she doesn't, Vick," Nancy says. "Ashley knows that normal babies have a mommy and a daddy who are married and love each other."

"Not always. Sometimes there are two mommies or two daddies," Ashley argues.

"See, Joe?" Vickie calls to her husband. "This is why I can't have my kids spending time at their own grandmother's house."

Joe sits mutely on the couch, three feet away from his father-in-law. He sighs. "*She* gets to live here rent-free every time her life falls apart. *She* gets them to watch her kid for nothing. We have to pay strangers to watch our kids. We have to pay a mortgage. It's not fair."

Steph scoops Ashley and Rosie into her arms and hugs them tight. "Life's not fair," she says to the children, "but even when it's not fair, we always have choices. And we can choose to be kind," she says.

"No matter what," Sandy adds.

* * *

After a very tense and delicious dinner, Sandy calls a car to take her and Rosie back to Manhattan. Steph waits with them in the driveway. The fresh winter air is cold and reviving. The sky is as dark now as it will be at midnight, and a few stars are visible.

"I'm not saying everything was perfect before Mark died, but it wasn't like this," Steph says.

"I had a great time. I mean it. You don't have to apologize."

"I know. I just want you to understand."

"Then tell me. What was it like?"

Steph looks at the sky and smiles. "It was crazy and loud—that part's the same. But I had Mark. I could come outside here like we are now, and he would smoke a cigarette and I would lecture him to quit smoking and he would listen to me and just love me. And together we could laugh at how crazy they are, because back then they were funny-crazy, not tragic-crazy. Then he went and OD'ed like an idiot. He left me alone with those people. I hate myself for saying that, but I can't help it. After he died, everyone was so fucking sad. I was so fucking sad. And the worst part was that there was no one to talk to in the driveway anymore."

Sandy looks down at the driveway. It's painted in huge faded bands of white, red, and green.

"Did your dad paint the driveway for Christmas?"

"What? No." Steph is confused by the question. She looks down at her feet and remembers. "Oh, that. It's the Italian flag."

"Painted on your driveway?"

"Yeah."

"Like, permanently. And huge. Four times the size of an actual flag someone would fly from an actual flagpole."

"That is correct."

"I hate to be the one to break it to you, Steph, but I don't think your family has ever been normal."

Steph cackles like a witch. It's infectious, and soon Sandy is laughing, too. They become hysterical. Their laughter screeches and rises into the air, tearing a hole in the darkness. Pain and stress rise to the surface of their bodies and fizz away in a million psychic bubbles of laughter.

"You know, when I got pregnant with Ashley, I honestly thought it would fix everything." Steph wipes the tears from her eyes, takes a deep nourishing breath. "I really truly believed she would heal my broken family just by being born. Like, who could be angry and mean or depressed and numb when there was a cute little baby to hold? I was positive she would save us."

"I thought Rosie would cure me from missing my mom," Sandy confesses. "She made me miss her even more."

She looks up at the sky. Without trying, she finds Orion. His three-point belt twinkles brighter than anything else in the black night.

"But you know what?" Steph says. "Ashley fixed *me*. I know I'm not supposed to say that, and I get why. It's unhealthy to put that kind of pressure on your kid, to make it their responsibility to fix you. But she did. She saved my life. The moment I looked at her, I made a promise to us both: it stops here—the addictions, the secrets, the depression and rage. She would never live that way. We would be different."

Steph's head is turned up to the sky, looking at Orion, too.

"It worked," Sandy says after a long pause. "You changed."

"And them—" Steph gestures to the house. "They stayed the same."

"You know you don't deserve to be treated like that. At all."

"Free childcare, free rent, free food—it all costs something."

"We have choices," Sandy says. "Someone amazing taught me that today." Steph smiles. They don't know what their choices are in that moment, but the possibility brings them hope.

Justin calls Sandy the next day. A combination of fear and instinct tells her not to answer. He won't leave a voice message, she knows, but a barrage of texts will follow. And she's right.

Sandy is not ordinarily savvy in conflicts. She tends to buckle quickly, to run away and hide as soon as she can, and if she can't get away, she's trained herself to absorb a measure of abuse that allows the aggrieved party to get it out of their system then leave her alone. Her parents' marriage had been full of conflict and both of them dragged her into it. They would scream or cry, sometimes indicting Sandy for not taking a side, and she would let them. Looking at the clock, she would time their rants, which never topped forty-five minutes. The price to pay. It allowed her to go back to her room, log on to her computer, and chat with friends and boys about frivolous stuff as though none of this emotional turmoil were happening.

"You just made the biggest mistake of your life . . . you went over to the dark side . . . the enemy . . . your going to regret this for the rest of your life . . . your going to come crying back to me and you know what? I won't forgive you . . ."

If she actually loved Justin, it would have hurt a lot, but Sandy is able to read it all with clear, dispassionate eyes.

"No more money from Daddy. If you keep talking to that witch your on your own."

You're, dumbass. And You mean the paltry sum you sometimes give me on no kind of regular basis? Sandy does not say back. "It might be helpful to cool off before we make a plan," she texts instead.

"You broke my trust and this is the consequence. Mom is disgusted with you. She won't be coming over anymore either. No more free food and diapers. See how it feels to be BETRAYED."

Sandy makes a spreadsheet of every trackable monetary exchange from Justin (most of them were on her cash app) and then another list of all her expenses directly related to Rosie: health insurance, which she pays for on the market as she no longer has coverage through her job; monthly daycare; a compilation of all her grocery-store receipts; a digital record of online purchases at baby stores. Then she calls Steph.

"I'm so sorry I never told you before." She discloses exactly what she has gotten from Justin now that she has it all tracked and recorded. "I wasn't trying to be greedy. It wasn't an *if she gets money from him, it will mean less for me* kind of thing. I honestly felt so guilty that I was getting help from him and you weren't. I didn't know how to bring it up."

"Never in a million years would I think that," Steph assures her. "I'm sorry you didn't get more, and sorrier that you're in the same boat as me now and that you don't have parents helping you out."

"I don't know what I'm going to do. I've been demoted at the magazine. They're paying me freelance rates now, which means I don't get a salary. I can't afford daycare without Justin."

"You could totally use my mom anytime you want. She and my dad won't shut up about how cute you and Rosie are. They can be so nice to people who aren't me."

"Your parents are generous, but it's not exactly ideal for either of us."

"You're right."

"But we have choices!" Sandy laughs.

"We do!" Steph laughs harder. "If only we knew what they were...."

The first time Steph tried to move out of her parents' house, it was to Justin's apartment in Tara's basement. Pregnant and imperious, she threw out all the processed food in Justin's tiny fridge, insisting they become vegetarians. She succeeded only in sending him upstairs to his mother's kitchen, where she bought whatever he wanted. Tara did all the laundry for Justin, who was twenty-two and still claiming that he didn't know how. Tara would only call her *Stephanie*, no matter how many times this pseudo mother-in-law was corrected, and in return Steph always "forgot" to lock the front door, enraging the already paranoid widow, who was sure they would all be murdered by a serial killer one day because of the careless pregnant teen who lived with her son.

Steph returned home to her parents, too drained from first-trimester nausea and fatigue to really process the failed experiment. If she did, she'd have been sure that Tara and Justin were impossible and it was all their fault. She was better off with her parents, no matter how imperfect that arrangement was.

The second time Steph moved out was three years later. She had a toddler now and a minimum-wage job as an apprenctice at a trendy tattoo studio on the Lower East Side. She'd recently transferred from CUNY to NYU, with the high-interest loan to prove it. "Proving it" was her motivation at this phase of her life. She was behind normal girls her age in so many ways, decades ahead in others, and she just wanted the outside of her life to finally reflect her insides. Moving out was the only way to show that she was on the right path.

If she had been asked at the time who she was proving this to, she would have answered *herself*, which was mostly true; but beneath the dry and dismal surface of this lowercase truth were also her parents, who had no faith in her to ability to succeed, and her older sister, who had recently gotten married and acted like there was no greater achievement for a woman.

So Steph found an ad online for a "kindly old lady" looking for a housemate to do light cleaning, grocery shopping, etc., in exchange for a small stipend and a free place to stay. The woman's house was in south Brookyn and was big enough for Steph and Ashley to each have their own room. So she packed up Ashley's bed and toys and books, all their clothes and a few decorations, and moved into what she would soon describe as a lower-middle-class *Grey Gardens*. The kindly old woman turned out to be as mean as a snake. She was incontinent and refused to wear adult diapers, so Steph was doing laundry for her every day, including in the middle of the night, when she'd wake up screaming and wet. One day the woman's little shih tzu bit Ashley on the finger and the woman blamed Steph, whose job it was to walk the dirty, un-housebroken mop of a dog. Steph quit on the spot. Ashamed, she called her dad and asked him to come over with his truck and help her move all of their stuff back home.

"I knew you'd be back," her dad said as he helped her carry Ashley's bed up the driveway to their house. They hadn't done anything with her old room. It was ready for her to move back in. A relief and an affront in one punch.

The third time Steph moved out, she had a little more perspective. Ashley was four now, ready to start school, and that school would not be in Staten Island, where Steph had encountered so many forms of conformist suburban torture. She had started dating a woman she met at an Al-Anon meeting, a woman with a real corporate job and a real apartment in the West Village, a grown-up who had things figured out, who appreciated what an old soul Steph was and loved her despite her messiness. At least that's what it was like in the first three months of dating. Once Steph and Ashley moved in, her girlfriend became controlling and critical. She liked the idea of a step-child but not the reality, always suggesting that Ashley spend the weekends with Steph's parents if she wasn't with Justin. She also drank a lot more than Steph realized.

"I knew you'd be back," her dad said again. "That lady seemed nice, but no one wants a roommate with a kid."

Steph was too defeated to correct the bisexual erasure of *room-mate*. Of all her experiments in adulting, this one was the worst, because Ashley was old enough to remember. Not the girlfriend so much as her school, her teachers, her friends in the West Village. She had to start pre-K over in the middle of the year at the same school where Steph and her siblings had gone. Steph had to confront some of the same teachers she had once known, now as the single mom still working on that elusive undergraduate degree. She had to endure the sneers of her sister, who had become a mother herself and felt even more entitled to judge than before.

She vowed never to do it again. The most important thing in a child's life was stability, even if that stability meant a narrow-minded Staten Island school district and grandparents who loved her but couldn't help seeing her and their adult daughter as a problem and a mistake. She would prove to them all—but most important, to Ashley—that she was a sturdy parent. There would be no more bouncing around, no more changing schools in the middle of the year, no more romantic partners playing Mom or Dad in the short term. They would be stable. They would stay put.

Then she met Sandy.

"What if we move in together?" Steph says.

It is a few days after Christmas, a few days before the new year, a magical liminal space where everyone is half asleep and dreaming out loud.

"What if we can make our schedules work so that I don't need my parents and you don't need that daycare center? We could split expenses and Mom duties. We could make it work."

The jump in rent from a one-bedroom to a two-bedroom apartment is actually not that much, Steph explains, which various real estate apps confirm, and when split between two people, rent could actually be cheaper than what Sandy is paying for her studio. They probably can't afford the Columbus Circle neighborhood where Sandy lives now, but in Washington Heights there are still some deals to be had.

"What do you think?" Steph says.

To make space for Rosie in her 380-square-foot studio, a pregnant Sandy had studied a reality show about the crew of a super yacht. She learned how to rig the walls of her apartment with hooks and shelves, converting every available surface to double as workspace or storage. She chops vegetables on her windowsill and stores her silverware in plastic jars hung with twine off the side of a bookcase; that same bookcase holds extra diaper wipes, towels, cardboard baby books, and the few remaining novels she hasn't given away. Preserving floor space had become more important as Rosie grew from charming-but-inert blob of infant to curious, crawling baby, and so Sandy downsized from a regular-sized trash can to a small one that fit under her sink, until that space was co-opted for pots and pans; now she reuses delivery bags, which requires her to take out the trash at least twice a day.

Is this the worst fate that has ever befallen a single mother? Certainly not. Sandy is able to solve all these problems with clarity of mind, not battling a brain on fire with mental illness or addiction, even if she's solving them alone. Both she and Rosie breeze in and out of doctors' appointments because they are fundamentally healthy and able-bodied, an unmerited gift. White privilege makes both their lives easier in countless invisible ways she can take for granted if she wants. There are women living a few blocks away from her who have to choose between buying diapers and buying food. Thatcher is a narrow-minded clown, but Rob makes sure there is enough work for Sandy so that she doesn't lose her income completely. As executor of her mother's estate, Sandy had to pay off some considerable debt her mother left behind. What remained of her life-insurance payout afterward has kept Sandy's head above water, whether or not Justin chips in. The hospital bill plus her six weeks of unpaid maternity leave had set a sizable chunk of that money on fire. That it was there in the first place was more than some people would ever have.

Sandy lies on her bed and watches Rosie snore in her spacesuit-looking sleep sack. The seals of her eyelids and lips make three perfect dashes across her face. Somewhere in the dream cycle, Rosie is tackling big things, and all of a sudden she sighs. Her nostrils, tiny as chrysanthemum petals, flare and then relax. The beauty of her brings Sandy to tears.

Somehow this twenty-three-pound baby will take up the majority of Sandy's queen-sized bed in the night. Another war of attrition. She had tried sleep training, and Rosie's screams were unlike any the baby had made before, a howl of existential terror so piercing Sandy vowed never again. Life became easier, sweeter, when she decided to keep her baby in the bed with her. It adds an extra thirty minutes of sleep when she can just roll over and plop a boob in Rosie's mouth rather than stand up, reach into the crib, lift her out, nurse, get her back to sleep, then successfully lay her in the crib again without waking her. The preciousness of those extra minutes is immeasurable.

She touches Rosie's chest, small and curved like the hull of a toy boat. It rises and falls as she breathes. The soft rabbit's foot of her heart thumps wildly inside. Sandy is alive and capable and present. What else could matter?

But it is only seven o'clock and there is so much to do, many more problems to solve today so that tomorrow might be less of a shit-show. She makes a grocery order on an app and double-checks to ensure the delivery window is a time she will be home. She doesn't know how much longer she will be able to afford this luxury, but for now it is a chore she can do on her phone in the dark, her baby sleeping next to her. She adjusts her diaper subscription to reflect Rosie's growing size, sends a few work emails, reschedules the pediatrician checkup on the portal, pays some bills. Whoever said "sleep when the baby sleeps" was not a single mother.

When all of this is done and she is sure Rosie is asleep for the long haul, another two hours at least, Sandy sneaks into the bathroom to take a shower. If Rosie keeps sleeping in the pattern she's maintained for the past few weeks, Sandy will have time to shampoo *and* condition her hair, shave her legs, thighs and all, maybe even exfoliate and gua sha her face. Like a day at the spa, except for the mildew blackening the corners of her shower and creeping up the grout, the ring of yellow around the tub, the occasional cockroach that climbs out of the drain, waving its spindly antennae at Sandy's naked body.

She lifts the bathmat off the tub floor to assess just how bad the situation is. The suction cups release with a rude succession of loud pops. Sandy holds her breath, counts *one, two, three, four* . . . The baby does not wake up. The white-noise machine roaring at her bedside has protected her in a blanket of sound like a good mama jet engine.

There is a pattern of brown circles on the bathtub floor where the mat was. She throws the water valve to its hottest level and fills the bathroom with steam. Perhaps the scalding water can kill some of the germs crawling around her feet. The water feels good, purifying. She shaves one leg, then puts her foot on the tub's rim to the shave the other when the water sluicing beneath her loosens her hold and she slips.

She falls down hard and fast. Her arms slam on the insides of the tub, sparing her head the trauma of hitting the tiles or the floor. Her tailbone takes the impact instead. Pain strikes her coccyx and zaps her spine. For a moment Sandy cannot breathe.

Is this it, the moment it all comes crumbling down? What if I'm paralyzed; what if I never get up again? What would happen to Rosie? How long would her baby have to cry before a neighbor called the cops and the fire department broke down the door? A long time. Too long.

The hot water feels too hot now, and Sandy is relieved—if she can feel the water, she is not paralyzed. Slowly, carefully, she lifts herself. Slowly, carefully, she limps out of the bathroom, pain shooting down her legs and up to her neck, her towel dragging behind her. She lies on the bed next to Rosie. Her wet hair soaks the pillow. She wraps the towel around her like a skimpy blanket.

She finds her phone charging by the bed and holds it to her chest. Her sad, pathetic lifeline. The truth is, to be a single mother of an infant is to live in a state of petrifying vulnerability twenty-four hours a day.

"Would you be willing to put something in writing?" she texts Steph. "Like some roommate ground rules. That we could have notarized, just in case?"

Steph is able to line up viewings for apartments that are all a little cheaper than their maximum hypothetical rent. The first place they look at is a sixth-floor walk-up in south Harlem with beautiful cityscape views and architectural details that make a Midwesterner like Sandy swoon.

"Built-in shelves!" Sandy says. "Pre-war crown molding!"

Steph points out that it will be a long time before Rosie can reliably walk up those stairs on her own. "Then add a bag of laundry to that hike. There's no laundry in this building."

They both agree: pass.

The second place they look at is deeper in Harlem and huge only by New York standards, clocking in at seven hundred square feet. But a mega luxury condo is under construction across the street.

"That means jackhammering for at least a year, probably more. It's not rent-stabilized, so rents will definitely go up when all the rich people move in across the street, bringing their nannies and dog walkers with them," Sandy says.

Over the course of two weeks, they look at five more apartments. Some are perfect and snatched up before Sandy and Steph can get an application in. Some are terrible and also get rented before they can make the first move. When they finally manage to file an application, Steph's credit score gets them rejected. That they are two single mothers living together as roommates excludes them from another listing.

"Is that legal?" Sandy asks.

"Do you have the time or the money to find out?" Steph answers.

At last they find a building in Washington Heights whose manager is either too lazy or corrupt to ask for a credit check. The rental is a ground-floor apartment that gets a surprising amount of natural light. It's pretty dumpy on the outside, small on the inside, but is a short walk to a park with a playground.

There is a Dominican chicken restaurant on the same block, so after touring the apartment, the moms and kids settle into an orange Formica booth to eat dinner and discuss. The menu is entirely in Spanish, with pictures they can point at. Rotisserie chicken, brown beans, yellow rice, green sauce, Steph tries to say in bad Spanish. The waiter, a boy with pretty eyes and long lashes, not much older than Ashley, laughs at Steph, says something to his mother, his boss behind the counter, making her laugh, too. Ashley watches him with longing as he sits down in an empty booth and plays a video game on his Nintendo Switch.

The food ends up being the most amazing meal of their lives. They devour it like wild animals, their hunger for this life together so much bigger than any of them realized.

"This whole meal is under thirty dollars."

"I'm sold. I'm in. Let's do this," says Steph.

"Let me do a search of the local public school." Sandy whips out her phone.

"Those school ratings systems are so fucking racist."

"Mom, you said *fucking*." Ashley holds out her hand to receive the ever-inflating swearing fee.

"You're allowed to swear if you're talking about racists or tourists." Steph pushes her daughter's usurious hand away. "Seriously," she says to Sandy, "don't look at the school ratings—it's like Yelp for neurotic white parents. Look at the programs the school has. Check out the ratings for this restaurant, too, as an experiment."

Sandy does. "Well, the school Ashley and Rosie would go to has a meditation class for K–5 and an after-school program with capoeira and coding lessons. All free. And this restaurant isn't rated on Yelp."

"Have you had better chicken in your lifetime?" Steph asks her.

"Never."

"There's your answer."

"Ashley," Sandy asks, "how do you feel about moving here and going to a new school?"

"Can I cut my hair?"

"Of course," Steph says. "That's your biggest concern about moving?"

"I want to shave it off. Like his." She points to the little waiter playing his video game, his hair buzzed into a military-style high-and-tight.

Steph pauses. A twinge of fear glimmers in her eyes. "Sweetie, you can do that now if you want."

"No." She stares the boy. There is so much she isn't saying, not yet. "I want to do it before I go to my new school."

"I'll buy some clippers," Sandy says. "It's a deal."

Sandy scrutinizes every word of their lease and negotiates a new fridge and a fresh coat of paint for a February 5 move-in. Establishing their rent due date a little later than the first of the month will safeguard both women with time for their measly paychecks to clear. Then she drafts a roommate agreement for her and Steph to sign and have notarized.

"This is really good," Steph says of the document. "You should go to law school."

"All the smart girls I knew in college went to law school," Sandy says. "I'm not that smart."

"Do you know how many morons go to law school? The only requirement is an ability to read huge-ass boring books as fast as you can without falling asleep. You could so do that."

Sandy wipes out the rest of her mother's money to cover both her and Steph's share of first, last, and security for the new apartment, her safety net officially gone. Steph hires professional movers to take a couch from her parents' basement along with all their other things. Afterward the truck will go to Sandy's apartment and load her furniture in, so that everything arrives together. Having boxed and labeled her entire apartment, Sandy meets Steph at the Santorellas' to help her finish packing.

When she arrives, there are half-eaten boxes of stale cereal under both Ashley's and Steph's beds. Sleeves of cookies litter the tops of bookshelves, alongside sticky bowls and spoons. The cleanliness displayed over Christmas had been a special-event performance.

Steph stands in the middle of her bedroom with the jittery affect of a runaway, throwing clean and dirty clothes into the same duffel bag along with books and shoes.

"We have time to organize and, like, sort stuff," Sandy tries to soothe her. "The movers won't be here for another two hours."

"I don't want to be here when my folks get home." She stuffs some stray unmatched socks inside a coffee mug, then wraps the whole thing in a T-shirt. Her eyes scan the room and settle on a half-full box of books, which is where this coffee mug eventually lands. Then she sits on the floor, immobile. "Do you mind supervising this part of the move for us? I can take Ashley and Rosie with me to the new place and start cleaning."

"Sure, okay," Sandy agrees. Steph calls a car and leaves with the two kids.

The movers are loading Ashley's mattress onto the truck when Nancy and Vickie pull up in the driveway.

"She's moving *again*?" Vickie asks. "No wonder her kid is so weird."

"Don't say that, Vick. Ashley's not weird," Nancy replies, a tremor in her voice. "She's a good girl. Oh, hi, honey." She kisses Sandy on the cheek, then walks wearily into the house.

"I don't know why she bothers," Vickie goes on. "She's just gonna end up back here."

Their belongings fit together like long-lost puzzle pieces. The Santorellas' old couch is poufy and beige, with a sunken spot where Steph's dad used to sit. Ashley and Rosie roll themselves into the dip over and over again, the thrill everlasting. The couch becomes the nucleus of the home, gathering all of the other objects mechanically into its orbit, as though it had always existed in this spot, as though all four of them had. Sandy has a meticulously restored dining room table that she bought as a present for herself when she moved out of Alex's apartment, but it never fit in her studio, where she had to shove it into a corner and remove all the extra leaves that made it a work of art. Here she can display it in all its glory.

As a surprise, Steph buys a brand-new TV for the living room.

"Can you afford this?" Sandy asks.

"Given the state of my student-loan debt, this TV is only one percent of that, so who cares?"

"Okay," Sandy says, feeling anything but okay, but also not wanting to deflate Steph's joy. "I guess the more important question is, how do we hang it up?" The answer is frustration, laughter, tears, and YouTube tutorials.

Steph's clinical adviser finds a bunch of unused shelving units in the department overflow office that they can take for free. Their bedrooms are on opposite sides of the kitchen-dining-living room, so that if Rosie wakes up crying at night, Steph and Ashley won't hear it. Sandy is not a great cook, but she has the most amazing kitchen gear from her years of working at a food magazine. Steph is especially impressed by the porcelain Dutch oven.

"I've always wanted one of these," she says.

The night before Ashley's first day at her new school, Steph puts a towel on the floor beneath a chair and Ashley hops on, giddy with excitement. Steph hands the clippers to Sandy.

"You know how to do it?"

"I watched a bunch of YouTube videos last night, so maybe?" Sandy leans over and whispers into Ashley's ear, "Ready?"

"Uh-huh!"

"I don't know how good the fade will be."

"I don't care," Ashley replies, beaming.

Sandy shaves a swath of hair from the nape of Ashley's neck first, in case she has second thoughts. She doesn't. Her feet swing happily from the chair, a smile glowing on her face. Sandy shaves some more on the sides until only the very top remains. She runs her fingers through the short fringe on top.

"More," Ashley says.

"You got it, kiddo."

Rosie plays with her sister's hair on the floor, swirling it around like coppery-brown confetti. When it's all done, Sandy gives Ashley a hand mirror. She looks for a long time, rubbing her hand up and down the back of her scalp, luxuriating in the soft fuzz.

"Can my name at my new school be Ash?" she asks her mother. "But not like my nickname. Like, don't put Ashley down at all."

Sandy and Steph look at each other. "Honey." Steph kneels on the floor, at her child's feet, and takes her hand. "Are you a boy? Is that what you're trying to tell me?"

It is a question she has asked her kid before: at three years old Ash cut her own hair with kitchen shears and refused to let it grow back; at six Ash crumpled up the few dresses remaining in the closet and hid them at the bottom of the trash can. Both times Ash had answered no and seemed confident in that answer; both times Steph assured her child that there were lots of ways to be a person and you never needed to pick a team.

This time Ash doesn't answer right away. She takes her customary time, killing her mom with a long silence. "I don't mind when people think I'm a boy, but it's not who I really am. I just know I'm not a girl."

"Okay," Steph says.

"Okay, Ash," Sandy says.

"Will you tell my teachers for me? Tell them not to call me a girl?"

"Of course, baby."

Later that night Sandy and Steph have a glass of wine on the couch, admiring the new TV hanging on the wall.

"If only we could afford cable," Sandy jokes.

"Oh, I will happily go into debt to pay for cable. Anything to keep Ashley off YouTube. She's about two clicks away from stumbling into a snuff film."

"Ash. And probably *they*. We should ask."

"Shit! Yes. Ash. My baby's name is Ash. My baby's name is Ash." She repeats it a couple more times, trying to teach herself. "*Ash* feels so right. I named her Ashley after the girl I thought was my best friend in high school. She was sleeping with Justin the whole time I was pregnant, and now she's married to a guy who tried to storm the Capitol."

"Named *them*," Sandy corrects.

"Fuck! Why can't I get this? I never screw this up out in the world. Why now, with my own kid?"

"It's okay. We'll keep practicing until we get it."

"Okay." She stares at the blank blue screen glowing dumbly on the wall, then starts to cry. "What if something happens to them? What if someone hurts them?" Steph whispers. "What if—" She stops. Fear grabs her by the throat and won't let go.

"Well," Sandy says, "my mom had a saying for whenever I spiraled onto what-if island. *Honey, we'll jump off that bridge when we come to it.*"

Steph stares at her for a moment, making she's heard it right. Sandy waits for her. "Oh!" Steph says, finally getting it. The two of them burst out laughing. "I love your mom so much. Is that weird?"

Sandy throws her arms around Steph and holds her. "You have no idea how good it is to hear."

They giggle on the couch, imagining a life where, maybe, just maybe, it will all be okay as long as they can keep giggling on a couch together.

"My god, couldn't Ash have done this sooner? So we had time to prepare? I don't even know who their new teachers are."

"Kids have genius comic timing."

With that, the TV they had worked so hard to hang comes crashing to the floor.

Neither of the mothers hears a peep from Justin. "If he wants to see his kids, it is his job to reach out and find them," Steph justifies. She sees no reason to tell him that she has moved out of her parents' house and into an apartment in Washington Heights with his other baby mama. Underneath that lies the real fear: she doesn't want to tell him about Ash.

Sandy waits a moment, looks into Steph's eyes, allowing her to arrive at the truth on her own. It doesn't take long.

"I can't handle it if he fucks it up," Steph admits. "And I know he will."

"We don't know that yet. We should give him a chance."

"Sandy, please, think about it for a minute."

She does.

"Yeah, he'll fuck it up."

"My baby is being so brave and authentic at their new school, and I can't handle whatever idiocy he or Tara will bring to the situation. Not yet."

"Aren't you scared he'll flip out at you?" Sandy asks.

"Eh." Steph shrugs her shoulders. "Not really."

It's laundry day. Gone is the luxurious wash-and-fold service Sandy used to rely on; gone is the in-home washer–dryer at the Santorella house. Now the two women confront a wrinkled mountain of

clothes they have paid to wash with quarters scavenged from beneath every bed and couch cushion in their apartment. They sit on
the living room floor, separating the mega heap into four smaller
piles for each member of the family.

"I never appreciated how much his occasional cash helped me,"
Sandy says, holding up a pair of underwear with no more elastic in
the waist.

"Those are mine." Steph grabs them from her.

Sandy makes a neat stack of folded T-shirts that Rosie stomps
through like Godzilla, reducing it to a pile of rags.

"I've never seen him really mad before," Sandy whispers so Ash
won't hear. "I guess I'm just afraid of what he would do if we made
him really, *really* mad."

"As someone who has done just that multiple times in the last
decade, I can tell you exactly what will happen—nothing. He's a hys-
terically barking dog behind a big door. Open that door and you find
a scrawny little puppy pissing on the rug."

Once upon a time Steph and Justin were young punk-rock kids
picking fights with skinheads; afterward they went home to their
parents' houses like the children they still were. The only fights in
Sandy's personal history *were* her parents.

"I looked it up and, legally, if we had any kind of court-ordered
custody agreement, we would have to tell him about a change of address within thirty days. You can do what you want, but I'm going to
text him my new address."

Steph huffs. "Okay. Fine. I will, too."

"I didn't say you have to."

"I know. I just love to make him suffer. The pained look on his
face when he realizes he's not in control—it makes my heart soar.
But you're right." Steph slingshots a lacy thong at Sandy's face. "Don't
start thinking you're the boss of me now!"

"Wouldn't take that job no matter how much it paid."

"Okay, good." She shakes out a pair of Ash's jeans and attempts to
copy Sandy's space-saving method. Sandy takes them from her and
smooths the jeans into a tidy roll. "I swear to god, if he fucks up Ash's

name or their pronouns, I will crush his balls into pesto and serve it to Tara with linguine."

"I'll buy the Parmesan," Sandy promises.

That night, they both send texts stating their new address.

Sandy's: "Because of the financial burden of raising our daughter without your support, and because of my desire for our daughter to know and love her sibling, I have chosen to share this apartment with Steph."

Steph's: "Obviously I can't afford to live without a roommate, and though you are a congenital shit-for-brains, your taste in women is impeccable. So my roommate is a woman you've already vouched for. Thanks for that, you little bitch."

There is no word from Justin the whole next day. Sandy does a little work early in the morning before Rosie wakes, then takes over the kids' morning routine for Steph, who has a full day at the clinic. Sandy keeps her phone in her hand like it holds an intravenous drug she needs to survive. At one point she tries to change a diaper while still holding it, with predictable results.

As soon as she's gotten Rosie and herself and her phone cleaned, she gets a text alert that makes her leap. But it's Steph.

"Oh, hi, full-blown psycho here, checking my phone twenty-five times a minute. Like, I could get fired because of how much I am looking at my phone."

"I can beat that . . ." Sandy replies.

The Museum of Natural History hosts a Valentine's Day program that year called "Touch My Heart." To illustrate the evolution of the circulatory system, a display of real hearts—from worms and fish to humans and whales—is on exhibit, with some preserved in resin that visitors can actually touch. The moms wake the kids early that morning to get a head start. They arrive at the museum to find a line already reaching down the stone steps, along the sidewalk, all the way to the corner of 81st Street. Rosie is not bothered in the least. She races past all the other people in line heading straight for the granite steps, climbs up to the landing at the top, and does a dance to a song only she can hear. Sandy chases after her and carries her kicking and screaming back to the line, where Ash is glued to their mom's phone, watching clips of teenage boys analyzing the latest serial-killer video game.

"We look like the bad moms here," Sandy says.

"I'm taking the day off from self-criticism," Steph answers.

"Should we, like, monitor Ash's search history?" Sandy asks.

"I'm sick of them punishing me with the sullen silent treatment," Steph says. "But I'm choosing not to view this as giving in. Maybe this is what supportive parenting looks like? One day, when they become a forensic scientist, they'll thank me?"

"You're the therapist."

"I work with queer elders navigating homophobia and loneliness in their assisted-living homes. Not kids. Kids are terrifying."

Rosie escapes her family's clutches again and races back up the stairs. This time she tumbles head over feet, a fall that looks a lot worse than it is. Sandy dashes to her, lifts her up, hugs her. For a moment there is silence, Rosie's face frozen in anguish, her mouth wide—a quiet all parents know well, the calm before the storm.

"Here it comes," Steph says, leaving Ash in line and running toward them.

Rosie lets out a shriek that can be heard from blocks away. She is fine—no scratches or bruises—but the shock of her body not doing what she wanted is enormous, and her screams convey this at maximum volume. Sandy holds her in her arms and sways from foot to foot, like she did when Rosie was a newborn. This seems to soothe her, but, sensing an audience, Rosie gathers steam for a second wave.

"I fall down," she wails into her mother's shoulder, wiping her face on Sandy's neck. Steph dabs them both with a tissue. Many people stop and stare; one of them moves closer and taps Sandy on the shoulder.

"Sandy?"

"Oh my god, Berkeley?" Sandy says. "Hi!"

Berkeley was the first of the squad to leave the city after getting married, though she made the monthly girls' nights with fanatical regularity even after she had kids. They had not seen each other since Sandy's baby shower, something they both acknowledge too cheerfully, as though no other emotions surround that fact. *I used to love you so much,* they both want to say. *I used to tell you things late at night that I never told anyone, and now we're practically strangers.*

Instead, they suck in their stomachs and fall into a familiar choreography: flattery ("You look *amazing!*"), deflection ("*Please,* I haven't showered in *days!*"), doubling down ("Shut up, you're *gorgeous!*"), and finally . . .

"Is this your baby? She's basically a teenager now!" Berkeley says, not remembering Rosie's name.

"I cannot believe how big these two got!" Sandy says of Berkeley's son and daughter, maybe five and four years old, maybe older? She can't remember their names, either. "What are you up to?"

"There's a race in Central Park today. Both our husbands are trying to qualify for the New York City marathon." Berkeley introduces her friend, a woman in the same black leggings and brightly colored puffer coat as Berkeley, maroon to her peach, the same brand of "it" sneakers, clocking in at $275 a pair, that Steph pretends to disavow but secretly follows on resale sites.

"We're marathon widows," Berkeley's friend laughs. Her baby naps peacefully inside a goose-down sleeping bag strapped into her stroller. "It's like this every weekend until November."

"Then it starts all over again in January." Berkeley rolls her eyes.

Sufficiently starved of attention, Rosie stops crying. She reaches for Steph, who takes over holding her. "I fall down," she informs her calmly.

"You sure did, chickpea," Steph says, kissing her forehead. "Should I be mad that Ash has yet to come and check on their sister," she asks Sandy, "or glad that they're holding our spot in line?"

"Do you want to stand out here another forty minutes? I say we let them watch whatever neo-goth animation they want as long as we get in before eleven A.M."

The cogs turn slowly as Berkeley and her friend try to make sense of Steph and Sandy. Berkeley gives Sandy a quizzical look that begs for an explanation. Sandy takes a deep breath.

"This is Steph, the mother of Rosie's sibling, Ash," Sandy says, "that grumpy tween over there hypnotized by the YouTube algorithm."

"Okay," Berkeley says, at a complete loss for what else to say. "Okay!" she tries again.

"So what are *you* up to, Berk?"

Of all the perfectionists Sandy had known, Berkeley was the most committed to the act. No matter how drunk she got, Berkeley did her five-step skin-care routine every night. She was their sorority chapter president, a full-time job that paid nothing, and still graduated with honors. She went straight to law school after college, where at orientation she met the man who would become her husband. They both got jobs at the same firm after graduation and registered their relationship with HR. At a girls' night years ago, Berkeley, three margaritas deep, confessed to Sandy that she had been offered a more senior position than her then-boyfriend and was rising in the firm faster than he could catch up. Berkeley had wondered if that was why it was taking him so long to propose to her. After she quit and started over at a new firm, accepting a pay cut, a big fat diamond and half-page spot in the *New York Times* "Vows" section soon followed.

". . . and we're still debating about baby number three. He wants one more, but I'm on the fence. His parents are so good about watching Lila and Matthew when the nanny can't, I don't want to push my luck. We're making it work," Berkeley concludes. She looks at Sandy and smiles sadly. "I just know things are going to get better for you, girl," she says. "You were always so good at making the best of a bad situation."

"What?" Steph has watched this dance silently, intrigued by the sociology of it all, but she has reached her limit. "When in this whole vapid dialogue did anyone say things weren't working out for Sandy?"

Berkeley is aghast. She looks to her friend for help, but the woman backs away slowly, pretending to shush her already napping baby to sleep. "I didn't mean to imply it's her fault or anything . . ."

"Fault? Sandy is the most amazing person I have ever met. She is strong, and loving, and loyal, and beautiful without Botox. You probably waited around for the Prince of Mediocrity to buy you that big fat blood diamond. You're actually super hot, in a Lululemon cult kind of way, and somewhere in that park is a human potato in Hokas who probably thinks he *settled* for you. And now you have the audacity to act like you won a prize that Sandy lost?"

Berkeley squirms under Steph's breath of fire. Sandy considers apologizing for Steph, who definitely didn't need to get so specific and harsh. And accurate—Berkeley's husband *does* kind of look like a potato.

"Take care, Berk," she says instead. "We need to get back in line."

They walk up the steps to the stately columns at the entrance, where Ash is now standing.

"I don't care," Steph huffs, already feeling guilty. "I'm not sorry." Her jaw is tight with self-righteousness, and Sandy's stomach flips noticing for the first time how striking Steph's profile is.

"Thanks for sticking up for me." She holds Steph's hand. "Come on, kiddos, let's go touch some hearts."

March is a season of revelation in New York City. The gray snow-banks begin to shrink, and little by little all the soda bottles and lost hats, the spent vape cartridges and stray gloves, resurface in the dwindling mounds of ice and soot. The slanted rays of sunlight are not enough, not yet, but the promise is there, lingering a minute longer in the sky every night.

Steph splurges on another new TV and hires a professional to hang it properly. She buys a huge throw blanket for the couch with the softness and texture of sealskin. The four of them cuddle beneath it and watch baking shows in high-def, their brains tickled by each shake of sifted flour, each stir of golden batter.

Steph starts seeing her first clients one-on-one at the clinic, and Thatcher is pleased with Sandy's increased availability. The commute from Sandy's office to their new home is longer, but if she catches the express train it's possible to do it all, door-to-door, in just forty-eight minutes, which isn't bad. Catching the local isn't so bad, either, as it provides something every working mother craves: a peaceful stretch of time alone to sit and think.

Sandy walks home from the subway at an easy pace one chilly night in March. The sky above her clings fast to a dramatic shade of blue, rich and tranquil, a lullaby color. For the whole first year of Rosie's life, Sandy was too frenzied to notice anything of beauty in the world around her. She was so tired and hungry and lonely and drained that she didn't realize it was summer until she was drenched with sweat, didn't notice the autumn leaves until they clung to the soles of her shoes and she had to wipe them off on her doormat. Now she is able to look at the sky and register its color. She is able to do this because for the first time in two years there is no anxiety in her heart, no race to get home and pay someone before she gets charged extra, no tinge of guilt for leaving her daughter with strangers juggling five other babies' needs. When Sandy walks through the door of her apartment, Rosie will have been fed, bathed, and put to bed by a mom and a half-sibling who love her. The next night it will be Sandy's turn to do this for Steph, who will make her own observations of the sky, the world, without the crush of guilt or fear or dread to rob her of it. Sandy will not have to face the bleak loneliness of her old apartment; Steph will not have to force herself or her child to conform. They will be safe.

A rat skitters across the front step of their building. Sandy steps back and allows it to run from their huddle of trash cans to the one next door. In the vestibule, she checks the mail and hears the sound of laughter coming from her apartment. Like an animal in the wild, she can identify each member of the family by ear: Steph's laugh is a breathless whistle, almost asthmatic; Ash's is bubbly and liquid, rising up and down like rapid piano scales; Rosie has a low little monkey's grunt that pitches into a screech.

Inside, Ash sits on the floor, wearing Sandy's donut-printed pajama top. Steph and Rosie are on the floor next to them, huddled around a large white bowl of melted chocolate, which is nearly tipping over. Their faces are sticky and smeared. Every cabinet in the kitchen is open, the counters covered with toppled bags of flour and sugar. All the pans, all the utensils, make a mountain in the sink.

The three of them look at Sandy standing in the doorway and start laughing even harder. Rosie watches Ash closely, her eyes full of worship, chronicling every detail of the nine-year-old's behavior so she can mimic them a second later.

"What happened?" Sandy says, smiling.

This makes them laugh more. Steph's eyes are closed, tears streaming. She flaps her hands in front of her face. "I can't . . ." she gasps. "Ash, explain it to her!"

"Okay." Ash tries to calm down. The giggles creep back in like a cough. "We made a mirror glaze, and . . ."

Apparently this is the funniest thing in the world. They collapse in hysterics again.

"Okay," Steph says, trying to breathe deeply. "We were watching the baking show. And the challenge this week was these cakes with a mirror glaze. So we wanted to try it, but we decided to start with the glaze first."

"We thought, who needs cake?" Ash chirps.

"That's so cute," Sandy says.

"No, that's not the funny part." Steph has calmed down the bare minimum. She wipes the tears off her face, leaving a big smear of chocolate on her cheek. "On the show, the test of your mirror glaze is that you have to be able to see your reflection in the cake. So we tested it and—"

She loses it. It's over. The laughter is so intense it looks like pain.

Ash steps in to explain. "You look into the bowl and say, 'How do I look?'"

"And then—" Steph gasps for air. "And then—you say, 'Deeeeee-licious!'"

The three of them are no longer able to sit upright. Their spines collapse from the weight of this joke. They lie on the floor, on top of one another, shaking with laughter.

"Deeeeee-shushus," Rosie says, entwined in the knot of Ash and Steph.

"I don't get it," Sandy confesses.

"I guess you had to be there?" Steph tries.

There's no need to explain. This is what a family is at its very core—a codex of inside jokes, held with both arms forever.

At long last Sandy's boss is hosting a work-pretending-to-be-social event on a Saturday afternoon. Never mind that the timing of it totally screws up Rosie's nap schedule. Never mind that it is a two-hour one-way trip with multiple transfers. Sandy is going.

The stakes are high, and so, in obedience to her most powerful instincts and fears, Sandy goes shopping. Since it is much cheaper to splurge on a baby than an adult, she buys Rosie an adorable bonnet that makes her head look like a begonia.

"It was thirty dollars on sale at that cute little baby consignment shop I was telling you about," Sandy tells Steph as Rosie rips the bonnet off her head for the third time.

"You got a lot riding on this bougie party, don't you?" Steph says. It's a question as well as a warning. She'd clocked Sandy straightening her hair in the bathroom despite a forecast of light rain.

"I want my old reliable paycheck back. Not this freelance bullshit."

"Bullshit," Ash says, hand outstretched.

"You know it defeats the purpose if you repeat the swears every time you extort us." Sandy hands them two dollars.

Ash crinkles their nose. "That's all you got?"

"Were you not listening? I need money. We need money. This party is my chance to show my boss how great I'm doing while also being an amazing single mom to a stunningly beautiful daughter."

"Sweetie, if he can't see that already, maybe the problem is him, not you."

"I don't need empowerment. I need a promotion."

Steph gives her a hug, then helps restrain Rosie while Sandy ties the bonnet under her chin. There is no time to argue. She has a train to catch.

Rosie loses her thirty-dollar hat somewhere between transfers on the Long Island Rail Road. Sandy is too angry to cry. "How could someone so cute and small be so evil?" she asks her daughter. She leans into the stroller with the intention of biting the child's head off, chewing it, and spitting it out like a wad of gum, but Rosie takes Sandy's face in her sticky hands.

"Mama!" she says, and pulls Sandy in for a drooly open-mouth kiss. It is borderline romantic. Sandy has certainly fallen for much less.

Rob, his wife, Maggie, and their son, Xander, are waiting at the station to pick them up. Sandy detaches the car seat from the stroller base and latches it on to the hooks in Rob's SUV. Xander refuses to give up his window seat. Motion sickness, he claims, and his parents co-sign, forcing Sandy to squeeze into the middle back seat. Wedged between a seven-year-old and her baby, Sandy feels like a thirty-five-year-old teen mom.

Thatcher's house in Northport is huge, elegant, and rickety, with gray weather-beaten shingles and voluptuous hydrangea bushes out front. Rosie totters across the gleaming parquet floors of the foyer and sings a baby version of Taylor Swift's "Anti-Hero," which Thatcher and his husband find charming. Everything is going according to plan. All Sandy has to do is make her way next to Thatcher for a solid twenty to thirty minutes, say one smart thing, one funny thing, and one work-related thing with as much enthusiasm as she can fake, and this whole odyssey will have been worth it.

Soon after everyone arrives and the caterer has finished laying out the buffet, the men gather together as though magnetized by the invisible forces of sports, the market, and prestige-television dramas, and the women form their own circle, hovering over a communal fire kindled by body complaints, retail therapy, and reality TV. The binary is as stupid as a middle school dance and makes even less sense now among adults in middle age.

Sandy and Jess have a lot more in common with the men, who are their actual colleagues, and yet both are subsumed by the wives' circle. Jess compliments everyone's outfit, a bored smile plastered on her face. Once again Jess crosses the finish line while Sandy is still lacing her sneakers. But Sandy has Rosie, who grants her admittance into the mothers' club, where there is never a shortage of things to commiserate about.

"How old is she?" Sandy is asked about six different times, and each time she answers in both months and fractioned years, unsure of which is less annoying.

"Is she sleeping through the night?" No fewer than four women ask this. Women with children. Women who should know better than to flick this particular match at the powder keg of a new mother with dark circles that foundation can't hide.

"Did you sleep-train? We did Ferber and loved it."

"We did the extinction method."

"Which one is your husband?"

Maybe membership in the mothers' club has some contingencies Sandy hadn't prepared for. When she explains that she is a single mother, there is a collective in-suck of breath among the nice married women. How is this still shocking in the twenty-first century?

"*How* do you do it?"

"I can't even imagine. I could never."

"I could *never!*"

"I was a single mother last weekend while Ramon was out of town. By the time he came back Sunday, I was *exhausted*."

"Yeah," Sandy says, "it's like that. Except every single weekend and weekday, forever."

Here is where the tone always shifts, and the nice married women drop their thinly veiled disgust and fear and pick up the pom-poms.

"Oh my god, you are a rock star!"

"Such a badass!"

"Seriously," Rob's wife, Maggie, exclaims, "single mothers are such superheroes! Are you dating anyone?"

Sandy almost spits out her mint julep.

When the fuck do you think I have time to date?

"Not at the moment," she answers.

"Good!" Maggie says. "I have the perfect guy for you." She screams across the room, "Rob! Don't you think Thom would be so perfect for Sandy?"

Rob hears nothing. He smiles and raises his glass to her. It's all the encouragement Maggie needs.

"What dating apps are you on?" she asks.

"None," Sandy says.

"No problem. I'll just take a picture of you now. This is a really flattering outfit. You've lost nearly all the baby weight."

"What?"

She takes a bunch of pictures of Sandy, who angles her body, right foot pointed out, sucking the last two years backward through her belly button. Maggie swipes through the dozen or so drunken shots she's snapped, until she finds one that's in focus. She lets Sandy have a quick look. In the picture, the compulsion to be a nice agreeable woman and the desire to hurl Maggie's phone into the sea are at war on her face.

"You don't have to—" Sandy begins, but it's too late. Maggie is texting away, as modern cupids do.

Showing up to one work gathering in over a year does not magically save Sandy's career. In fact, it amplifies how shaky her position is. Hours after Sandy left Thatcher's weird and Waspy spring revel, Jess vomited in his prizewinning hydrangea bushes. Everyone who remained at the party saw it happen, and yet Thatcher was himself so drunk by this point that he referred to the woman who threw up as "Sandy," proving once again how faceless and interchangeable the two women at the magazine are.

That is the buzz at the office on Monday. Sandy is too depressed to be outraged. How does someone go about correcting something like this? She sidles up to Rob's desk, prepared to beg for help.

"Oh, good," Rob says. "I was just about to come find you."

"Thank you. It's so embarrassing. I don't know how to approach it—"

"No, no, no. Don't be embarrassed. I'm happy to help. I didn't realize you were on the market."

"What?"

"Our friend Thom. Maggie said you're interested in him."

"No! I mean, sorry. No, thank you. I'm not. Interested. I was hoping you could tell Thatcher that you dropped me off at the LIRR hours before Jess puked in his bushes."

"I don't know what you're talking about. Listen, Thom is some kind of lawyer. A boring kind, too boring to remember, but he pulls in a boatload of money. You should let him buy you dinner. It would make my wife happy, and when she's happy, I'm happy, if you know what I mean."

Rob makes a hand gesture indicating some kind of sex act, in the sad shared language his generation of straight white men uses.

"Ew. Rob, no. You're my work husband, I guess, but that is not our dynamic."

"Sorry. Don't tell HR?"

"I think, technically, you're HR."

"Oh, good. So you'll do it? It would be a huge favor to me. My wife is obsessed with fixing people up. She said it's her new brand."

"Like, professionally?"

"No, I think in life? All her friends are branding themselves on social media. It's a weird, unspoken, competitive thing her friends do. I stay out of it. Can you just call this guy? For me?"

"If you talk to Thatcher, tell him it *was not* me who puked at his party, tell him who I am, put in a good word for me, I'll text your lawyer friend."

"Great!" Rob drums a happy beat on his desk. "I'm telling Maggie right now. Love is in the air, Sandy! I can feel it!"

Again Sandy goes shopping with money she doesn't have, this time to buy a new outfit for her date. She finds a last-season blouse she doesn't hate on the clearance rack at Nordstrom, then splurges on a heavily padded bra to support the illusion of normal-sized breasts.

"How do I look?" she asks Steph.

"Bit of false advertising here," Steph says, rubbing the silky neckline of Sandy's shirt. "But you look gorge. If Lawyer Man doesn't fall madly in love, give me his address and a fire burns tonight."

"I don't know if I want to have sex or if I just want someone to want to have sex with me. I honestly think that would be enough."

"You don't have to go."

"I'm in too deep now. I can't stand him up."

"Tell him your kid is vomiting. Rosie, do gross."

Rosie hops up and starts making long, ornate puking noises.

"I wish you'd never taught her that."

Sandy flips her hair so that the part falls on the not-usual side. It gives her about thirty seconds' worth of bounce and body before falling flat again. She flips it back to her normal part. "Steph," she whispers, "I have to ask you something."

"Are you okay?" Steph says. "What's wrong?"

"Nothing. It's nothing. I just ... Is my vagina like the Holland Tunnel after having a baby? Tell the truth."

Steph spits out her kombucha. She laughs until the look of anguish on Sandy's face tells her to stop. "Sweetie," she says. "I can't speak for anyone else's vagina post-pregnancy, only mine. I have had sex with a couple of people since having Ash—that guy who was in Justin's band; that woman I lived with, who turned out to be an alcoholic. Another woman who turned out to be an alcoholic. A guy in my stats class, who was addicted to Adderall. Noticing a pattern there? That's why I'm single. Oh, wait—I think one more person?"

"Steph! Come on. Help me."

"Point is: all of them loved my vagina. I think you'll be okay."

In their text exchanges leading up to the date, Sandy very clearly told Lawyer Thom that she doesn't like beer. And yet the menu at the restaurant he chose lists only craft beers and homemade sodas. Sandy has plenty of time to peruse this menu as Lawyer Thom is more than forty-five minutes late. She sits at the table alone, straining to smile as the waitress refills her water glass again.

"Traffic," Thom texts, which Sandy accidentally anoints with a heart.

"Fuck," she says a little too loudly. An elderly couple sitting at the next table look up at her. "Sorry," she mumbles to them. "I meant to give this lawyer guy's text a thumbs-up, not a heart. I'm always doing this."

"You've been waiting a long time," the woman observes.

"I know," Sandy groans.

"He's a bum!" the man says. "You should leave before he gets here!"

"I'm trying to be positive," she tells them. "You know, give him a chance."

The man and woman look like they have been together since the Reagan administration, blissfully ignorant of the technological complexities of dating. Sandy debates amending her heart, but before she can, Lawyer Thom texts her back, this time a single red emoji heart. "Fuck," Sandy says again, softly this time.

She reviews their exchange while she waits and confirms that, yes, he had explicitly asked her if she liked beer, and she had very clearly told him she did not. "I'll keep that in mind . . ." was where they had landed on the subject, Lawyer Thom's ellipses about as coy and cute now as a string of spittle.

Be positive, she scolds herself. *I'm not hot anymore—if I deserve a chance, so does he.*

Lawyer Thom arrives dressed in a suit. He kisses Sandy on the cheek and she bristles. His hair is the color of dirty water, and his skin is a shade of pale that makes every imperfection seem to glow in contrast—the tiny dots of blood from shaving nicks, the blue veins at his temple. Taking the seat across from her, he removes his tie and folds it neatly into his jacket pocket. On his right hand is a big gold class ring. Sandy reads the alma mater: Boston University. She files that away as something to ask him about.

She won't need to. Lawyer Thom is perfectly comfortable supplying her with information about himself. He talks so much that he forgets to look at the menu. The waitress arrives and Thom waves her away, saying they need more time to order.

Sandy does not need more time. Sandy is starving and knows exactly what she wants. She sucks on the lime in her water.

"You're not going to get a beer?" Thom smirks, his pale eyebrows arched.

"Yeah, about that," she says in a disarming tone. "I thought we talked about beer. Pretty sure I told you I wasn't a beer drinker?"

"I know." Thom laughs. "I'm trying to get you out of your comfort zone."

"Okay."

He snaps his long white fingers in the air, flagging down their waitress, and orders Sandy an Irish stout. Sandy sneaks in an order for a burger, rare, just so it will come out faster. Without so much as a nod of encouragement, Thom launches into another monologue. As Sandy sips the bitter, frothy beer, he tells her all about his trip to Machu Picchu last year, about the boxing gym where he works out, his plans to learn how to surf this summer—all examples of courageously getting out of his comfort zone.

"It's sort of been my theme lately," he expounds as he finishes his beer. A line of foam clings to his mustache. "Going on a date with you," he adds, "is another example."

"How so?" Sandy manages to insert.

"If you told me five years ago I'd be dating a woman with a kid, I would have said, 'Hell no.' But after all my recent adventures, I've realized life is about taking risks. You're about my age, right—thirty-eight, thirty-nine?"

"I'm thirty-five." She takes a big wolfish bite of her burger, trying to make it disappear.

"Exactly. We're at the age now where we have to wait for the first round of divorces to get anyone of quality. The trick is not to be the first person they date post-divorce. Been there, done that. Too much baggage. You're the first single mother I've dated. Definitely out of my comfort zone."

Sandy hunts for the waitress with her eyes. She prays to her like the patron saint of microbreweries: *Please, please bring the bill now.*

There are some dates so awful that the best part is realizing the other person is taking a different subway line home, sparing you the torture of standing on the platform together. Sandy is Thanksgiving-grateful to learn that Lawyer Thom is getting the 2 train to Brooklyn. He walks her to the uptown A station, prattling away about estate law, new inheritance-tax codes he'd learned, all the challenges in his challenging and courageous life outside the *comfort zone.*

Just as Sandy is about to say good night, he grabs her by the arms, pulls her in, and kisses her on the mouth. It isn't a bad kiss. If only she liked him, it might have been a good kiss. Then she imagines the big gold class ring on his long finger sliding into her underwear and pledges a life of celibacy.

But Sandy is a woman, which means she is someone who could be murdered for appearing rude to the wrong man. Back when she was on the dating apps, simply saying, "I don't think we're a match" could wound men so deeply they became ghastly and offensive.

"I don't like flat-chested girls anyway."

"You're too old for me." (This from a man ten years older than her.)

"Ugly bitch."

What if she pulls away and Thom gets offended? She doesn't know what cruelty he is capable of, only that she is not ready to deflect it tonight, in person, when she is already so tired. So she puts Thom's kiss on a countdown, waiting for the appropriate amount of time to pass before she can stop, so that he won't feel rejected. The official rejection she can handle later, via text, when she is safe at home.

It is an awful lot of consideration for a man who has not once in two hours considered her feelings at all. It is not how she'd want Ash or Rosie to react in a similar situation. And it feels like a betrayal of Steph and of the authentic, funny, and courageous woman she is when they are together.

Sandy pulls away and takes three steps down toward the subway station.

"Thanks for dinner," she says, making a point not to smile.

"I'll call you," Thom replies, beaming.

"No," Sandy says. "Please don't." Then she runs to catch her train.

They hadn't discussed it, but Sandy knows Steph will be waiting up for her. She will come home and Steph will be there, working at the beautiful dining room table. Sandy hopes she'll be up for having a glass of wine with her, but it doesn't matter what they do. Just knowing she will be there after this ridiculous night is enough. Sandy can feel Steph's presence, her warmth, before she slides her key into their door.

Steph is indeed at the dining room table. She is close to finishing some insurance claims for her clients and has opened a bottle of wine. She pours a glass for herself and one for Sandy. A jingle outside the door catches her attention, and she looks up as Sandy comes in.

"Hi!" she says, in the soft nighttime whisper they use once the kids have gone to bed.

"I was going to text you to open that exact bottle on my walk from the subway," Sandy whispers. She kicks off her low-heeled Chelsea boots and sighs with relief. "If I never, ever go on a date with a man for the rest of my life, I would not only be fine, I'd be happy."

"The logic of this is unassailable," Steph says. "I've been on dates like that." She hands Sandy's glass to her. "I let it breathe first, like you taught me."

n April, a reused Amazon box arrives in the mail. It is from Tara and is addressed to "Ashley and Rosie Murray." Ash's dead name, Justin's last name, even though both kids have their mothers' last names hyphenated before his. There are two pink plastic baskets, a mess of shredded green plastic grass, a lot of chocolate bunnies and little foil-wrapped chocolate eggs, the usual Easter fare, all purchased from the dollar store Tara loves. This is nothing new. Beneath the faux grass in each basket is a wooden crucifix, about the size of a hardcover book, with fake mother-of-pearl inlay, upon which a gold-painted plastic Jesus writhes in everlasting agony.

"Uh-oh," Steph says to herself.

"It is technically a Christian holiday," Sandy says when she gets home later that night.

"In ten years of holidays, no one in that family has said Jesus's name except to swear," Steph replies. She bites the head off a chocolate bunny. "Now he's our lord and savior? Read this."

She shows Sandy two identical greeting cards, written to each grandchild but with their mothers as the intended audience. On the front of each card is a sunrise scene with big sweeping scripture quotations. Inside is a preprinted message about the miracle of resurrection, etc., etc., and a handwritten note from Tara. "Hang these crucifixes in your bedroom and He will watch over you," the note instructs.

"You haven't told Justin about Ash being nonbinary, have you?"

"I'm waiting," Steph admits. The chocolate bunny is hollow on the inside. Steph flays the rest of the pastel foil from the decapitated body and spoons some peanut butter inside. Her mouth is sticky and her head surges with sugar. "Tara and Justin are so goddamn coda."

"Coda?" Sandy asks.

"Codependent. Haven't you noticed? It's like they're on this sad little team, just the two of them versus the world."

"Totally. But I don't see what that has to do with this."

"This is what they do," Steph explains. "Whatever Justin is into, Tara gets into. And Justin goes through phases like people go through tissues. There was his hardcore-punk phase, which Tara didn't co-opt for herself exactly, but she did *hand-wash* all his ripped T-shirts. She even hung them up on hangers in his closet, which is the least punk thing in the world. I guarantee you if we opened the trunk of her car, it would be filled with merch from all the different bands he's played in. When he was into tiger preservation, the two of them took a trip to Florida to volunteer for a long weekend at this fucked-up illegal zoo. There is no doubt in my mind this Jesus kick is something Justin got into first."

"I can't see Justin getting religious."

"Justin has a big Daddy-shaped hole in his heart," Steph explains. "Who's better equipped to fill that than the Big Daddy in the sky?"

On Easter, Sandy and Rosie wake up to an outbreak of itchy red welts on their skin. At first Sandy suspects chicken pox. There had been outbreaks in certain neighborhoods in the city where vaccinations rates were low. Because the same welts are on her, she assumes she's lost her immunity, compounding the viral load for both of them, rendering it lethal. She lies paralyzed in bed, holding Rosie—who has no fever and seems fine—and googles herself into fantasies of hospitals and funeral homes. It doesn't matter how many times the internet steers her headfirst into certain death, she always returns to it.

There is a knock at the door. "Happy Easter!" Steph says. She and

Ash have repurposed a baking sheet into a tray. A single daffodil droops brightly over the rim of a recycled jelly jar. Eggs in purgatory, toast, coffee, and juice—a breakfast for the four of them—fills the tray. They climb onto Sandy's bed and start eating.

"Don't look at the kitchen right now," Steph warns. "Sauce got everywhere."

"It looks like a bloodbath!" Ash says, delighted.

Rosie crawls across the bed to Ash's lap and rubs her hand on their fuzzy shorn hair.

"Mom, look, she has them, too." They lift the hem of Rosie's pajamas to show where the welts are.

"Oh shit," Steph says, taking Rosie's chubby ankles in her hands for a closer look. "That means they're everywhere."

"Oh shit," Ash repeats, casting a wary eye first at their mother, then Sandy, to see if this will slide.

"Oh ssit!" Rosie echoes, and Steph pinches Ash lightly on the shoulder.

"Bad example!"

"Do we all have chicken pox?" Sandy asks.

"Worse," Steph says. "Bedbugs."

Sandy has never dealt with bedbugs in all her years in New York City. Living with her parents in Staten Island, Steph has also escaped this particular menace, but she knows enough people to be familiar with the protocol.

"We have to put everything, and I mean *everything*, in sealed plastic bags. It's a whole saga," she explains.

"Where did they come from?"

"Anywhere," Steph starts, then gasps. "Oh my god, Tara's package!"

"What package?" Ash asks.

"Oh shit," Steph says.

"Oh sssit," Rosie says again, this time with more assurance.

"Bad example," Ash gloats.

Steph retrieves the Easter care package from its hiding spot on a high shelf in the kitchen and tries her best to assemble the baskets and grass with the chocolates she managed not to eat in secret.

"Grandma T usually gives me way more candy than this on Easter," Ash notes.

"Yeah, there must have been a supply-chain issue," Steph replies.

Sandy volunteers to negotiate with their building manager about fumigation. He texts back demanding proof of a bedbug infestation before he will make a call to an exterminator.

"Our welts aren't enough evidence?" Steph cries.

"I texted him pictures of our ankles and back. He's ice-cold. Said it could be anything. He wants us to trap the bugs and have them verified as the species *Cimex lectularius* first."

"The fact that he knows the taxonomical name means he's done this before."

"Yup. But what is our alternative?"

"Call an exterminator ourselves? Foot the bill and hope he pays us back?"

"With what money?" Sandy says. "You're on SNAP, and I'm buying generic-brand food to stretch my grocery budget."

"I only have a hundred fifty thousand dollars of debt at the moment. What's a thousand more?"

"You say that a lot," Sandy observes. Steph doesn't answer. She is already pulling the cushions off the couch to catch a *Cimex*.

They vacuum and bleach and wash everything they can in scalding-hot water, meanwhile setting little bowls of sugar water under their beds in the hopes of trapping a specimen and proving that their plague is real. When at last they have a few bugs to show, Sandy texts the landlord pictures of them, alongside screen grabs from Wikipedia of *Cimex lectularius*.

The problem, their landlord replies now, is not the bedbugs but their allergy to them.

"He said not everyone is allergic to bedbugs, so it's our problem, not his," Sandy reports.

"Is that legal?"

"Definitely not. I'm doing some research about how to scare him into action."

Sandy emails their landlord three separate times, studiously reminding him of theirs rights as tenants. There is no response. Sandy and Steph try scorching their mattresses with hot air from Sandy's blow dryer, dousing everything in lavender oil. None of it works.

"Maybe if our kitchen wasn't a biohazard zone," Sandy says one rainy spring morning. She had scrubbed the entire kitchen spotless the night before and woke up still feeling heroic about it. Everything in their life is a mess, but they can at least wake up in a clean house. By 8 A.M. there are grease slicks and honey smears across the kitchen counter. The floor has more crumbs than a bakery.

"What are you talking about?"

"What the hell did you make for breakfast?"

"Toast," Steph snaps back. "Oh, and coffee. Is that okay, your majesty? I made some for you, by the way."

"How is it that when you cook, literally every single pot, pan, bowl, knife, and spoon gets used and stays out all night, and when I cook, the kitchen is already clean by the time we sit down to eat?"

"First of all, 'when you cook' is practically never. And if you're so good at managing a kitchen, go ahead. I don't need to make nutritious food for our family. We can eat McDonald's."

"Oooh! Yes! Can we have McDonald's?" Ash asks.

"No," both mothers reply.

"I feel like I could vacuum twice a day every day and still not keep up with the trail of crumbs you leave behind. You're worse than the kids. No wonder our apartment is infested."

"Bedbugs eat blood, not dried cereal," Steph argues. "Our house has life in it, and life is messy."

"Our house has bedbugs!"

"That is not my fault, no matter how much you want it to be!"

For the next week they avoid each other. Steph feeds the kids dinner early and puts Sandy's portions in recycled take-out containers in the fridge, eating her own dinner alone in her room. Sandy moves her hair products and several steps of her skin-care routine into her bedroom so that she doesn't have to share the bathroom mirror with Steph in the morning.

Very quickly, Ash and Rosie learn to exploit this schism. "Can I sleep with you tonight?" Ash asks, holding Rosie in their arms, looking too theatrical to be convincing. Steph makes Ash read before bed, while Sandy is willing to spoon and fall asleep to the flickering light of sitcom reruns on her laptop. When Rosie wants a cookie, she bypasses her mother completely and runs straight to Steph's room. She takes her hand, pulls her away from work, saying, "Cookie pwease." Steph is constitutionally incapable of saying no when children ask for food. It could be 3 A.M. and she would fry an egg for the kids if they asked her to.

The moms attempt to reconcile, but every well-intentioned conversation ends in a fresh wound. It's like a sinkhole in the middle of the apartment they keep skirting, falling into, helping each other out of, then tumbling back into.

"...You always ask the kids if they want to stop watching videos. It's not their choice. You need to learn how the hell to set a boundary..."

"...You're incapable of the most basic planning. They went to school in snow boots and hats yesterday when it's almost seventy degrees outside. You never remember to check the weather before school, which is wild for someone who is always on their phone..."

"Why do you always throw away perfectly edible leftovers that I rely on to make lunches?"

"Because you never throw anything away and our fridge smells like a dumpster."

With *always* and *never* as their swords, they lock themselves into a fight no one can win.

One night Sandy gets a text from Justin. He misses his daughters, he says. It's the first time he's admitted to having two kids. Sandy chooses to see this as a milestone. She shows the text to Steph.

"Don't get too excited." Steph hands her phone to Sandy.

"When are you gonna give up the game? Your being ridiculous. I have a right to see my kids"

Sandy makes a group thread for all three parents. She proposes a time on Friday to get together, which Justin declines. He's busy, he says. She gives him another option. Nope, he is booked then, too.

"Why don't you tell us what works for you, then?" Sandy texts, trying to sound as cooperative as possible.

He wants the kids every other weekend, but he can only take one at a time, he says on a group chat. "Rosie Friday night, Ashley Saturday night." The moms have to meet him halfway for pickup and drop-off.

"Cool, should we pack extra diapers for you, bc you're acting like a big fucking baby," Steph responds.

"This is a good start," Sandy says.

The night Justin takes Rosie, Sandy cashes in a coupon for a high-intensity workout, then comes home and collapses in her bed, still in her sneakers, where she cries herself to sleep. She's blindsided by the ache of missing her daughter, even the way Rosie jackknifes her body in her sleep and does an Irish step dance on Sandy's back.

"I know that was hard," Steph says the next morning. She gives Sandy a fancy Japanese bath bomb that smells like the forests of Sandy's childhood, tangy and crisp with a hint of deer fur. "For next time. It will still hurt. I've never gotten used to it, not in nine years. But a nice bath does help, I promise."

Weary and relieved, Sandy accepts the olive branch. The next day Ash comes home and the four of them are together again. Despite Steph's barrage of questions, Ash says nothing about the weekend or their dad's fluency with pronouns. They just sit in the dip of the sofa and watch a creepy YouTube video about long empty hallways that lead to rooms speckled with blood. Rosie rests her head on their shoulder, watching with morbid fascination, repeating each time her sibling whispers, "Whoa."

"Ah, how I've missed this idyllic scene," Sandy muses.

"I've been complaining for so long that he's a deadbeat, but if I'm being honest, I actually prefer when he bails."

"I missed Rosie so much I think I would die if he made this a regular thing," Sandy says. "Do you really think he'll keep this up every other weekend?"

"No way," Steph promises. "He never has and he never will."

They eat dinner and clean the dishes, make lunches for the next day, and draw baths. Steph continues to ask Ash about their night with Daddy. Every time, Ash replies with monosyllables. It's not until they are all sitting on the couch, reading bedtime stories, that they say, "Daddy kept calling me Ashley."

"Did you correct him?" Steph asks.

"Yeah. He said sorry. But then he'd do it again. He said not to tell Grandma T."

"That motherfucker," Steph whispers under her breath as she leaps up from the couch. She grabs her phone and begins pounding a screed to Justin with her finger: "I've seen tree stumps hollowed out by rot and used as toilets by the houseless that have more decency than you, dickwad . . ."

"Grandma T loves you," Sandy assures Ash. "It might take her a minute to get on board, but it will happen, and Mom and I will handle her if it doesn't."

"Promise?" Ash asks.

"A million percent," Sandy tells them.

That night, Rosie can't fall asleep. "Tell a story," she says to Sandy in their darkened room. Slivers of spring light beam through the gaps in the curtains. Rosie clutches each of Sandy's ears with her small hands and won't let go. Sandy keeps her head still and close, feeling the little puff of warm air escaping Rosie's mouth against her face. Finally her eyelids flutter and fall, her breath gets low and hard. It happens slowly, then all at once, like a sunset, ordinary and miraculous. Even sound asleep, she will not let go of her mother's ears.

Beneath the comforter, Sandy's phone starts to buzz. She reaches to find it. Shielding Rosie from the light, she checks the new message. It's from Steph.

"Come out to the couch. You have to see this."

Slowly, Sandy twists out of Rosie's grip and tiptoes from the room. She finds Steph sitting on the couch in the dark, a stunned look on her face.

"What did he say about Ash?"

"Nothing. Not a word from him. But I got this."

She gives Sandy her phone.

"Hi, I'm Kaya. I was Justin's girlfriend. I'm pregnant and now he's not speaking to me. I was wondering if you would."

There's nothing mystical about coordinating a trio of mothers and their children. Three work schedules, three school and daycare schedules, an assembly of prenatal checkups, playdates, coding classes, and dance lessons become a puzzle made of calendar pages. But it's hard to call it a coincidence when the first time in their collective lives that the three women meet is on Mother's Day.

Since Kaya is pregnant, Steph and Sandy insist that they will come to her in Queens. Kaya tells them to meet her in a grassy field by the tennis courts in Astoria Park, which is fairly close to her house. Steph and Sandy promise to provide lunch. All Kaya has to do is show up.

"She cried so hard I couldn't really understand what she was saying," Steph reports after talking to Kaya on the phone. "The takeaway is exactly what you'd expect: Justin is a shithead. Let's pick up some banh mi and Vietnamese coffee on the way," Steph says. She straps Rosie into her stroller. "Do not poop until we get to Queens, do you hear me, you little demon baby?"

Rosie shakes her head no. "I poop on *you*," she declares. Steph hangs a diaper bag on the handle of the stroller.

"Don't you think something plain, like burgers and fries, might be better? She's pregnant and could be sensitive to strong smells right now."

"Wow, racist?!" Steph replies.

"You're being selfish," Sandy says. "You've been craving banh mi since last week. You wouldn't shut up about it. This is about you, not her."

She hangs the picnic bag on the other handle of Rosie's stroller and the whole thing, Rosie included, flips backward.

Another petty argument degenerating into low-grade character assassination. It is stupid and unnecessary and both women want it to stop, but they are so stressed from the overwhelming ickiness of bedbugs that they can't help turning on each other. They have both grown to hate the apartment that just three months ago seemed like the answer to all their problems and are equally afraid to admit this.

The weather on Mother's Day is perfect. The sky is movie blue with big puffy clouds that look painted by hand. Like any good idea for a nice Sunday in New York, ten thousand other people have had it, too. They step carefully through a patchwork of blankets spread across the grass. Kaya texts a hint to finding her in the crowd: "I got big hair, big tits, big ass, and freckles." She would be in a red tank top. Her five-year-old daughter, Kayla, will be wearing pigtails and "something chaotic idk picking clothes is her journey now I can't fight that fight anymore."

It is her energy that calls them in first, the description of mother and child matching up afterward. They find Kaya and Kayla on the grass, cuddling and watching a video on Kaya's phone. Kaya is breathtaking, traffic-stopping, freak-of-nature beautiful. She has long, dark, curly hair and flawless skin with a spray of light freckles over the bridge of her nose. Her lips look like a cartoon of pretty-girl lips: naturally pink and bowtie-shaped.

Sandy's first thought, Steph's first thought, something they won't share with each other until later that night: *How did Justin ever get a woman this hot?*

They all hug hello. Steph shakes out a few blankets for them to sit on and a bunch of toys to keep Rosie occupied. She pours each of them a cup of Vietnamese coffee from a thermos. (She won that fight.) Sandy puts a bouquet of flowers in the middle of their picnic. "To be festive," she says brightly.

"He said he had two *daughters*," Kaya floats the last word out cautiously.

"Justin is struggling with the nonbinary thing," Steph groans.

"Is he a good dad? He said he was, but now I don't know what to believe."

"He's a—" Steph begins.

"He tries," Sandy interrupts.

"Can't be worse than Kayla's dad," Kaya whispers.

There's so much they need to say without the children hearing. Steph searches her bags for the toy she bought for just this purpose, an alligator that is basically a machine gun that shoots bubbles. She loads it with a fresh bottle of bubbles and new batteries. It should secure them a good fifteen minutes of adult conversation.

"Doug left me a month after Kayla was born," Kaya continues once the two older kids are out of earshot. "I don't know what's wrong with me. Guys always fall so hard at first. Then they disappear. I thought Justin was different. He wrote a song about me."

"*What can I say, girl,*" Steph sings in a low, groaning voice, "*you got good bones under that dress, you got good bones, good bones, stand tall.*"

Kaya and Sandy gasp.

"Familiar?" Steph asks.

"That motherfucker," Sandy says.

"He said he loved me," Kaya says. "Why would he say that if he didn't mean it?"

"Because you're gorgeous?" Steph says.

"That's true," Kaya agrees.

"And men lie, especially to gorgeous women," Sandy adds.

Kaya got her education on the New York City MTA, where boys and men were always mooning over her. *I think I just fell in love,* these idiots would say, knowing nothing about her. *I'm gonna marry you,* they'd slur, drunk with desire. She was the scrim on which so many morons projected a two-dimensional illusion of love. Kaya slapped these boys and men away like mosquitoes. It was more annoying than flattering, as the power that came from such hotness was brief and pathetic in the grand scheme of things. Sometimes it was a liability. It took a little time to figure out, but by the end of high school Kaya learned to avoid eye contact with her friends' boyfriends, and then to avoid friends with boyfriends altogether, until there were very few women she could call friends. All because of these guys who were a whole lot of nothing.

So many men talked a big game about the luxury they would put Kaya in, but like their supposed love, it was all empty promises. Doug showed up with gifts in hand. In their whirlwind courtship, he bought her a Coach bag, limited-edition Jordans that matched with his, and lingerie from La Perla—not the stuff on sale. When Kaya was growing up, her parents would wake her and her brothers in the middle of the night to move apartments. They hopped from one home to another across the Bronx and Queens to avoid paying rent. After all this financial chaos, Kaya's love language found an easy translation through gifts.

She loved Doug so much it physically hurt, even when things were good. A red flag, for sure, one of many that Kaya stomped past. Like her, Doug had lived his whole life being looked at, always being smiled at, getting things for free, just because he was beautiful. Un-like Kaya, who had worked every weekend of her life since the age of fifteen and forty hours a week since graduating high school, Doug was chronically laid off, or between jobs, or waiting on a guy to pay him soon. He had that handsome white guy's expectation that the world would be his forever. At the peak of Kaya's powers, when men were putting hundred-dollar bills in her G-string, she still had to work for it.

Then Doug moved to North Carolina and changed his number. Kaya vowed never again. She had a baby to protect now. Her stan-dards had to be higher. Flashy presents were about ego; they weren't enough. A real boyfriend had to buy her tampons and French fries when she was on her period. He had to pay for dinner *and* a babysit-ter. Most guys bailed on this project. Justin was game. He bought her and Kayla pizza and garlic knots for dinner on school nights. He paid the past-due amount on her cell-phone bill and her gas bill. Why would he do that if he wasn't planning to stick around?

"I should have known not to fall in love with a Gemini," Kaya tells the two other mothers. "After all the scumbags I'd dealt with, I thought I was finally calling in the One, you know?"

"You thought Justin Murray was the One?" Steph cannot hide her disbelief. Sandy glares at her to shut up.

"He has his own business, his own truck, he takes care of his mother, he's so good with Kayla, and his dick is perfect. Long, straight—"

"Mommy! Come push me on the swings!" Kayla comes running from across the lawn. Both Steph and Sandy offer to take playground duty for her, but Kaya insists she's okay, she can do it.

"Poor thing," Sandy says.

"I know. She is in the midst of one of life's most painful reality checks—that the person she thought was her soulmate is nothing but a fuckboi."

"Tale as old as time," Sandy agrees.

"Justin sure doesn't have a type," Kaya says when she returns.

"That's true!" Sandy says with a laugh. "Three baby mamas and not one of us looks like the other."

Sandy is tall and big-boned. Before Rosie, she was so flat-chested she could get away without wearing a bra in public. Steph is tiny and muscular and would need to double up sports bras if she went running, which she would never do unless someone was chasing her with a knife. Kaya is somewhere between them in height and nothing but big soft curves.

"This is so good," Kaya says, inhaling a second banh mi.

Steph gives Sandy a look that says, *See?*

"I never had one of these before," Kaya goes on. "I'm basic to the core. I could honestly live on burgers and fries."

See? Sandy's eyes shoot back at Steph.

"I craved them when I was pregnant with Ash. Here, have the other half of mine." Steph gives Kaya the sandwich. "Is your family in Queens, too?"

"Just me. I grew up all around the area, but my grandparents were always here in Astoria. I'm living in their house now. My brothers and I inherited it when our yiya died last year. My brothers are in California, parents in Florida."

"So you're on your own?"

"Pretty much. A lot of my girlfriends disappeared after I had Kayla."

"I can relate." Sandy nods.

"Working full-time and getting Kayla to school and dance lessons and birthday parties and stuff . . . I don't know, maybe it's me, but it's been hard to make friends as a single mom. Like, I can't just pop out for a drink on Saturday night. That drink would cost me an extra twenty dollars an hour in babysitting. Besides, the other mothers are all, like, suspicious of me. They think because I'm single I must be so desperate for a man I'll snatch their doughy-assed husbands right out of their beds. They're nice to my face, but let's just say no one invites me to brunch, you know?"

"I do," Steph says. "I've been going through that for years. I think we threaten the married moms, the *normal* moms. It's not just the husband-stealing. We threaten the whole idea that they have to put up with a mediocre man at all."

"Or they think it's contagious," Sandy chimes in. "They'll catch what we have and end up single and it will be too hard."

"Every once in a while, I'd meet another single mom in the pickup line at school and we would have this amazing, hilarious, life-affirming conversation for five minutes," Steph goes on. "But then, because we were both single moms, we could never find time for more than that. It's half the reason I roped this lady into moving in with me." She throws her arms around Sandy. "I knew if I didn't lock her down with a lease we'd never see each other."

Steph is laughing as she looks at Sandy. Her dark-brown eyes twinkle. Sandy feels a lovely shiver over her body, like when a stylist runs her fingers through freshly cut hair.

"I'll take the next shift at the playground," she says, giving Steph's shoulder a squeeze.

"You're so lucky you have each other," Kaya says to Steph. "I'm shocked by how lonely it can get when Kayla falls asleep. That was the thing with Justin—I just wanted to matter to someone else, a grown-up. Yeah, the sex was good. But I'm a grown-ass woman. I need more. I told him that, no sugarcoating, daring him to bail like everyone else. But he didn't. He showed the fuck up. He was so good with Kayla. She fell in love with him, too."

"He is pretty good with kids," Steph grants. "He and Ash eat pizza all weekend and play extremely violent video games for hours, which is not the kind of fun I generally bring."

"He used to take Kayla to McDonald's. It was their little thing. She looked forward to it. One night last week I was super busy and I tried to stop there on our way home to grab a quick dinner. She said, 'No, I only eat here with Justin.' I can't believe I let this happen to her."

"It's not your fault he's such a shit," Steph says. In the distance, Sandy pushes Ash and Kayla on a tire swing. Her blond hair escapes the ponytail she tried to "elevate" with an organza bow and now falls prettily around her face. When the tire swing comes her way, she bends down to blow raspberries on the children's cheeks, making them scream with delight. "How did you meet him?"

"It was like a fairy tale. I've been a stylist for almost five years now and I've never met a man at work. Then one day someone hired Justin to wash the windows of the building where the salon is. My chair is right next to the window. Every time I looked out, I would see him looking at me. Finally I waved, as a joke, and he waved back. And—" She breaks down in big heaving cries. "Things were so good before. I'm an idiot. I thought he'd be happy when I told him I was pregnant."

"Have you met his mother?" Sandy asks, returning to the blanket. The bubbles have been reloaded for round two. Kayla sprays Ash with rapid-fire iridescence while Rosie chases them down and tackles them like a football player.

"That's part of the whole drama—I've never even met this woman, but she thinks I'm evil. Apparently, I'm some kind of bad spirit? She told Justin to stay away from me."

"That's Tara," Steph and Sandy say in unison.

"He spent every second he could with me. Like, he really made the effort, and it was hard, because he's so busy." Steph rolls her eyes. "After about four months I asked him if he wanted to move in with me, which I know sounds unhinged but it felt so real. I really truly expected him to say yes. I have this big house all to myself and Kayla now that Yiya Devine is gone. As soon as I said it, he got all distant. He broke up with me for a week, then changed his mind and we got back together. But it wasn't the same. He was checked out. Then I found out I was pregnant. When I told him, he begged me to have an abortion. That's when I found out about you two for the first time. He broke down crying and finally told me that he already had two baby mamas, who refused to let him see his kids—"

"Lie!" Steph snaps. "Sorry, go on."

"He said you two were sucking him dry financially."

Steph snorts.

"Also not true," Sandy says.

"I blamed you for making him this way. Like, he would be able to commit to me if he wasn't traumatized by you two. I think I needed it to be your fault. So I hacked into his phone and sent your contact info to myself while he was in the bathroom. I was planning on calling you to chew you out. Then he dumped me again. This time for real. I haven't been able to get him to talk to me for weeks."

The children gravitate back to the blanket and find their way into their mothers' laps. Kaya dries her eyes and puts on her brave face. "Are you having fun with our new friends?" she asks her daughter.

"Yeah, but it's really hot," Kayla says. "I feel so sweaty. I think I need an ice cream to cool off."

Kaya pulls out a wad of cash and peels off some ones, hands them to Ash. "You're the oldest. Can you handle taking these two across the lawn to the ice-cream cart?" Ash's chest swells with pride. They nod. Kayla grabs their hand, Rosie the other, and the three of them walk away. "Oh, wait, I should have asked first. Are they allowed to eat ice cream? You're not organic gluten-free moms, are you?"

"I really wanted to be, but then I got too tired," Steph laughs.

"I was all about that homemade-baby-food life when I was pregnant," Sandy says. "I got this special little blender that came with these silicone ice-cube trays to puree asparagus and freeze it in perfect portions. I used it once."

"We all fall for those silicone baby-food ice-cube trays," Steph adds.

"The second you pee on a stick, social media starts blasting you with ads for those things," Kaya says. "Bitches make it look so easy to just freeze up a meatloaf."

In the distance, Ash hands two ice-cream cones to Kayla, then pays the woman at the cart.

"Sometimes, a big horrible breakup is the thing that sets us free," Sandy says.

"I hope you're right," Kaya says sadly. "It took me so long to put myself back together after Doug left. I don't want to go through all that again. I can't."

"You won't," Steph says. "This time you have us."

The three women pack up their picnic and wrangle their sleepy, sweaty kids. "You're welcome at our house anytime," Sandy says, hugging Kayla goodbye.

"We'll have a slumber party at our place," Steph tells Kaya. "Give you a little break."

It is an absurdly long ride back to Washington Heights. Both Ash and Rosie fall asleep on the subway. Sandy and Steph fall into a drowsy silence themselves, until Steph cries, "How, in all this time, has that man not learned to pull out?"

The trip between the apartment in Washington Heights and the house in Astoria never gets any shorter, but the three mothers vow to get together as often as possible, and when they can't, they treat each other to Mom's Days.

It's Kaya's invention, in honor and defiance of the day they first met. Mother's Day, Kaya says, is too loaded. It connotes clichés and formality, obligatory brunches, useless flowers, sappy cards.

"*Mothers* are fancy bitches who wait all year to get theirs. We need Mom's Days, and we need them, like, once a week minimum."

"I love the macaroni necklaces," Steph says, "the pictures with the Popsicle-stick frames, all the glittery goddamn cards. So much glitter, my god, does Ash love glitter. But I do get jealous of the moms—the *mothers*—with partners who send them to the spa for the day."

"It's going to be years before I get a macaroni necklace," Sandy adds. "Sometimes I wish I could fast-forward to the day when Rosie's old enough to bring me a cup of coffee. That would be everything."

"I don't even want a spa day," Kaya says. "Okay, that's a lie. I do. But I'd settle for a morning in bed without hearing *Mom?* a thousand times."

So the three women pool their resources and take turns treating one another to simpler things more often, because Kaya is right: once a year is too little, and elementary school crafts, precious as they are, are not enough.

On a random Wednesday morning, Kaya orders bagels and coffee to be delivered to Steph and Sandy's apartment for breakfast. Sandy picks up Kayla for the day so so that Kaya can have a couple hours to lounge and nap. A new cell-phone case when the old one is looking raggedy, a fifteen-dollar manicure, a rotisserie chicken so no one has to cook dinner: these are the little things they can give one another, the unnecessary indulgences that fix none of their bigger problems but make them easier to face.

"Should we just buy a car?" Steph says to Sandy one sweltering Saturday in August. Kaya had invited them to come over and spray one another with a hose in her backyard—her private backyard, with lovely shade trees and fragrant rosebushes—but it was too far to schlep. Rosie and Ash beg to go to their neighborhood playground. Sandy and Steph try to explain that it's too hot, the equipment will be scalding, but the kids aren't hearing it. They trudge to the park as if walking through mud. The air is thick and smells like boiling expired milk; it seems to push back at them. Heat rises from the concrete and warps their vision. At the playground, the slides and swings are indeed so hot they burn the backs of the kids' thighs, and Ash and Rosie demand to go home. Staying inside the air-conditioned apartment with the bedbugs is the lesser of two evils.

"If we had the money for a car, we would have the money to move to a place without bugs," Sandy says. She isn't trying to be bitchy. They had settled into a frustrated truce. The bigger enemies—bedbugs, patriarchy, Justin—are more than enough.

"I know," Steph laments. "I just sort of hate it here now."

"Me, too," Sandy says.

They jack up the AC and watch a movie on the couch, all four of them falling asleep in the hazy afternoon light. Two hours later they wake up in a sweat slick, their bodies sealed together. Their hair is matted to their faces, and their clothes are damp with perspiration.

"Why is it so quiet?" Ash asks.

That's when they realize the AC unit has stopped.

Sandy leaps up to turn it back on. The machine sits mutely on the windowsill, doing nothing. She pokes every button, unplugs it, and plugs it back in. Tries a different outlet.

"It's broken."

"No!" Steph starts to whimper. "I can handle anything, just not this!"

"It's okay," Sandy tries to comfort her. "We can . . . we can . . ." But it's too hot to think.

Steph's phone dings with a message. "Whatever it is, I don't care," she groans.

Sandy's phone dings from the kitchen table soon after. "Ash, I will pay you to go get the phone for me."

"I can't," Ash pants, sprawling out between them on the couch. "It's . . . too . . . hot."

Steph's phone rings now, which alarms her. Everyone in her life texts—even her mother has been trained to—so a phone call can only mean someone has died. She gets up to answer but misses the call. Sandy's phone begins to ring in the kitchen. Steph looks at the screen and decides to answer it for her.

"Okay," she says calmly. "Okay. Honey, don't worry about any of it. We've got you." She hangs up.

"What's going on?" Sandy asks.

"It's Kaya. She's at the hospital. She's in labor."

"But she isn't due for another ten weeks!"

"I know," Steph says. "She's going in for an emergency C-section like now."

"Where's Kayla?"

"With her at the hospital."

"I'm ordering a car."

"Pack a bag, kids. We're going to Queens after all."

Mykayla Ash Rose Devine is three pounds of pure fight. She relies on machines to breathe and eat, and her skin is so thin you can see all the blue veins branching down her limbs like an old lady. In the picture Kaya sends, the baby's fists are the size of peanut shells and balled so tight they wonder if there are fingers inside. But already there are glimmers of Kaya's beauty in her face.

"Ash and Rose after her siblings. Mykayla after me and Kayla. I'm cheesy, I know."

"It's beautiful," Sandy writes back.

"It's perfect," Steph agrees.

"I don't know how long I'm going to be in here."

"It doesn't matter," Steph replies.

"We're not going anywhere."

There must have been a sale on pistachio-green paint in 1971. The hallways of Sandy's old apartment building and the basement of Steph's childhood church had been painted this exact color, now covering the first floor of Kaya's house in Astoria. The walls, the moldings, the doors and doorknobs. Green everywhere, like a perpetual St. Patrick's Day.

"Yiya Devine was a Greek Jew. She came over from Athens when she was nineteen and married my grandpa when she was twenty," Kaya explains. "She got a little excessive trying to fit in with her Irish Catholic in-laws."

The little brick house is typical of those built in the 1920s: two stories on top of an unfinished basement, four bedrooms and a bathroom upstairs, and a tiny water closet under the staircase on the first floor. While it's outdated and small, there is a feeling they always get as they walk up the steps to the front door, a feeling of being *home*. The curved front window has a ledge that Kaya has covered with throw pillows. Sitting there, looking at the street, Sandy and Steph unclench their fists for the first time in ages.

The backyard is where Yiya Devine's authentic vision took shape. Seven rosebushes line the chain-link fence. Fragrant, hearty, unstoppable—the more they are cut, the more they grow. Their bloom season seems to last longer than any natural one should, and on cooler days when the windows are open, their perfume drifts into the house.

Steph, Sandy, Rosie, and Ash live at the house in Astoria and take care of Kayla while Kaya and the baby are in the hospital. They stay there the night Kaya comes home from the hospital and hold her as she cries for her infant, still in the NICU. They stay the following night just because. On the third night, Kaya's C-section stitches get infected and she has to go back to the hospital, so they stay longer. It's the dog days of summer, when time drips slowly as a bead of sweat. The days seem to come to a standstill under the weight of all that heat, and nights stop moving when you close your eyes. Ash's summer camp in Manhattan was free, so Steph doesn't care if they stop going. Rosie is happy anywhere Ash is. Kayla thinks her life is a nonstop slumber party. And the lush backyard that Kaya's grandmother had cultivated is an oasis for them all.

Justin had paused visitations for six weeks that summer while he was on tour with a new band. According to Kaya, he is still claiming that Mykayla is not his baby.

"I'm going to fucking kill him. This time I mean it," Steph says.

"Shhh," Sandy says. "Ash is quiet, but they listen to every word you say."

"Fine." Steph loads plates into Yiya Devine's ancient dishwasher. When the wonky door refuses to close, she shoves her hip against it until it clicks, locks, and groans into action. "If you won't let me pour sugar into his gas tank, can I please tell him what a loser he is?" Steph begs.

"Let's wait. We need to be smart about this." Sandy wants to do some social-media sleuthing first. Maybe there is an explanation for this particularly heartless turn of events.

"Oh my god!" She grabs Steph's arm. "So Justin is having a great time on tour. Good for him." She taps and scrolls. "He is in a new band, as we know. Don't hold your breath for fame and fortune just yet. His new band is called Bathed in His Blood, and it appears—wait, let me confirm . . . yep, it's Christian rock."

"What?" Steph takes Sandy's phone out of her hand. She swipes and taps and expands various pictures. "Holy shit. It's Christian *metal*," she cries.

"I didn't know that was a thing."

Steph reads aloud all the Bible quotes in the captions of his band's posts. "Bathed in His Blood does sounds pretty metal."

"Somehow I have a feeling this is going to come back to bite us."

"I'm not worried," Steph says. "He's a chihuahua. All bark, no bite."

Kaya's infection clears up and she comes home, but Mykayla will be in the NICU for another four weeks. Walking up the stairs to her bedroom is too painful, so Kaya sets up camp on the living room couch. It is clear by the next morning that she needs more help. She sits on the sofa, forcing droplets of breast milk into flimsy plastic bags every three hours, looking at pictures of Mykayla on her phone and weeping.

"Please don't leave," she begs Sandy and Steph. "Whatever you're paying for rent now, I'll match it."

They tell her their rent in Washington Heights. Kaya spits out her water.

"How does anyone live in Manhattan? If you paid me half that, I'd be happy. Or stay for free. I don't care. The mortgage was paid off years ago. I just pay taxes, insurance, and utilities. My brothers and I own it, but they don't care what I do. There's room for all of us. Please stay."

"I already uprooted Ash in February. If we move again, Ash will have been in three different schools in one year."

"They hate their school in Washington Heights," Sandy says.

"What? They never told me that. They said they loved their teacher," Steph replies.

"They loved their teacher, that's true, but the girls in their class were cliquey and the boys didn't know what to do with them. No one bullied them, but no one made them feel welcome, either."

"They told you that? And not me?"

"Aren't you glad they told *someone?* Instead of keeping it all in?"

"Good point," Steph agrees.

"My commute is the same distance, so staying here doesn't affect me, but your trip to the clinic is going to be a haul."

"I think I'm willing to take it on in exchange for that backyard."

"And no bedbugs."

So it is decided. The three women agree on a rent that feels fair, and what is fair is significantly cheaper than the Washington Heights apartment. With the money they're saving on rent, Steph and Sandy are able to hire a professional pest-control company to bag up their stuff and fumigate so they don't bring insects into their new home. Steph gets a spot for Ash in the fifth grade at the same school where Kayla is registered for first grade. Sandy finds a sweet in-home day-care for Rosie, run by three Uzbekistani women just down the street from Kaya's house. It, too, has a nice backyard for the toddlers to play in.

"I never knew how much I missed having a yard," Sandy says. She rocks on a rusty metal sliding chair in the backyard and sips a chilled pinot grigio. Ash, Kayla, and Rosie are drawing with chalk on the flagstone patio. Rosie grabs a piece of chalk right out of Kayla's hand with the righteousness of a toddler. Ash grabs it back and returns it to Kayla, a perceived injustice that makes Rosie howl with rage.

"I wanna go *home*," Rosie says, hugging Sandy's leg.

"Baby, this is our home now," Sandy tells her, forcing a little too much brightness into her voice.

Rosie surveys the scene—the three women drinking wine in plastic cups, the two big kids coloring rainbows on the ground, the rose-bushes, the sunset, and the big brick house.

"This is our *home* house?"

"Yes, this is our home house," Kaya answers. Rosie looks around and sighs, annoyed that she had to ask.

The owner of Kaya's salon threatens to give up her chair if she doesn't return to work, so a mere two weeks after her emergency C-section, she resumes cutting hair full-time Tuesday through Saturday, going to the hospital NICU every day to see Mykayla, then working late at the salon to make up for the long lunch breaks.

It is cruel that of the three mothers she is the one having to put in the longest hours at work, so Steph and Sandy agree to let her have control of the TV once the kids are in bed for the night. A simple kindness too small to be considered a Mom's Days gift. For Steph, though, it is an epic sacrifice.

"Please, Kaya, I am begging you, can we watch something written by writers? Or anything without the words *Real Housewives* in it?"

"I'm saving the *Housewives* for Ash," Kaya says. "That's our show."

"Ash watches the *Housewives* with you? My Ash?"

"They're *my* Ash on Wednesday nights, and yes, I got them hooked. Can we watch *The Bachelor*?"

"Are you allergic to scripted drama? What's the issue here? Talk to me, Kaya. Have you heard of HBO? They've had some really good shows these past few decades."

"I know, I know. I've tried all those shows. I couldn't get into any of them except *Sex and the City*," Kaya says. She settles on the couch between Steph and Sandy and drinks the herbal tea Sandy bought her from a social-media influencer. It's supposed to naturally stop milk production without the painful swelling, and it tastes like freshly mowed grass. Kaya adds heaping spoonfuls of sugar and milk to make it go down.

"To be fair," Sandy says, "*The Bachelor* is not *un*scripted."

Steph makes a gagging sound. "Whatever, I give up." She opens her binder of casework and pretends to tune them out, but she keeps looking up at the TV, raising her eyebrows.

"Look at her," Sandy says to Kaya. "She won't admit it, but she loves this show."

"Gross! I do not. That woman right there—" Steph points her pencil at the screen. "She's a goddamn lawyer. She took the LSATs, did three years of intense study, got a law degree, and passed the bar. And yet here she is spending whole weeks in a bikini, getting a UTI, and trying to convince Zach from Finance to fall in love with her. Know your worth, Aimee!"

"Aimee is in it for the wrong reasons," Kaya points out. "Sarah F. is the one who really loves him."

"Sarah F. wants to be the spokesmodel for a flat-tummy tea company."

"No, she's in love," Kaya says confidently. "You can see it in her eyes."

At the end of the episode, when Sarah F. does not get a rose, Kaya bursts into tears.

"Oh my god, you know what I just realized?" she says, recovering from the vicarious heartache. "Remember that Mormon reality show where the women all lived together with one husband? That's the show we should be on!"

"*Sister Wives!*" Sandy cries. "I loved that show!"

"Yes!" Kaya laughs. "We're like that minus the husband."

"Okay, first of all, that community wants to be called Latter-day Saints, not Mormons. And not *all* LDS practice polygamy," Steph instructs. "In fact, most don't—so it's insensitive to make a generalization like *We're just like the Mormons.*"

"We get it," Kaya says. "Hashtag not all Mormons."

"What we're doing is more like a feminist collective—"

"Steph will be the annoying but lovable social-justice warrior on our reality show," Kaya says.

"Totally!" Sandy says. "Which ones are we?"

"I'll be the hooker with a heart of gold, the sweet slutty one—"

"You're not a slut," Sandy says. "Not that there's anything wrong with sluttiness . . ." She turns to Steph, who is too conflicted to speak. Her respect for Kaya's right to own the label slut is at war with her compulsion to liberate these women from internalized misogyny. Kaya notices all this happening in real time on Steph's face. She giggles.

"Steph's chyron will be, 'Therapist Who Needs Serious Therapy.'"

Sandy's stomach cramps from laughing. "Now do mine!"

"You're the stable, balanced one. Your chyron will be, 'Sandy, Libra, Everyone's Rock.'"

"Aw, thanks, Ky!" Sandy leans over on the couch and hugs her. They give Steph, indignant on her corner of the sectional, a taunting look.

"She's so cute when she's trying to be mad at us," Sandy says.

"You know you want in on this sister-wife action," Kaya says to Steph.

"You can't keep saying that!"

"Okay, we promise we'll be good citizens. Now come hug it out with us!"

"And we have to reinforce healthy sexual esteem for our kids and teach them there is no such thing as a slut, only a spectrum of choices, all of which are valid with consent."

"Okay, Mom."

"We promise."

Steph puts down her binder and crawls across the couch toward them.

"I didn't go to college, but this is what I imagined it was like," Kaya says. "Hanging out with a group of girls you could say anything to and they'd love you no matter what."

"I went to college, and I can promise you that's not how it went down. I had a whole crew of supposed sisters, but it was never like this," Sandy says.

"I have an actual blood sister," adds Steph, "and it was never like this, either."

Kaya strokes Steph's hair. Her split ends are disgusting, but she chooses not to ruin the moment by mentioning it.

Justin is a fool. He is stupid and selfish, childish and stubborn, gullible and annoying. But he isn't cruel. As frustrated as both Steph and Sandy have been with him, they can't bring themselves to hate him, because he has never done anything truly hateful. The way he is treating Kaya, though, makes it hard to maintain this position. When Justin returns from his tour, he refuses to visit Mykayla in the NICU. He ignores most of Kaya's calls and texts, only occasionally responding with, "That's not my kid."

"What the actual fuck?" Steph screams. "This isn't a daytime talk show. Is he serious?"

"He said with a whore like me, anyone could be the father," Kaya tells them.

On top of all this, Kaya is on her feet at the salon eight hours a day, wearing a special compression belt to ease the pain of her C-section, and trying not to cry in front of customers.

"Even if I had maternity leave, I'd have to go back," she explains to her new housemates. They are assembling cheap metal bunk beds in Kayla's room for Rosie and Ash. Rosie is obsessed with Kayla's vast collection of dolls, and Kayla is loath to lend them out for a whole night, so the toddler who could not close her eyes without holding her mother's ears has decamped happily to the room across the hall. Ash turns their nose up at these childish obsessions and looks forward to doing so from their perch on the top bunk.

"The salon is full of vultures. It's so competitive. Like, cutthroat. There was this one stylist, Mara, who used to sabotage our color mixes, then when the clients got pissed off, Mara would use it as an opportunity to lure them in. Someone brought in a nanny cam, and we finally caught her pouring extra pigment into a mix another stylist had prepared. She was fired that day. But that's the work environment of my salon. It's so toxic. In the two weeks I was recovering, bitches already started poaching some of my regulars. I have a few loyal clients but not enough to earn a living."

"You do not need all this stress. Not ever but especially not now," Steph says.

It all feels so hopeless that hating Justin gives them a little taste of power. Of the three mothers, Sandy is on the best terms with him. In person, because their kid is there, Steph manages to be civil, even kind, but over text she is ruthless. If he is running late to meet them for a weekend pickup or drop-off, she fires back, "oh no, was there a nü metal crisis and you had to drop everything and sing about it?"

Sandy remains diplomatic. When Justin runs late, she simply waits and says nothing. Because of this, Justin is more likely to give her basic info, like whether or not Rosie ate, was bathed, or pooped when she was with him. She has a tiny bit of leverage, so she elects herself to speak up for Kaya.

"Mykayla is just a baby," she texts him. "She's our daughter's sister. She needs you right now."

"That kid's father could be anyone. She doesn't even look like me."

"How can you tell from a picture of a preemie covered in tubes?"

"You think your so smart. Ask your new landlord how she makes her money."

"Your baby is in the NICU and she needs your help."

"Stay out of my business. End of discussion."

For the second time in her life, Sandy blacks out while totally sober. Just as Alex's breakup had swept her away, Justin's words now knock the color out of her world. She feels dizzy. Her vision gets blurry. After a few seconds that feel like hours, she comes to and rises out of her stupor to go find Steph.

Sandy is afraid of what she's going to say when she knocks on the door, when Steph says, "Come in," when she opens that door and steps inside. Part of her is plotting Justin's murder and how to get away with it, which means implicating Steph as either an accomplice or a witness, a horrible place to put someone you love.

The kids are home, watching TV in the living room, and she is also afraid that the words she is about to say about Justin, words she has no control over at the moment, would be traumatizing for them to hear. She is flaming hot with rage. At Justin. At everything he represents. The unfairness, the irresponsibility, the damage and chaos people like him cause. It is everywhere in this world, and she's sick of it. She wants to punch him in the face. She wants to scream and swear about how much she hates him. But instead, she blurts:

"I want to go to law school."

If it is a surprise to Sandy that these words came out of her mouth, it isn't to Steph. "Welcome to your destiny!" she says.

"Really?"

"Really. I love this for you."

Sandy sits on Steph's bed and fills her in on her exchange with Justin. "I'm sick of pretending that it's normal not to have maternity leave. I want someone who's actually been through this to help women like Kaya. Like us. There are so many of us out there, and we're all so busy working and giving our kids a good life that we don't have time to fight back. I think this is my calling."

"I am *so* here for this late-in-life awakening!" Steph all but squeals.

"I'm not even thirty-six yet!"

"Whatever, keep going, I'm listening."

"I never thought I was very smart. My college boyfriend was brilliant and I was always struggling to keep up with him, so that confirmed it. But that girl on *The Bachelor* didn't seem smart at all, and she's a lawyer. I know this is stupid, but I thought, if she could do it, maybe I could, too?"

"Okay, first, Aimee is a woman, not a girl. Don't infantilize. Second, many women get the message that they can either be pretty or they can be smart, but they can't be both. You chose pretty. And who can blame you? Pretty offers the most immediate rewards. But, Sandy, you're both gorgeous *and* smart."

"You think I'm pretty?"

"Not pretty. Gorgeous." She puts her hand on Sandy's face. "You have to know that."

"No one's ever said that before."

"What?" Steph shakes her head. "They were obviously stupid or blind or self-absorbed or I don't know what, but you are one of the most beautiful women I've ever met in my life. *And* you're also smart. Definitely smart enough for law school."

"You really think so?"

"Are you kidding? Of course!"

"Can I tell you something else? It's super cheesy."

"Tell me."

"My mom named me after the first woman on the Supreme Court. I know this sounds ridiculous, but, like, maybe that's a sign?"

"I don't think that's ridiculous at all."

The mention of her mother makes Sandy cry. Steph pulls her in close, strokes her hair, and listens. This makes Sandy cry even harder—the love she feels for Steph is something she never could have imagined in her life. Just as she is thinking this, Steph reaches out and wipes her tears. Sandy leans closer and kisses her on the mouth.

It is a long, deep kiss. Steph takes her neck in her hand, and they kiss faster. It feels shockingly familiar, as though they have been in love for decades and this is just another ordinary moment of passion in a long life of passionate love, old and new at once.

Soon they are lying on Steph's bed, taking off each other's clothes. This used to be the moment Sandy dreaded, when her head would swirl: *What comes next? What is he thinking? What does this mean?*

Two things are different about this kiss: the softness of Steph's lips and the absence of fear. She isn't afraid of Steph pulling away first or of what game they are playing and if she is winning it or not. She is simply in the moment, and in this moment, she is making out with her best friend in the world and her lips are so soft.

Why are secrets so much fun? The tension required to keep a secret deepens release, catapulting an average orgasm into a full-body event, fingers and toes and the tops of the ears and scalp and knees and spine and all the organs of the pelvis as well as the stomach and heart, all of them shuddering and relaxing together. So, yeah, that. Then, someone you think you know, a body you've sat beside doing normal, boring things, becomes a whole new world once naked, a world only you have access to.

Over the next few weeks, Steph and Sandy fall into a pattern of sexting, sneaking handwritten love notes into each other's purses, and leaving tiny presents in each other's bedrooms. Sandy comes home from work to find the newly released print edition of *People* magazine slipped under her door, with an article about *The Bachelor* fully annotated by Steph's hot-pink gel pen. Steph finds a fancy chocolate bar on her pillow one day, a couple of tubes of a hard-to-find flavor of lip balm a day later. Then one morning Sandy finds an LSAT prep book waiting for her next to a cup of hot black coffee in her favorite mug. She can't help crying a little. It is confirmation—all of this is really happening.

Studying for the LSATs becomes their cover for hooking up. It's boring enough to drive Kaya into her own bedroom, where she can fall asleep to the stylized combat of *Real Housewives* on her tablet, leaving the living room couch for the lovers. Until one night when she doesn't leave after the live broadcast of the finale and all its ensuing commentary shows.

"Who wants to check out the new Jane Austen series?" Sandy asks.

"There's another new Jane Austen series?" Steph groans.

"This one's different—it's not an adaptation of her novels. It focuses on her real life before she was a writer, when she was a teenager."

"Is it funny or serious?" Kaya asks.

"It's a fictional interpretation of a true story about her drama with this guy she loved but couldn't marry because of money issues."

Steph is aghast. "So it's both a teenage drama and a period piece?"

"I tried to read those fucking books in high school," Kaya says. "All my teachers were like, *Ooooh, it's so modern,* even though it's all old and British and shit. I was always like, why you playing this stupid game, Lizzie Bennet—just be a whore, you know?"

"I would rather die of syphilis in the poorest brothel in London than spend five minutes with the Bennet sisters," Steph agrees.

"I can watch it alone," Sandy says to them, eyeing Steph.

"I'm gonna self-soothe with some old eps of *Housewives.* Good night." Kaya kisses them both on the forehead and walks slowly, carefully, up the stairs to her bedroom. When Steph hears the door shut, she hops on Sandy, straddling her lap.

"The things I do for love."

In bed alone when the house is empty, they can be naked and athletic and loud, but what is inexplicably hotter is when they snuggle under a blanket on the couch, the LSAT book and some papers and pens performatively arranged on the coffee table, hands jammed down each other's sweatpants, shirts and socks still on. The need to be quiet has Sandy biting Steph's shoulder. Steph presses her face into the faux-suede couch cushion and moans. They come as hard as teenagers afraid of getting caught.

It is one of the miraculous things about love—the way time explodes and the lovers get to re-create all the years before they knew each other. Steph and Sandy become little kids who play and tease and tussle, teenagers who lie and scheme, young adults who dream big, parents who solve problems together. All of this, all of time, compresses inside the container of new love.

"We should tell Kaya," Sandy says when they're done for the night.

"Yes," Steph agrees, "but not yet. There's so much going on, and I kind of want to enjoy this as it is. Does that make sense?"

"It does, actually," Sandy says after a thoughtful pause. "It's just about us right now. Soon it won't be. I mean, in addition to Kaya, we have to tell the kids. And our families and all that. But this time belongs to only us, so let's savor that while we can."

"Exactly."

A secret is also a lie of omission. If they are being honest, both Steph and Sandy are afraid of what their new relationship will mean for their home in Astoria. Will Kaya want to live with a couple? Will she ask them to leave? There are enough new feelings to process without adding another relocation to the mix. Somewhere inside, however, they both know this is an excuse. The one they are really hiding from is Justin.

At the end of September, baby Mykayla is finally released from the hospital. Her homecoming is a grand event. Ash and Kayla attack several poster boards with all the glitter in the house and paper the doors, the walls, and the front bay window with WELCOME HOME signs. Steph makes her mother's meatloaf recipe with a generous side of collard greens, protein and iron her truest love language for this family. Sandy cleans the whole house top to bottom and puts fresh flowers in Kaya's room.

"You're home now, Little-little. This is our family," Kaya says, weeping. She hands the baby to Steph, who nuzzles her face into Mykayla's thin black hair and inhales deeply. "If we could bottle this new-baby smell, we'd be billionaires."

She hands the baby to Sandy. "Ohhhhh," Sandy coos. "I love her so much!" She cries like a fool looking at Mykayla's preemie nose. "Should we have another?" she says to Steph.

"What?" Kaya asks.

Steph and Sandy look at each other. No, they agree instantly, silently, now is *not* the time. This is Mykayla's moment, not theirs.

"I'm a one-and-done mom," Steph says, recovering quickly. "That I got three more bonus kids in this lifetime is already better than I could have hoped for. Besides, we are running out of bedrooms."

Once all the moms get to hold Mykayla, the siblings clamor for their turn.

"She's *my* sister," Kayla says, "so I get to hold her first."

"She's my sister, too," Ash fights back. "I'm older and more re-sponsible. You don't even know how to hold a baby. I've been holding babies since Rosie was a baby, so I'm experienced."

"My baby." Rosie stomps her foot.

The moms set up all the kids on the couch with pillows to support them while they hold the tiny baby, who is still only five and a half pounds. Everyone is so in love they learn to wait their turn.

Life is different with an immunocompromised newborn at home, but it is also comforting in its sameness. School, work, groceries, laundry—the perennial quartet plays on. The women and their kids dance through the days in various combinations, following a rhythm that is constantly in flux.

As a preemie, Mykayla still needs a lot of extra care. She has an apnea machine and a rigorous feeding schedule to catch her up on weight gain. "I could never do this without you," Kaya says to Steph and Sandy, and the guilt strikes them too much to ignore.

"We have to tell her," Steph says.

"I know," Sandy says.

"Okay, so when?"

"Let's wait until things settle down a little more."

It is cowardly, but they agree to let the justification stand. Kaya spends more time in her bedroom with the baby, trying to teach her how to sleep outside the hospital, where the noise and light made day and night harder to distinguish. Kaya staying in her room means more time for Steph and Sandy to be alone in one of their rooms. This is also convenient and something they selfishly want to hold on to.

Their street in Queens is lined on both sides with maples and elms that one by one ignite with color that fall. The air smells fresh with autumn's decay. Rosie's second birthday has come and gone;

then, on the weekend of Sandy's birthday, Justin announces he will be taking both Rosie and Ash for the entire weekend and every other weekend thereafter. He constructs a whole narrative around being excluded from his daughters' lives.

"I invited him to the party we had for Rosie in the backyard," Sandy says. "I have texts to prove it. Now he's saying I excluded him? He's trying to stage something."

"He's a big baby," Steph replies. "Wait, did he say *daughters?*"

"Yeah."

"How many times do I have to explain it before the village idiot understands? How hard is it to say *kids?* It's a spelling word on his grade level."

"It's my fault," Kaya says sadly. "If it weren't for me, he probably would've come to Rosie's party."

"No, he was pulling this bullshit before we even met you," Steph assures her. "Give me that baby, hon." She takes a bleary-eyed Mykayla from Kaya's arms and settles on the couch with her. "Go take a nap. You need one."

"I'm so tired I can feel the individual creases under my eyes getting deeper. I feel like I'm made of paper and someone just scrunched me into a ball."

Sandy massages Kaya's shoulders. "This is the beauty of the formula-fed baby. We can take care of her while you sleep as long as you need."

Since Kaya has to work all weekend, they make her Friday afternoon off as easy as possible. Steph consults the parent phone list for Kayla's class and arranges a playdate after school. Sandy packs bags for Ash and Rosie and agrees to be the one to take them to Union Square for their meetup with Justin.

At the drop-off, Justin looks different. He's in his Jesus era, hair parted in the middle and striving to reach his shoulders, his beard thick and professionally groomed. He wears a lot of chunky silver rings, and the barbed-wire tattoo that used to ring his left bicep has been updated into a crown of thorns above a mournful-eyed Jesus.

He looks squirrelly, his eyes darting around the station, avoiding Sandy's face as she tries to explain Rosie's current potty-training status.

"She will sit on the potty to pee, but if you even suggest that she try to poop on the potty, she will hold it in for *days*. So offer her a diaper like forty-five minutes after breakfast and then again right before dinner. . . ."

If he's absorbed any of this, he doesn't show it. Justin scoops a wiggling Rosie into his arms. He scratches his fingers under the rings and keeps glancing around as if he's being stalked. Sandy would have been stressed, too, but on the ride down she gave all the same information to Ash, and she is both relieved and depressed that a fifth-grader is going to be the reliable caregiver this weekend.

Justin's phone beeps constantly, and he puts Rosie down to check it.

When she spies a woman selling candy farther down the platform Rosie tries to make a run for it. Sandy grabs her with jaws of life ferocity, which Rosie does not appreciate. Her shrieks echo for all to hear.

"Everyone is staring," Justin says. "Let's go, Ashley."

"It's Ash, Justin."

"Come on. We're still on this phase?"

"Hey, honey," Sandy says to Ash, "I saw the churro lady at the other end of the platform. Go get some for us to share with Daddy and Grandma T, will you?" She hands them a twenty-dollar bill. She gives Rosie her phone and cues up a revolting video of a kid opening boxes of doll accessories.

"It's not a phase," she says once Ash is out of earshot. "This is who they are, and it's unlikely to change no matter who stands in their way. It's honestly easier if you get on board than if you fight it."

"*Who they are* . . . She just turned ten years old this summer. She has no idea who she is!"

"Look," Sandy tells Justin, "I know this is hard. I get it."

"No, you don't. She's not your kid."

This is not true. In biology, sure, but in spirit, hell no. Sandy has clocked more hours with Ash in the last year than Justin probably has in two years. It's almost crass to hear him say they are not her kid. She has loved Ash in the unconditional way she loves Rosie from the moment she met them and has felt like a stepparent since they moved in together, before she and Steph became a thing. None of this is admissible at the moment.

"Okay, you're right. I don't understand. So explain it to me."

"She loves glitter!"

"Glitter is awesome, Justin. It belongs to everyone."

"She was always a tomboy, but that doesn't mean she's a boy."

"They're not a boy."

"This whole nonbinary thing is some bullshit a therapist invented to make money."

"It's not something we talked about when we were kids, except in hideous, not-funny jokes, but I promise you it's real and it's not new."

"She and my mom are obsessed with that ballroom-dancing show! One time Ma watched it without her, and Ashley flipped out and cried. Now Ma won't watch it unless she's there. I can hear them upstairs screaming and cheering and pretending to do the moves."

"All of that is still who they are."

"And her hair—" At this, his voice cracks. "It was so pretty. When she was little, people used to stop me all the time and ask to touch her hair."

"I can imagine."

"It's my dad's hair. The color, the shine. Never seen anything like it except on him and her."

There it is—the wound beneath the armor. He loosens his fists, lets his phone slip back into his pocket. He looks at her for the first time.

"I know," Sandy says. She touches his arm and he flinches as though zapped by static electricity. He looks around the station warily. Sandy withdraws the gesture but not the kindness. "It's hard letting them grow up and become these people we didn't expect they would be. You and I will probably go through this in some other way with Rosie when she gets older. It's all part of parenting. But you've got to understand: kids like Ash who don't get support from their families and communities, they kill themselves. Like, at an alarming rate."

Maybe it is fear, a fear so big he can't bring himself to acknowledge it. A loss so devastating it is unthinkable, and so, to protect himself, he doubles down on dismissal, holding on to whatever is convenient to justify his protective armor. Or maybe he is just a self-centered simpleton. Who knows? Justin's face winces in disdain. The angry rumble returns to his voice.

"You sound like Steph. I knew she'd poison you. I should have never allowed you two to meet."

"You don't control us," Sandy snaps. "And you never will."

Ash returns with a greasy paper bag of churros. Justin grabs their hand, scoops up Rosie, and starts to walk away. Separated abruptly from the videos on Sandy's phone, Rosie goes boneless and howls.

"Justin, you're forgetting something," Sandy says coyly. She holds up the kids' backpacks of clothes and stuffed animals. Justin turns around and marches back toward her, dragging Ash with one hand, holding the fish flop of Rosie in his other arm. Sandy asks Rosie for one more kiss goodbye, which calms her. She bends down to kiss Ash.

"Bye, Other Mother!" Ash says proudly.

"Don't call her that," Justin grumbles as they walk away.

"Why?" Ash says. "It's true."

With both kids gone for the weekend, Steph and Sandy can sleep in the same bed without any fear of being interrupted, going downstairs to breakfast separately to keep up the charade for Kaya. Sunday is Sandy's birthday. Steph has bought her a buttery leather tote bag big enough to fit her LSAT book but structured enough to be stylish doing it. Sandy looks at the label—a brand way out of anyone's price range—and opens her mouth to argue, but Steph shuts her up with a kiss.

"Don't you dare start about the price. I bought it used from this fancy consignment store where rich women get rid of practically brand-new stuff."

"I love it. But do you know what I really want for my birthday?" Sandy says.

"Tell me."

"I want to tell Kaya about us."

"We'll do it tonight. After family dinner."

Justin texts to say that he is too busy to take the train to the meetup spot at Union Square, that his mother will drive the kids to Queens instead. About an hour and a half later than their agreed-upon drop-off time, Tara's car pulls in to the driveway. Tara is in the passenger seat and another woman is driving. The woman appears to be in her thirties but weirdly resembles Tara, with the same pinched mouth that looks like it is both searching for and rejecting a cigarette at the same time.

"Is that her . . . niece?" Sandy asks.

"I've met the whole family. There are no nieces," Steph says.

Sandy opens the back door and unbuckles Rosie from her car seat. "Hi, I'm Sandy."

"I know," the woman says.

Ash gets out of the car, wearing a pink cotton dress. A thick plastic headband studded with rhinestones wraps uselessly around their close-shaved hair. Rosie is in a matching dress, her hair in French braids so tight they look painful. Tara gets out of the car, kisses both kids goodbye, and nods at their mothers. For a moment she stares at the red-brick house, sizing it up, then shakes her head and gets back in the car.

"Get me out of this friggin' thing," Ash says, pulling the dress over their head as they stomp up the stairs. The headband flies off. They pick it up and snap it in half.

"Who was that in the car with Grandma T?" Steph asks.

Justin has never forced Ash to wear anything they didn't want to wear before. This mystery woman might be the one behind the forced girl-drag.

"That's Mara," Ash calls down the stairs. "Daddy's fiancée."

"She's what?"

"Daddy's getting married."

"Honey, what you're experiencing right now is emotional whiplash," Steph says, slowly and deliberately. She's holding both of Kaya's hands, alternating a light squeeze of one, then the other, to keep her in her body before she flies away into a full-blown breakdown. "It's like a car came out of your blind spot and hit you. It's okay. Just breathe."

"How could he? How? He found someone else and *got engaged*? So soon? How—"

While Kaya hyperventilates on her bed, Sandy sets up the kids in the living room with tablets disabled of any restrictions. The nuclear option—it would keep the kids quiet for a scary amount of time.

"He's probably just 'engaged' engaged," she hears Steph saying as she comes back into Kaya's bedroom. "Some stupid declaration to get attention on social media. I'm sure they haven't set a date. People do this all the time, and that would be the most Justin of moves."

"Er, no," Sandy says softly. She flashes her phone at Steph with an image of Justin on bended knee and the woman from the car staring down at him. The caption reveals that their wedding date is December 31.

Kaya gets under her comforter. Her hands burrow deep into her thick curly hair, absently plucking out strands one by one. Steph feeds Mykayla a bottle, then takes her to her room, lays her down on her bed, and turns on the white-noise machine.

"I'm thinking now is not the time to tell her," Sandy whispers to Steph as they pass in the hall.

"Yeah, we're pushing that back a few weeks."

They return to Kaya's room and sit on the end of her bed. Kaya lies motionless in the fetal position. Her eyes are glazed over from crying.

"Justin dumped me because I'm a prostitute."

"Do *not* say that."

"No, it's true. I used to be a stripper, right? Well, let's just say there are always opportunities, you know? And before my grandmother died and I moved into this house, I was paying rent for this shithole apartment and paying for daycare for Kayla and paying for hairdressing school. It was a lot. My parents couldn't help me. Both of my brothers paid their own way through college. My parents love us, but they're morons with money. That's why Yiya left the house to my brothers and me. She knew my parents would piss it away. Anyway, before I got the house and got on my feet again, I took advantage of some opportunities. Honestly, I never felt bad about it. The money was good and I only worked with guys I knew from the club, guys I genuinely liked and trusted. A lot of the time I worked with my friend Tasha, before she moved to New Orleans. We could charge twice as much for half the work. I know how to be safe, and the money got me through some hard times."

"Sex work is work," Steph says. She's been dying to use that line in a real-life setting for a long time. Her face is pink with self-righteous anger. Sandy swoons a bit watching her. "You don't have to justify it or minimize it or qualify it at all. It should be legal and unionized and stigma-free."

"I hate the term *sex work*. It makes me feel like an old lady in a hairnet clocking in at the dildo factory. I was a stripper and an escort, which is something only very hot people can do."

"How much did you make?" Sandy blurts.

"Sandy!" Steph balks.

"No, it's okay." Kaya tells them, and they sit back in amazement.

"Do you know how many tables I had to wait to get that kind of money?" Steph gasps.

"I know. I haven't done it in a while. My passion is hair. You guys know that. Once I got a good clientele at the salon, and my grandma died and Kayla and I moved in here, I was financially okay for the first time in my life, and I didn't need to see my guys anymore."

"Again, you don't need to justify—"

"Let her finish," Sandy says gently.

"Sorry."

"People get so weird about sex, never mind *sex work*." She looks at Steph, who flashes a tiny smile of approval. "So I never told anyone. Except Justin. You don't understand. We were really in love. I felt like I could tell him anything. But it made him hate me. If I'd known . . . I'm such a—"

"No," Steph interrupts. "There is so much that is lovable about you. The list is endless."

"Endless!" Sandy chimes in. "You are so funny and kind and generous and literally the hottest person I've ever met in my life."

"He didn't fall out of love with you because of how you made money or anything else you did. He love-bombed and gaslit you. That's what he does!"

"Hello!" Sandy says. "You're sitting here with not one but two of his ex-girlfriends. Clearly the guy has commitment issues."

"But he's committing to *her*," Kaya weeps. "Whoever she is. I have to see her. I have to know what's so great about her."

"Think before you do this," Sandy says. "Do you want to make a bad day worse?"

"I'm choosing violence," Kaya replies.

"Fair enough," Sandy says. Steph bows to Kaya to offer her respect.

Sandy shows Kaya the engagement post she found on social media. Kaya lets out a gasp and throws the phone across the bed.

"That's Mara!" she screams. "That bitch who used to work at my salon. The one who was fired for sabotaging another girl's color."

For a few days, Kaya is ablaze with conspiracy theories. How did Justin meet Mara? Had they been together all along? Was *Mara* the one he was really staring at when he was washing the windows of the salon? Was it supernatural? Is Mara a demon from hell sent to punish Kaya? Was Kaya cursed at birth like a fairy-tale princess? Is Mara her fate or her comeuppance? Is it possible they had met randomly? Is the world really that small?

"Honey, this is getting unhealthy," Steph says kindly.

"You're about two theories away from getting your own Netflix series," Sandy adds.

"I just need to know *when* they met. Like, was it while we were dating, before, when we were taking that break? It would explain everything."

"No, it wouldn't," Steph says. "It would only make you doubt yourself more."

"But if I knew—"

"I promise," Sandy says, "if you knew every single detail of how, when, where, had transcripts of every conversation, every text, HD video footage, all of it, you would still be left with the hurt."

"There's no getting around the heartache," Steph agrees. "You have to let your beautiful perfect little heart grieve." She cuts a thick slice of sourdough and slathers it with butter. She puts the bread in

Kaya's hand. "And let us love you and take care of you in the mean-time."

Kaya lets out a big shuddering sob. It is a cloudburst of grief, hard and fast. A cleansing storm, she is herself again afterward.

"It would be great for my healing process if we could order Greek appetizers for dinner."

"*Fine*," Steph concedes. "Which ones?"

"All of them. And extra pita."

The mothers doubt Justin's ability to handle both Ash and Rosie at the same time on a regular basis, but for several scheduled weekends—for the first time since becoming a father—he does. Mara does not make another appearance, but every other Sunday when Rosie and Ash come home, their hair is braided or curled or shellacked into a new style that looks repressive and severe. Ash is forced into a frilly exaggeration of girlhood, and Rosie always matches. The clothes their mothers pack for them remain untouched in their backpacks.

As soon as they are home, Ash runs to their bedroom to change. That school year, they had asked Steph to start buying boxer briefs, and even those are replaced with girly panties on their weekends with Justin.

"I fucking hate Mara," Ash says, slamming their bedroom door.

"This is what I've been trying to tell you people," Kaya says. "You can only poke a July Cancer so many times before they will literally snap." She pulls all the dollar bills from the swear jar, then scoops out the change. "I'm giving all this money to Ash—they deserve it," she says, thrilled to hear Mara's name smashed to the ground with such violence.

"Honey?" Steph pads up the stairs and stands at Ash's door. "I know you're upset, but you have to use your words."

"I *am* using my words," Ash shouts back. "My words are: I. Fuck-ing. Hate. Mara."

They emerge from their bedroom in their favorite hoodie, the one with the disturbing stoned-looking unicorn on it, and a pair of cutoff sweatpants. A tie-dyed baseball cap is pulled low over their eyes. They thunder back down the stairs, wiping tears on their sleeve. The only thing worse than watching a kid cry is watching them try not to cry, and it kills the three mothers to see Ash this way.

"Daddy never used to care what I wore. Now Mara buys me this shit and he makes me wear it, and if I don't she locks herself in the bathroom and cries."

"It's your body, Ash. Your life, your choice," Steph says. "You can wear the clothes I pack for the weekend."

"I know." They collapse on the couch and hunch over a tablet, knowing full well that no one will contradict this move, not right now. "But when Mara cries, Daddy yells at Rosie and me and tells us we're stressing him out, and then he takes off in his truck and leaves us there with her, and it's just easier to do what she wants until I come home. But I still hate her."

"So tell me, lovey, what does Mara look like when she cries?" Kaya says, cozying up next to Ash on the couch. "Like, does her nose get all red and puffy? Do her dark circles get more pronounced? Paint a picture for me."

"She looks like actual *trash*," Ash declares, blues eyes gleaming with petty joy.

Kaya takes their feet in her hands and starts massaging them. "You are my favorite person in this house," she says.

"Interesting bit of intel," Steph says to Sandy later that night as they study together on the couch. "I have so many questions."

"Me, too," Sandy says. "I was kind of hoping Mara would be cool, like the three of us, like maybe we could recruit her to join our side. But she's in too deep."

"And it seems like Justin is, too."

* * *

A few days later, Sandy and Rosie are walking to the park when Rosie stops and pretends to puke on the sidewalk.

"Sweetie, are you okay?" Sandy asks.

"I okay. I puke like Mara."

"Does Mara puke . . . *a lot?*"

"She do this," Rosie says, and walks down the sidewalk a little farther. Suddenly she stops, clutches her stomach dramatically, puts her hand over her mouth, then pauses. With a great surge, she bends over the curb and pretends to vomit on the street.

It takes all the restraint Sandy has to wait until Steph gets home to tell her in person, reenactment and all. At first, they laugh. Rosie has a flair for theatrics, this cannot be denied. The takeaway from the toddler's performance is interesting.

"Either she's bulimic or—"

"She's pregnant!" Steph screams.

That Christmas, Kaya takes her girls to Florida. No one in her family has met Mykayla yet, and she is excited to work on her base tan. Steph decides to skip her parents' annual party and stay home with Ash. After everything they've been through with Justin, she can't bear to subject her baby to more pain from ignorant family members, especially on Christmas. Sandy's father buys her plane tickets to Minneapolis.

"You still don't know how to say no to him, do you?" Steph says.

"I'm working on it," Sandy whines. "You and Ash should come with us!"

"Not this year," Steph responds. There are a host of good reasons: They still haven't told Kaya about their relationship, and she is their first priority, so it doesn't feel right to tell their families yet. She's never spent a holiday alone with her kid, whose tween attitude blossoms with more brutality each day. "I've been waiting my whole life as a parent for Ash to be old enough to appreciate Chinese food and the movies as a viable Christmas plan, and this is our year."

It all seems valid on the surface, but Sandy gets that feeling like a tiny bolt of lightning is cracking inside her. Just a little bit. A splinter of worry. And hurt. But nothing worth dwelling on. It is Christmas, after all.

* * *

Rosie sleeps the entire flight to Minnesota. "Why can't you nap this soundly at home?" Sandy asks her. Her legs tingle beneath Rosie's sweaty head. Once off the plane, Rosie turns into a little monster. Sandy wishes Steph was there. Her snack game would be weak—too heavy on the dried fruit—but she's so good at laughing her way through moments like this that they're almost fun.

That first night back home, Sandy tries to sneak out for drinks with some high school friends, but her dad and stepmother make it clear they will not be babysitting.

"I'm sure you could find a wonderful sitter online," her stepmother suggests.

The following day, her father and stepmother put on layers of heat-tech spandex and go out for a ten-mile run. Then they go to the gym and the grocery store, making themselves so busy that Sandy wonders why they invited her out at all. The only topic of conversation is what to eat for the next meal, a poorly camouflaged excuse for her parents to congratulate themselves on their austere wellness goals. They hate gluten with the fervor of religious people expelling Satan from their lives. For breakfast, overnight oats made with water and chia seeds; for dinner, a steamed or grilled fish with steamed vegetables.

"Steph always says I'm a foodie who can't cook. I guess this is where I get it," Sandy jokes. She pushes a forkful of salmon into Rosie's mouth. "Come on," she begs, "it's pink! Your favorite color!"

Rosie lets the food fall from her lips and glares at her mother. "It's too yucky for me," she says. "I want yogurt."

"We've cut out all dairy, gluten, and sugar from our diet, and it's amazing how much better we feel," her stepmother says.

"Really, Dad? Not even ice cream?"

Her father used to be a fiend for ice cream. Sandy remembers a snow day in third grade when her father discovered there was no ice cream in the house. He hauled Sandy in her snowsuit to the car and drove fifteen miles an hour in a blinding squall to buy an emergency quart of freezer-burned vanilla from the gas station.

Her father shuffles his napkin from hand to hand and looks down. "We feel so much better. So much more energy."

"You're saying if you died tomorrow you'd be *glad* you didn't eat ice cream? Like, on your deathbed?" Sandy pushes.

"Well, that's certainly morbid!" Her stepmother laughs. They drop the subject. Sandy starts telling them about her law school applications. Her LSAT scores are solid, though not excellent, but her essay, she feels, is the clincher.

"The law school at CUNY is designed for working adults. I'd be assigned an adviser who specializes in mentoring students like me— working mothers. It's a great program."

Sandy's dad and stepmom exchange glances. Her stepmom scrapes the last half of her salmon onto her husband's plate for him to finish.

"I'm just so full!" she chirps. "Did I tell you my niece Katie got engaged? Look at this photo from the proposal," she says, whipping out her phone.

"Yeah, I saw that. I'm so happy for her." Sandy had met this niece once, at her father and stepmother's wedding. They exchanged obligatory follows on social media and haven't spoken since.

"Poor thing had to wait eight years for that ring! Can you believe it took him so long? She nearly died having to wait all that time."

"She could have asked him to marry her," Sandy says.

"Huh?"

"If waiting was so painful, she could have proposed to him. It's not like she was waiting for a kidney donor. She had options."

"She's a neonatal nurse," Sandy's dad interjects. "Hard worker, that Katie. Taking care of babies. Says a lot about a person, that she does work like that."

"You sound really proud of her, Dad."

With a 6 A.M. CrossFit class on the schedule, they all agree to turn in early. Sandy makes a huge nut-milk smoothie for Rosie and her to share before bed. They are so hungry they lick every last drop, scraping loudly at the bottom of the glass with a spoon. Sandy's dad pads down the stairs and, finding them still at the table, starts washing the blender.

"Dad, I'll wash that later. You don't have to."

"I'll do it now. Peg needs it for her green shake first thing in the morning."

He unscrews the base from the glass jug and carefully washes the blades with a sponge. "You know," he says, his back to Sandy, "I never thought I had to worry about you. You were always so self-sufficient."

"Are you worried about me now?" Sandy asks.

"You're applying to schools? And living with roommates? You're not a kid anymore, Sandra. If you need money, you can ask. I can only help you so much—I have Peg to think about—but if it gets you back on your own two feet, I'll do it."

"It's like he's ashamed of me," she tells Steph later that night. She sits on the side of the bathtub while the shower fills the room with steam. "Why can't he believe I am able to live this life and make it work?"

"The better question is, why do you care so much what he thinks?"

This smacks of judgment, even if it is true. Sandy ignores it. "It's two more days until I'm home. I wish you would fly out here. I miss you so much."

"I miss you, too, babe."

"So get on a plane and fly out here!"

"That is an insane amount of money for what would amount to one night in a place that is colder than New York right now."

Says the woman who maxes out credit cards so fast the paint on the raised numbers disappears, which is saying a lot considering most of her purchases are online; the woman who put rent for their old apartment on her credit card, a choice so stupid even Ash would have known better; who bought a brand-new four-hundred-dollar television for their apartment, then bought another brand-new one to replace it when it fell and broke the very next day. *This* woman is suddenly fiscally prudent, suddenly unwilling to splurge to see her lover, who is lonely and sad and needs her?

"Are you fucking kidding me right now?"

"What?"

Sandy hangs up. In a flash, her brain weaves a story on the loom of catastrophe. It is ornate and realistic, spun from threads that sparkle with real-life texture: Steph is a commitment-phobe. Her past relationships, her past jobs, her history of moving and returning home—the warning signs have been there all along. Sandy is just another in a long line of experiments. This explains why she didn't want to tell Kaya or their kids or their families. It explains so much.

The only reason they even moved in together was fear. Sandy fell down in the shower and suddenly realized how vulnerable she was, living alone.

Something that started for the wrong reasons would surely end the same way.

Before she can decide what to do next, her phone rings. It's Steph.

Despite how much she wants to hear Steph's voice, she pauses. "I need some space right now," she texts instead.

There are a few correct responses, and she is waiting for one of them to pop happily onto her phone screen:

I just bought a plane ticket. Ash and I will be there tomorrow morning.
Come home! Minnesota is too far away and it's making us both crazy.
You need to eat 3–5 servings of gluten. STAT. Then call me back so I can apologize in a way you can hear.
I'm sorry. I love you. We'll get through this.

What Steph texts: "Okay."

Sandy wakes up the next morning in an empty bed. Her heart seizes—where is Rosie? She feels around the blankets, finding nothing. She looks under the bed and in the closet. The staircase at her dad's house is hardwood, and the railings are open. The best outcome of a fall down those stairs would be stitches. She races down and finds Rosie sitting on the kitchen floor, looking at YouTube videos on her grandfather's phone.

"There she is," her dad says, and Rosie gets up and hugs Sandy's knees.

"What time is it?"

"Late. We missed our CrossFit class," her dad says. He's smiling but not laughing.

"Why didn't you wake me up?"

Her stepmother buzzes around the kitchen, cleaning the few dishes in the sink and stacking them on a towel. She sips a mug of black coffee. "We tried. You were out cold."

"I'm—" She is about to say *sorry*. But why? She had slept. That was her big crime. They got to spend time with a gorgeous toddler, their only grandchild. There was nothing to apologize for. "I must have been so tired." She pours herself a cup of coffee. There is only enough left in the pot for half a cup.

"Thanks for watching Rosie."

"Well," her stepmother says.

"Okay, then," her father adds. The subtext is excruciating. Sandy stifles a laugh. "We'll get going now. See you at lunch."

"You betcha," Sandy replies.

Taking her own advice, Sandy searches the kitchen for sugar and starch. She finds cereals made of dried rabbit turds and thin brown crackers that taste like burned seeds. Her parents took the car with Rosie's car seat in it, stranding her in this gluten-free tundra. She would kill for a bodega bagel with a solid inch of cream cheese.

Finally, in the back of the pantry, Sandy finds a tiny packet of airplane pretzels from an airline that went bankrupt years ago. She pours the whole bag into her mouth, crunching happily.

"I need a reality check," she texts Kaya.

Kaya calls her immediately on FaceTime. "Bitch, this humidity is a hate crime to hair. You need a visual," she says. Kaya takes off her sun hat and swoops the phone around her head, giving Sandy a panoramic view of the frizz. They laugh as Sandy catches her up on suburban Minnesota life.

"Ugh, I wish you and Steph were here with me, having cocktails by the pool. You deserve this life. We all do. For a little bit. But you're right—then I need to come home. I cannot do this no-bodegas-on-the-corner joke of a town. It's not civilized. Lemme show you what I finally learned to do."

Kaya takes a big gulp from her fruity, boozy drink, then holds something in her mouth. "Mmmmm-hhhmm-mm-hmm," she goes on, lips shut tight, as though Sandy could understand every word. Then, "Ta-da!" Kaya spits out a cherry stem tied in a knot.

Sandy sits on the cold kitchen floor, spooning peanut butter from a jar into her and Rosie's mouths. She laughs and laughs.

"You still look sad. What's going on, boo?"

"I got in a fight with the person I'm seeing," Sandy ventures.

"You have a boyfriend? How did you keep this secret? When the fuck do you have time to go on dates? You a stealthy bitch. I love this."

"I think drunk Kaya might be my favorite Kaya," Sandy says.

"I got my mom here. She's crazier than me when it comes to being paranoid about these kids. So trust and believe I am enjoying this free babysitting while I treat myself to some day drinking." In reality she has had one cocktail, nursed slowly over the course of an hour. She tips it back to get the last of the juice, and all the ice comes crashing down on her face. "Wait, don't change the subject. You have a secret *lovah*. I have so many questions. Does Steph know?"

Ouch. Sandy isn't prepared for this. It hurts to say yes and hurts to say no, but there is safety in the lie, at least for the moment. "No."

"*Yes!* I'm the first person to know! I need to be the first to know. It's an Aries thing. Don't question me. I am truly at my best on the front lines of gossip. What did you have a fight about?"

"Do you think if something starts out fucked up, like inspired by fear, covered up in lies, that it can ever become legit? Or is it doomed from the start?"

"Oh my god, he's married."

"No."

"No judgment! I love you. I will do some fucked-up shit to his wife if you need me to. Anything short of murder. I will take a shit in a box and leave it at her doorstep if you want."

"Kaya, in what world is that a solution?"

"I don't know! This is your journey. I'm only giving you options." Kaya crunches the ice between her teeth and gazes at the turquoise pool. In the shallow end, her dad and two brothers are playing catch, using Kayla as the ball. They hurl her into the air, catching her just as she hits the water. She shrieks with terror and joy each time.

Oh god, Kaya thinks, *I hope Kayla doesn't think all men will adore her like this.* She eats the rum-soaked wedge of pineapple at the bottom of her cup. *Actually,* she decides, *I hope she does.* Kaya adjusts the wide brim of her hat to shade out the new angle of the sun hitting her face.

"Here's what I know," she tells Sandy. "There are no rules in love. I honestly wish there were. Some relationships start out super fucked up, then turn out to be amazing. And some things are all rainbows and unicorns in the beginning, then turn to shit. We make rules about how it should be because it's too scary otherwise. Love is crazy, girl. But you'll be okay no matter what."

That night Sandy goes with her parents to Christmas Eve mass. During the long homily, Rosie takes all the hymnals out of the metal brackets in their pew and slides them down the bench like a train. Her stepmother looks disgruntled, and her dad acts like he doesn't notice. The choir sings about comfort and joy. The irony is stupid and annoying.

In her boredom, Sandy reflects on what her life was like before Steph. It was okay. She would have eventually found kindred spirits to replace her old friends. She would have found a partner that made her excited about sex again. No doubt she would have found love.

And the best versions of all that would not be as good as five basic minutes with Steph. That feeling of love filling her up. Of being so fully seen and held and adored by someone extraordinary.

Is that selfish? Is it sustainable? Is it enough?

Like a sorceress, Kaya chooses this exact moment to text her, "Don't forget you are a Libra who can talk herself out of anything."

"I love you, Ky," Sandy responds.

Kaya sprays her with a heavy stream of pink hearts and dancing girls holding hands, repeating in a thick column of emoji love on her phone, then, accidentally, a snail. "I'm still drunk."

After mass, when Rosie is asleep, Sandy calls Steph.

"I don't need you to make me feel safe or to help pay rent or to be happy or even okay," she says. "I don't need you for anything. But I want you."

"I totally need and want you," Steph says. "Like, very much both."

"Okay, yeah, me, too."

"I'm sorry I was bitchy on the phone last night. I didn't mean to be. I was just mad at my family for sucking, and then I was mad at you for not being mad at your family for sucking."

"It's okay. I'm sorry, too."

"And the plane ticket—I was dying to come with you, but I'm trying to save money. I want to buy you an engagement ring that astronauts in space can see. Which is so heteronormative it's embarrassing, but I love you so much it's made me want to do fairy-tale shit. I never used to care about my debt. I was all punk rock, eat the rich, debt is not real. Then I met you, and for the first time in my life I care about being responsible, because I can't drag my wife into my financial ruins. I'm trying to sort my shit out, Sandy. That's why I'm not hopping on a plane."

In her past life, Sandy would have pretended to be surprised, shocked even, like she had never entertained the possibility of marrying Steph. In this life, there is no need for a performance. Her first item of concern is locked and loaded:

"In *Hamlet,* his mother was accused of incest for marrying her brother-in-law," she responds immediately. "What will people say about *us*?"

"That we're not Shakespeare."

"I'm sorry I hung up on you. I thought it was over."

"Sandy, I love you in a way that will never be over."

"Okay," Sandy says, because she believes her, and, "I love you, too," because it is true.

They have another Christmas celebration for the four kids, with a surprise visit from Santa on the morning of December 28. Ash is deeply critical of the scam.

"You expect us to believe this shit?"

"I'll give you twenty bucks if you just go with it," Kaya says to them.

With alarming speed, Ash changes their tune. They postulate the route Santa must have taken and the weather conditions over the last few days leading up to their late Christmas.

"Gotta respect that kid's hustle," Kaya cries.

"So easily bribed. This must kill you, Steph," Sandy says.

"It's their Italian side." Steph shakes her head.

Justin's wedding is imminent, and Kaya is still in emotional shambles, so the family keeps the holiday spirit going as a distraction. Chanukah treats, movies nights with themed snacks. Sandy and Steph study up on the contenders of the various reality dating shows that Kaya loves and discuss them at dinner with the passion of sports fans at the playoffs.

Kaya remains strong. She has to. As a mother, she knows what's coming, and she's steeling herself. When the day finally arrives for

Steph and Sandy to drop off their kids for the wedding, it is Kayla who is in shambles.

"I want to be a flower girl, too! Please can I go to the wedding? I have a pretty dress I can wear!" Steph holds Mykayla so that Kaya can cradle her heartbroken girl in her arms. She hugs Kayla tight and rocks her as she sobs. "I know, baby," she whispers. "You are so angry and sad right now. I got you, baby. I got you."

"I hate him," Steph whispers, her breath so hot with rage she feels like a dragon holding back fire. "I hate him so much. He will need a GoFundMe for his scrotum when I'm done with him."

Sandy and Steph aren't allowed to know where the church is, nor the reception, only the address of a salon in Bay Ridge where Tara is scheduled to meet them.

"Does he think we're going to be those people who stand up and say something when the priest asks if anyone objects?" Sandy says.

"God, if Mara's crazy enough to do all this, she deserves him." Steph rolls her eyes.

"Stop bashing him," Kaya says. "It doesn't help."

"Sorry, hon," Sandy says. "When we get back, let's get some champagne."

"Yeah, as soon as Kayla and Mykayla are in bed, we're partying."

"You mean drinking champagne on the couch while watching TV in sweatpants?"

"That is exactly what I mean."

"Then, yes, I'm down to party."

They arrive at the salon on time, but Tara is running late. No problem, they learn, because the stylists and nail tech have been informed by Mara precisely what to do. Sandy has to hold Rosie down to get a coat of polish on her nails. The nail tech makes it clear that she is not paid enough for this drama, so when Ash asks for black polish instead of the burgundy color Mara had stipulated, she agrees. Small victories, full of grace, will get them all through this day.

"Gross," Sandy says. "It just hit me: Mara. Tara."

"Oh, Justin. You sad little man."

Tara shows up about an hour into the appointment, wearing a silk maroon dress, her own hair done in all its layered glory. It is obvious that she has been crying. Her eyes are red and puffy.

"You look lovely, Tara," Sandy says.

"That color's really great on you," Steph adds.

"By order of the bride," Tara explains, a note of resentment in her voice. She keeps tugging at the hem of her dress, pulling up the neckline, never satisfied with how it hugs her body. "What she says goes."

Saying this releases something inside Tara, and she begins to cry right in front of them. She produces a wad of tissues from inside her sleeve and dabs at her cheeks, trying not to smudge the professional makeup job.

Sandy lays a hand gently on her shoulder. "Is everything okay?"

"Yes, it's fine. It's fine," Tara says, staring at her shoes, a horren-dous pair of maroon slingback kitten heels with rhinestones on the toe. "They're moving out after the wedding. I offered them my house and I'd live downstairs in the little apartment, but they say they want a fresh start."

"Oh, Tara," Steph says. "I'm sorry to hear that." It was ancient his-tory, but during the short time Steph lived in the Murray house, she was able to piece together the family history that predated her ar-rival, that the Murrays were unable to admit let alone say: when Pat-rick Murray was out drinking, Justin was the man of the house Tara needed, and when Patrick died, the role became even more impor-tant. Justin was Tara's whole world.

"It's fine," Tara insists again. She smooths out the plastic garment bags holding Ash and Rosie's clothes. "Here." She hands Sandy a maroon velvet dress for Rosie. "You need to get her dressed. She never listens to me."

"She's a wild one," Sandy admits.

"Hey, Peppermint, I got something I think you'll like," Tara says.

Sandy and Steph look at each other, confused. Who is she talk-ing to?

Ash skulks over from the nail dryers, and Tara hands them the garment bag. They lift the dark plastic, and a smile creeps across their face. They don't say anything; they just hug Tara's waist and hold on tight. Tara pats their head.

"All right, all right, go get dressed now."

A few minutes later Ash emerges from the bathroom in a dapper little suit, charcoal-gray, with a maroon bow tie. "Thanks, Grandma T," they say.

"I couldn't find one exactly like Daddy's," she says, "but this is close enough."

"Mara's okay with this?" Steph asks.

Tara doesn't look at her. A wry half smile cracks open her face. "I guess it's too late now."

Over champagne and Doritos, the three women scour social media for pictures of the wedding. Ash looks miserable in the staged photos, but there's a glint of mirth in their sneers, as though pleased with their ability to ruin Mara's dreams. Rosie looks cute but also fails to be the model child, and all pictures of her blur at the edges, barely capturing her before she runs out of frame. Mara is a huge and swollen mess. Her updo is sweaty, and her makeup fails to hide the hormonal acne on her chin. Justin, his face practically green with nausea, looks worst of all.

School starts up again in January and takes over their lives once more. Ash has a big concert coming up, a fundraiser for their school's music department. The honking of their clarinet is threatening to drive them all crazy, but at least they are practicing. They play the same eight notes of a hard-to-distinguish melody over and over again in their room. They play it after school; they play it on weekends. One night Steph catches Ash playing their clarinet while sitting on the toilet.

"What song is that supposed to be?" Kaya whispers the morning of the concert as the mothers are stuffing kids into coats and boots.

"I can't tell," Steph confesses. "They told me twice, and both times I wasn't paying attention. I don't want to hurt their feelings by asking again."

That day at work, Thatcher humiliates Sandy in a group email for forgetting to follow up on an article she is not technically in charge of. Behind Thatcher's back, the staff jokes that the core readership of the magazine is dead and the ones still living are too senile to cancel their subscriptions. In a desperate attempt to reach a younger readership, Sandy has been DM'ing food influencers, while her colleagues go out to five-course meals until late in the night. Sandy is juggling so many different roles at work, only some of which are actually her responsibility, that it's hard to keep track of the deliverables. Was this latest error hers? Yes, sort of. But the high of moral indignation is the only thing getting her through that slushy January day.

Then she gets the email. The law school of her dreams, the one she didn't think she would get into, is accepting her. They are sending her another email later with the details of her financial-aid package, the email promises. In a personal note from the dean, he says that a single mother starting over in her mid-thirties is just the kind of student whose trajectory they want to nurture.

This is not the life I thought I would be living ten, five, even one year ago, Sandy whispers to her mother, wherever she is. *It's so much better than I could have imagined.*

She flies out the door after lunch and doesn't look back. She is so excited she can't sit down the whole train ride to Queens. Her feet barely touch the ground as she walks home from the station. She opens the door, kicks off her wet boots, drops her bags, and yells at the top of her lungs:

"Guess who's going to law school in the fall?!"

Kaya comes running down the stairs and almost knocks her over with a hug. Ash, Kayla, and Rosie jump up and down and cheer in the kitchen. Steph rises from the couch, baby Mykayla in her arms, a sheet of paper in her hand. She walks slowly over to Sandy. Her eyes are shining with love, but her mouth is tight, tense.

"Perfect timing," she says soberly. "Because I'm being sued."

"By who?"

Steph shows her the summons from Justin Murray. "I got served today as I was picking up Ash and Kayla at school."

Sandy reads the document slowly. "He wants *full* custody?"

"He won't win," Kaya says. Her voice shakes. "He can't. Right?"

"What happened?" Ash asks.

"Nothing, baby."

"We dancing!" says Rosie. Kaya puts a dance song on her phone and twerks all the way to the kitchen, the kids copying her every move.

"He can't really do this, can he?" Steph whispers. Brazen Steph. Big-mouth Steph. The woman who used to beat up skinheads twice her size when she was a little teenage punk sneaking into clubs. The woman who made it an art form to humiliate Justin over text. The woman Sandy thinks of as older and stronger even though she's eight years younger. Her face is still, searching Sandy's eyes for reassurance.

Sandy looks at the summons again. Steph has to appear in Kings County Family Court in three weeks. That isn't much time to prepare.

"We'll think of something."

They don't have time to dwell. The concert is in forty-five minutes, and they have to get three women, two kids, a toddler, and a baby dressed up in their cutest outfits and out the door. They make it out of the house in record time, only to discover that Ash has forgotten their clarinet. So they all walk back to the house and start over.

"As long as we catch the four-twelve bus, we'll be fine," Kaya says.

On the walk back to the bus stop, they watch in horror as the 4:12 P.M. bus splashes through a puddle and drives past them.

"Tell me this isn't an omen," Steph says.

"It's not an omen," Sandy says.

"Come on, fam!" Kaya cries. "It's ten blocks to the school. We can do this! Let's race!"

They run. Ash makes it to the corner first and waits for Kayla and then Rosie to catch up. They take the younger ones' hands until the moms arrive and give the okay to cross the street. Kaya power-pushes Mykayla's stroller. "We got this! We got this!" She chants it louder than she needs to. Like a spell—if she keeps repeating it, maybe it will come true.

They get to the school auditorium with a minute to spare. Ash kisses all three mothers and runs to take their seat with the other woodwinds in the school orchestra. The moms find two seats for Rosie and Kayla in the back row, while they stand behind them with other late parents.

The school orchestra is awful. They sound like a group of hungry shorebirds squawking over dead fish on a pier. No one is on beat. No one is in key. And if they are, they are drowned out by the forty other elementary school musicians who aren't. It is a glorious mess of songs none of the moms recognize.

"I think that one was . . . 'Old MacDonald,' maybe?" Steph says.

Kaya screams her head off after each song. "That's *our* baby on clarinet!" she yells.

"We've saved the best for last," the orchestra teacher says, a huge grin on her face. She lifts her arms. The students, poised, lift their instruments. There is a long pause, then the notes that Ash had been practicing so obsessively begin to fill the auditorium.

"I know what song this is!" Steph finally says.

"Is this—

"Yup."

"Oh, I love this song!" Kaya's eyes flood with tears. "I love this song so much." She reaches into Steph's bag in search of tissues.

The chorus to Katy Perry's "Firework" blasts through the confusion. The brass wobbles and the woodwinds honk. Six kids all play the drums and none of them at the same time.

"*Do you ever feel already buried deep?*" Kaya sings along, a little too loud. A tall thin mom with chiseled biceps and a crisp long bob swivels around in her seat to glare at her.

For a moment, Sandy is filled with shame. She feels like a troublemaker about to get detention. She feels poor and out of shape, a failure at life. She looks at this woman and thinks, *This is what I should look like, what I would look like if I had done things the right way.*

Steph clocks the Apple watch on the woman's wrist, the big, fat, irresponsibly sourced diamond on her finger and the sparkling wedding band to match, the tasteful athleisure ensemble whose price tag equals a week of groceries for her family, and she wants to punch the woman in the face. Instinctually, she takes off her earrings. "You got a problem?" she growls at her.

"There's no singing in this show," the woman hisses.

"Whatever, gentrifier!" Kaya tosses out this word with pride. Steph has recently taught her what it means, and she is thrilled for this perfect opportunity to use it right now.

"Excuse me?" the woman says.

Sandy feels Steph's fists ball up. She feels Kaya radiating with grief and rage. She grabs Steph's hand, grabs Kaya's hand, and sings.

"Come on, show 'em what you're worth . . . "

Steph and Kaya join her for the next verse. They are loud and confident and, to their surprise, infectious. Other parents in the audience join in, then the teachers and the kids, until everyone in the auditorium is singing.

"Is this really happening?" Steph asks Sandy.

"What do you mean?"

"Court. Lawyers. More money we don't have, stress we can't afford. And what if he wins? What will happen to Ash in that house, where they don't 'believe' in gender diversity? I'm really fucking scared."

Sandy can't think straight. The wild, defiant howl of the fifth-grade orchestra stuns her rational thought. Which is maybe a good thing. "I think we should just keep singing," she says.

After the performance, the orchestra teacher makes an impassioned plea for all the parents to donate what they can to keep the music program going. The school cannot afford to employ a music teacher full-time, and the department of education deems it unnecessary, leaving the PTA responsible for raising the funds. A poster of a large thermometer hangs on the wall behind the concessions table. A red Magic Marker squiggle reaches up to three of the ten thousand dollars they still need.

"It seems like so little to ask for, and so fucking impossible," Steph mutters as she buys coffee and cupcakes for her family.

They find Ash and hug them until, mortified, the kid pries themself away. This ragtag team of moms and little sisters is so weird, so unlike anything the other kids at school have. But nothing in the world makes Ash feel safer. In a corner of the auditorium, the family sits cross-legged on the floor. Steph feeds Mykayla a bottle. Kaya takes out and refastens the barrettes in Rosie's hair. Kayla lets Ash eat the frosting from her cupcake, and Ash picks the raisins out of their oatmeal cookie and gives them to Kayla.

"I keep wishing my mom were here to fix it," Sandy says to Steph and Kaya. "Or that one of your moms would just drive up and command us all to get in the car in that definitive mom way. Then I realized—I *am* that mother. All three of us are."

"We are."

"We are."

Sandy is served her summons while at work a week later. It's just a piece of paper, and the person Justin hired to deliver it is polite enough, but the whole experience leaves her shaking. How did Justin know her office address? His lawyer has clearly done his research, which implies a lot of other unsettling realities: The man who constantly evaded child support has money for a lawyer. Sandy and Steph don't. Do they have court-appointed lawyers for custody cases, or is that only a criminal thing? Sandy wishes so badly she could fast-forward to the day she graduates from law school and knows better how to defend her family.

After an hour of her stomach churning and her bones rattling, Sandy takes an early lunch at the park across the street. She sits down on a bench damp with melting snow and cries.

"Justin, what is going on? Can we talk about this like adults?" she texts. She feels sick. She can't eat her sandwich. She keeps staring at her phone, waiting for his response.

He doesn't reply until later that night, when she is home. Getting served her court summons at work had felt like an attack, but the house in Astoria is a fortress, where assaults merely ping the brick walls and never reach inside.

"Children need and deserve a stable, healthy home with a mother and a father who are married to each other," he texts. "I want what is best for my children and I will fight for them."

* * *

The balance of seven schedules is a complex and delicate house of cards, and Steph's first appearance at court hurls a brick at it. To survive the day, all three women have to take off from work—Steph to go to court, Sandy to go with her, and Kaya to watch the kids.

"Even on my day off, I have to do someone's hair." Kaya sips her coffee and mists Steph's hair with detangler. She starts combing out the mess carefully with a wide-toothed comb. Kayla and Rosie crawl around on the floor of the bathroom, directly under Kaya's feet, useless and adorable as kittens. "Are all these varying lengths . . . a choice?"

"I'm capable of doing my own hair," Steph says, blowing away the pink frizzy ends Kaya has trimmed.

"Ew. No." Kaya puts down her coffee and whips Steph's hair with a paddle brush. "You know you have naturally gorgeous hair. Like, these follicles are healthy as fuck. But you dehydrate it with that all-natural Dr. Boondocks dish detergent you use to wash it. And that home hair dye you used is gross. If you took care of it, you'd look amazing."

"Don't start!"

Sandy comes in, Mykayla draped over her shoulder with a pink pacifier bobbing fast in her little mouth.

"Is that a sandwich?"

"What? Where?"

"On the back of the toilet."

Kaya restacks the mess of magazines and books on the toilet tank and discovers among them, indeed, a half-eaten peanut butter and Nutella sandwich.

"That's Ash's sandwich."

"How can you tell?"

"I made it for them. Yesterday."

Sandy shrugs and swipes some mascara on her lashes.

"You have to do that in here?" Kaya groans.

"The downstairs bathroom gets no light."

"This blowout makes me look like my mother," Steph complains.

"Exactly," Kaya says. "We're giving Staten Island housewife today."

"She's right," says Sandy, fastening fake-pearl studs in her ears. "We need you to look parental and reliable."

Rosie has gotten some of the trimmed hair into her mouth. Sandy wipes Rosie's lips with her socked foot.

"I have to poop," Ash announces at the doorway.

"Go downstairs!"

"That bathroom gets no light," they answer, squeezing themself inside.

Sandy and Steph put on coats at the door, kissing Kaya and the children goodbye.

"Wait, I almost forgot." Kaya hands them a tin of salted peanuts.

"Um, okay. Thanks?"

"Mara is deathly allergic to peanuts," she explains. "It's all she ever talked about at the salon. Fully fifty percent of her whole personality is this nut allergy. The other fifty percent is being a cunt. If shit gets real, you have a weapon."

In a windowless antechamber of Kings County Family Court, there is nothing but sadness and stone the color of piss. What architect decided this? What project manager signed off on it? The floors, the walls, the ceiling—everything is made of the same yellow granite, like a stone box of human misery.

Rows and rows of women fill the wooden benches. Mothers and grandmothers, ex-girlfriends and ex-wives. Many of them have babies with them. One woman has a black eye and an arm in a sling. Sandy and Steph listen to snippets of conversations, most of them one-sided on cell phones. These women are desperate for help, begging for support, pleading with men to show up.

"Just show up," says a woman with two kids in a double stroller. "Come here and let the judge do his job." She is stone-faced and listless. God only knows the fuckery she has tackled in her lifetime.

"I hate it here," Steph says, moping. She scratches under the neckline of her dour thrift-store dress.

Justin arrives wearing a charcoal-gray suit and a maroon tie. Mara, who looks miserably pregnant, walks behind him and whispers angrily to his lawyer, a man shorter than Justin with a gleaming bald head and a thin mustache hewing close to the border of his upper lip. They pass Sandy and Steph and take a seat on a bench several rows away.

"Look who's here? Jello Biafra!" Steph calls to Justin. "Hey, is that the same suit you wore to your wedding?"

"Shhh," Sandy scolds. "Be good."

Steph has known Justin for thirteen years. Is she supposed to pretend they are strangers meeting for the first time in this courtroom? Is that the protocol? She waves to him. He does not wave back, his gaze focused straight ahead. His lawyer does the same while Mara glowers.

At 9:30 A.M., Steph's court-appointed lawyer shows up. He is not much older than Sandy, though his face sags with stress. A day of beard growth covers his chin and cheeks like a stain.

"Hi." Steph reaches out her hand to shake his. "What's the plan?"

"Plan?" The lawyer pounds on his chest with his fist, suppressing a belch. The smell of alcohol hits them, sharp, unmistakable, oozing from the man's pores. He's either had a beer or two for breakfast or he's still drunk from the night before. "There's no plan. We just go in and do what they say."

"I think we can handle this on our own," Sandy says firmly. Steph looks at her, wide-eyed. Sandy takes her hand and squeezes it.

"Okay," Steph agrees.

"It's your funeral," the lawyer says, belching out loud this time.

"What are we going to do now?" Steph asks Sandy.

"I don't know, but it has to be better than what that guy would do."

It is almost 2 P.M. when they are finally called for their turn. They stand before a court clerk who sits at a desk looming several feet above them. After verifying several pieces of ID for Steph and Justin, the clerk goes through the calendar to set a date for the real hearing, which won't be for another month. All this for a mere formality. Justin's lawyer doesn't seem to understand. He keeps interrupting the clerk to deliver dramatic testimony.

"Your honor, these women, as you can see here—they came together—are living in a morally bankrupt household. They do not have secure housing, move from domicile to domicile as their whims so dictate. Their current landlord is a prostitute, and my client's young daughter is subjected to a life of chaos and instability."

"Sir," the clerk says, "we are setting the schedule today. That's all."

"I understand, your honor," his lawyer thunders, "but I was hoping you would hear our plea on behalf of the father, who is a happily married man, attends church weekly, is a small-business owner and taxpayer, and can provide the stable home his daughter has never had."

"Again, sir, I am the clerk, not the judge. All I do is consult the calendar and set the dates for hearings."

After they are dismissed, Justin's lawyer hands Steph a copy of Justin's petition for custody, along with his business card. His specialties include family law, entertainment law, corporate law, and personal injury.

"He's an ambulance chaser," Sandy says.

"Justin probably found him from a subway ad."

They read the petition on the train ride home. It details the moral degradation of their house in Astoria, making the claim that, by living with a prostitute, Steph is "grooming" their daughter for a life of perversion.

"Funny it doesn't say anything about how he fathered a child he's never met with that same sex worker or how he continuously invalidates his kid's gender. What about that?"

"He's an idiot, and so is his lawyer, but it's a smart tactic. This whole grooming thing is huge for some people. Hopefully our judge sees through it."

"We can't show this to Kaya," Steph says. "She feels bad enough already."

* * *

Knowing what to expect this time, Sandy insists that Steph go to work the day she has court. "I'll be fine." She kisses her cheek just as Ash is coming out of their bedroom.

"We're going to be okay!" Sandy says with too much gusto, covering up the kiss by kissing Ash, too.

"Why wouldn't we be okay?" Ash asks. "What's going on?"

Steph gives Sandy a look. "We are juggling way too many secrets," she whispers.

At Sandy's first court date, Justin's lawyer makes sure to mention that Justin is a happily married taxpaying churchgoing small-business owner, but he doesn't try to convince a powerless clerk to grant Justin full custody. After Sandy's court date is set, they are dismissed from the little windowless box within a box. Justin and Mara walk ahead of Sandy, but his lawyer stops and holds the swinging gate open for Sandy to exit. It is an odd moment for chivalry, given all the nasty things he wrote about Sandy in Justin's petition, but she accepts the gesture. She turns back to thank him when she sees his eyes staring at her ass. He smiles, his gross stencil of a mustache stretching thinner across his face.

"He checked out my ass. Like so conspicuously," Sandy reports once safely back home.

"That's sexual harassment. We should countersue or something," Steph says.

"It's a power move," Kaya explains. She is deep in a pile of perforated Valentine cards, tearing them out, signing her daughter's name, and putting them in individual envelopes that have to be personally labeled for each kid in Kayla's class. "That look the lawyer gave you was all about dominance and humiliation. My manager at the club used to do stuff like that. He wants you to think you're his bitch. Says the grown woman forging a six-year-old's signature twenty-six times." She caps Kayla's pen and zips it up in her pencil case. "I can't keep my eyes open."

"We can finish these for you, Ky."

"Would you?"

"No problem."

The mothers say good night and Kaya heads up the stairs. Once they hear her door shut, Steph and Sandy scooch their chairs close. Sandy lays her head on Steph's shoulder, and Steph wraps her arms around her.

"What a day."

"I can't believe this is only the beginning. We could be in court for months, maybe years."

"We'll jump off each bridge as we come to them."

"One bridge at a time."

They press their foreheads together and breathe. "I hate that you're going through this, but I'm so glad *we're* going through this."

"You read my mind."

Sandy sits up, touches Steph's cheek, runs her fingers down to her mouth. They kiss sleepily at the table, under the glow of Yiya Devine's green and black imitation-Tiffany hanging lamp. The toilet flushes upstairs and they pull apart. It's Kayla—they can tell by the way she shuffles her feet. The door to her bedroom closes. They begin again, kissing in a happy, lazy dream, too tired to have sex on the couch, too in love to go to their separate beds yet.

"Are you fucking kidding me?" Kaya says.

They jolt apart. Kaya stands in front of them, a slimy sheet mask clinging to her face, giving her the appearance of an unholy demon in booty shorts. She slaps two unopened sheet-mask packets on the table.

"I couldn't sleep, so I was gonna see if you two fucking bitches wanted to do some self-care with me, but looks like you're all set."

"Kaya—"

"How long has this been a thing? Wait, Sandy, is *Steph* your secret boyfriend? Or was that someone else?"

"That was Steph."

"You told her about us?"

"No. I mean, yes. When we were fighting over Christmas."

"Why didn't you tell me that?" Steph asks.

"Why didn't *you* tell *me* about *this*?" Kaya starts piling the unfinished Valentines into a bag. "The two of you always act like I'm some fucking moron for falling in love with Justin. Like you're so much smarter and superior to me because you had him all figured out. Or you think I don't know what real love is, not like you two. But at least I have always been honest and real with everyone. With Justin. With you."

In the fire of rage, inspiration hits. A little jar of glitter twinkles on the dining room table next to bits of construction paper and glue sticks. Kaya snatches the glitter and unscrews the lid. Looking Steph and Sandy dead in the eyes, she pours it all over Steph's binder of casework and inside Sandy's leather tote bag. After she has shaken out every last fleck, she wipes her hands on Steph's cardigan, hanging off the back of the chair, and retreats to her bedroom upstairs.

Rosie, Mykayla, and Kayla have all slept through the shouting, but Ash hasn't. They come down and sit at the table, observing the glitter bomb with a confused frown.

"What's going on?" Ash demands. "For real."

They are so gorgeously, perfectly ten going on eleven. Both Steph and Sandy cannot ignore this extraordinary fact. All Steph's hard work to create this independent thinker is now coming to confront them. So Steph and Sandy tell them the truth, too.

"... but you and Rosie always come first," Steph concludes.

"Always," Sandy reinforces.

Ash looks distracted as they listen. They pull at the dry skin on their foot, peeling thick layers off their heel and flicking them to the ground. A disgusting habit that Steph also has. Watching Ash, Sandy is queasy with love for these gross, gross people she has chosen as her family.

"Do you have any questions, honey?" Steph asks.

"Yeah, I do," Ash says.

No one is more prepared than Steph to deliver a speech on the spectrum of sexuality and all the ways it can be expressed. She has been laying the groundwork for years, studying the best practices. Ash is not a question-asker, not out loud, but every once in a while the portal opens, and Steph has made sure to be ready. Just not at ten o'clock on a school night.

Please, Steph prays, *let this be quick. We can have sex ed tomorrow, after coffee.*

"Anything you want, love," she says. "We're here for you."

"Now that you two are sleeping together, can I have my own room?"

A t Steph's first official hearing, the backlog of cases is so long that the judge adjourns for a later date. It buys them another month.

"At least we have the same judge. Plus, she is a woman," Sandy says, trying to shrug off the day. "I know she has to be impartial, but I saw the picture on her desk. She has three kids. She's a mother. She's got to have some sympathy for us."

"I don't know," Steph says as they ride the subway back to Queens. "Did you see those pleated pants she was wearing?"

"Yeah."

"Those weren't pants. They were *slacks*. We fundamentally don't vibe with the slacks-wearing crowd."

"Yeah," Sandy conceded. "Her haircut does have a real I-want-to-speak-to-the-manager number of layers. I wish Kaya was there to see her bangs."

"I wish Kaya would talk to us," Steph replies.

Like most people, Sandy and Steph's entire notion of court proceedings comes from TV, and nothing they've seen could have prepared them for the tedium and viciousness of a real-life court case. When Steph's trial resumes, Justin's lawyer seizes every opportunity to slam her, even when it is Justin who has made an obvious mistake. On a miserable day in April, assuming their case will not be called for hours, Justin leaves the court to go get something to eat. When the judge calls them into session before he's returned, his lawyer finds a way to shift the blame.

"Your honor," he says, "this is highly unusual behavior from my client, who is a happily married, taxpaying, churchgoing small-business owner . . ."

"Did you know that Justin was a happily married, taxpaying, churchgoing small-business owner?" Steph sneers under her breath.

"What a great guy this Justin must be . . ." Sandy whispers back.

"This absence is more like the kind of chaos this woman always creates. As you have seen yourself, my client has been perfectly prestigious and reliable throughout this trial, despite what this woman has . . ."

"Does he know what words mean?" Steph whispers to Sandy.

"I think he's on a slower learning curve than us."

He takes a different tack for Sandy's trial. There he tries to paint the portrait of Sandy, who in the first months of Rosie's life worked from home part-time, as "scantily employed."

Hearing him say this, Steph gasps. She doesn't yell or swear or argue. She doesn't bang her fists on the desk or flip the desk over in a fit of justifiable rage. She merely inhales some air a little louder than she meant to.

"If you can't keep ahold of your emotional outbursts, you can wait outside the chambers," the judge says to her sternly.

"All I did was *breathe*. So much for the sympathy of mothers," Steph groans later.

There are times when Justin's lawyer says things about the women that are not only insulting—"she's lazy"—but objectively untrue. He depicts Steph as a layabout trust-fund kid who flits from hobby to hobby, never committing to anything that could earn income to support her daughter.

"I've been working since I was sixteen years old!" Steph screams on the train ride home. A few fellow subway riders look up from their phones to see the commotion, then just as casually look back down. "Justin has known me since before that! He knows this!"

Sandy, the lawyer says, "is a jealous, vindicating woman who plays mind games to get more money out of my client."

"I think he meant *vindictive*," Sandy says later, laughing, when she is home in Astoria. She is forcing the laughter out of her stomach, chuckling like a mechanical clown. If she doesn't laugh, she will cry in front of all of them.

In court they sit up straight and listen to all this, their faces motionless, not defending themselves or arguing back and certainly not interrupting; that would make them *emotional, irrational, hysterical, untrustworthy*—all unsubtle code for *female*. They sit and wait for their turn to tell the truth, which should feel like a relief, but after a horrible first impression has already been made by someone like Justin's lawyer, the simple truth is an uphill battle.

"It is genetically impossible for me to keep being this quiet," Steph complains.

After a series of delays and early adjournments, Sandy finally gets her chance to speak on her own behalf before the judge in July. At home she practices her account of being a good mother and co-operative co-parent. She assembles pages and pages of printed, time-stamped text messages to back up her claims, collects affidavits from Rosie's pediatrician and daycare. She wears her mother's wedding ring on a chain under her blouse for good luck and braces herself for war. Steph comes with her, surreptitiously squeezing her hand under the table while they sit and wait. But Justin never shows up. The judge adjourns for another month.

"What the fuck?" Steph cries on the sidewalk outside.

"Nice language for a mother," Justin's lawyer sneers as he walks past.

Steph is about to jump on him and claw his eyes out when Sandy grabs her hand.

"I'll find out what happened," she says while Steph shakes the rage out of her body. "Hey, Justin," she texts, "we had court today. Just checking in to see if everything is okay."

He doesn't respond. Since the lawsuit began, he's replied only to texts about drop-off and pickup times and only with an emoji thumb up or thumb down.

"Try Tara," Steph offers. So Sandy does. Her phone dings. She reads the text and gasps.

"What now?" Steph groans.

Mara had gone into labor that morning and given birth to a healthy baby boy.

It's Steph's idea to buy a bottle of not-too-cheap champagne. "A baby is a baby," she says. "Our kids have a new brother, and that is a beautiful thing. Plus, Kaya loves champagne, so it will help the news go down easier."

"Technically it's a sparkling white. We can't afford real champagne," Sandy says.

"Technically I love you, so I'll let the snobbery slide."

It's a Wednesday night. Ash has a sleepover with a friend from summer camp, and Steph arranges for Kayla to sleep at a friend's house, too. Rosie is old enough to know that going to bed when the sun is still out is some unacceptable bullshit and she lets her thoughts be known to the rest of the house as well as some of the neighbors. By the time her shrieking protests subside, Sandy is ready to drink the whole bottle of not-cheap sparkling white herself.

Kaya and Steph are on opposite ends of the couch. Kaya is cradling Mykayla in her arms, feeding her a bottle, while Steph scrolls through her phone. Sandy gets out the champagne and Yiya Devine's green-studded wine goblets. She pours them each a drink.

"So there's some big news," Steph says gently.

"You got married and didn't invite me?" Kaya answers flatly.

"No, honey, we would never—"

"Just tell me. My stomach is in knots. I'm not in the mood for a big dramatic reveal."

"Mara had the baby today," Sandy says. "It's a boy. I don't know the name, because Tara won't tell me."

"Kyle Krystian Murray," Kaya replies. "I saw it on socials this morning. I'm furious they stole the letter *K*. That's my thing. But I'm happy for them. The baby is healthy. I wouldn't wish the NICU on anyone, not even Mara. And Mykayla has a new brother, if she's ever allowed to meet him."

"You're taking this very well," Sandy says.

"What the fuck, Sandy!" Kaya cries. Mykayla wakes up. Her eyes are changing from the stormy gray of her newborn days into an earthy green. At first they couldn't tell who she looks like, but now, except for her eye color, she is a tiny clone of Kaya. The baby lets out a little cry to inform them she does not appreciate being woken up.

"Give her to me," Steph offers.

Kaya hands over the baby, finishes her glass of champagne in one gulp, then pours herself some more. Steph gets Mykayla back to sleep, then lays her down in her crib upstairs.

"Okay," Sandy says to Kaya once Steph is back, "now you can yell at me."

"I don't want to yell at you. I just want us to be like we were before. I can't stand all these secrets and plans and conversations behind my back. You treat me like I'm a lost little girl, not a grown-ass mother same as you."

"We would never do that to you—"

"You just did."

"You're right. I'm sorry."

"I'm sorry, too."

"Before you two became Standy—"

"Standy?"

"Yeah, that's what I call you."

A moment of grace—there is a pause, a break in the momentum of justifiable anger and justifiable defensiveness; they all hear it at the same time, their ridiculous voices spewing ridiculous words, and they begin to laugh. Like they used to laugh. Everything is not okay, but in that laughter, something is released that lets them know they are on the road to okay.

"Let's put this on hold and go get some more champagne."

"And onion rings."

"On it."

Sandy runs to the liquor store to get another two bottles of not-cheap sparkling white. Steph orders a few baskets of onion rings with extra dipping sauces on her delivery app. Kaya goes upstairs and rolls an old-school joint so skinny it could be described as cute.

"All I want is for you to text me all day, all the time, about everything that happens, immediately," Kaya says, jutting her head as far as she can out the big bay window to exhale smoke. "No more of this Standy versus Kaya bullshit."

Steph sprays a lavender aerosol after every hit, and Sandy flaps a *People* magazine to fan any lingering smoke out the window. It is a clear night, and Venus is the sole speck of light they can see in the polluted city sky. It shines dimly above the apartment building across the street. They stare at it quietly with confusion and hope, mistaking it for a star.

"I would rather have a Pap smear than be Standy versus Kaya," Steph says. It has been a long time since she smoked pot, and she is extremely, profoundly stoned. "No offense, my love." She kisses Sandy on the mouth.

"Is *that* okay, though?" Sandy says. "Is it okay if we are affectionate?"

"Yes, that's what I'm talking about," Kaya says, refilling all their glasses. "I've been *dying* to know your fuck schedule. What positions you use. Who tops who."

"We don't have roles like that. We collaborate."

"Steph is a bossy bottom, isn't she?" Kaya asks Sandy.

"Sometimes," Sandy concedes.

"At first I was offended, but I've had a lot of time to think about it, and I actually understand why you never invited me to be your third. I bring a sexual electricity that neither one of you could handle."

"Who can argue with that?"

"And if we're all being honest now, I've been avoiding telling you something, too," Kaya says. Her two brothers have decided it is time to sell Yiya Devine's house. They have given Kaya the option to buy their shares at the lowest possible price, but there is no way she can come up with the money to do that.

"They've been super supportive and patient with me, but they are both ready to buy houses of their own and they can't afford to without this sale. You two don't have some hidden money somewhere, do you?"

"We're representing ourselves in court."

"I know," Kaya says. "I just wish we could all own this house and live here together and for all this to go away."

Satisfied that all the smoke has floated outside, Sandy shuts the big window so that the AC can cool the living room again. Kaya leans her head against the glass, and Steph leans her head against Kaya. It is an oppressively hot summer night. The sky looks like a black void smeared with dirty light.

"What are we going to do?"

"I don't know."

They sit on the floor, too stoned and drunk to get up. The house is silent. On the baby monitor, Mykayla lifts both legs together like a mermaid's tail and thumps the mattress. She twists her head left and right, then settles herself back to sleep. Kaya, Sandy, and Steph are thirsty for water, hungry for the remainder of the onion rings, but they don't move from where they sit against the curved bay window, looking out over the street. It is almost as if they are waiting for something.

After a long silence, Kaya gasps. "Did you see that?"

"See what?"

"A shooting star. I saw a shooting star out the window!"

"I am officially too old to smoke pot."

"It was probably an airplane."

"Oh god," Kaya says. "I tried to tap left on the window to make it play the shooting-star video again. You're right. It was probably an airplane."

They all laugh. The spell has been broken; they can move again. They clean up the evidence of their indulgent night and drift off to bed, still giggling like high school girls getting stoned for the first time. But secretly they all make the same wish. Just in case the shooting star was real.

Nothing is going to stop Sandy from taking Family Law her first semester. She scans the course listing and emails the professor before registration to say she is interested in taking his class. When she gets no response, she emails her adviser to let him know the same.

"Relax," her adviser tries to tell her. "You have three years to take all these courses. You'll get to Family Law later. Most first-year students take Civil Procedures, Contracts, and Torts. Not much room for flexibility in this."

There is a finite number of times a woman can hear the word *relax* from a man before she snaps. Especially from a man who barely knows her. Sandy is getting dangerously close to this number. She chooses to focus on the positive, the crack of light glinting through the closed door. "*Not much* room for flexibility" is not "*no* room for flexibility." She can wedge herself inside that class like she does on crowded subway cars at rush hour. She emails the Family Law professor again. Again no reply.

"Try going in person to his office hours," Steph suggests.

"Try showing a little skin," adds Kaya. The other two gawp. "What? Did you not see *Legally Blonde?*"

"Oooh, this is the perfect time to break out my first-day-of-school present," Steph cries. She bought Sandy a vintage tweed pencil skirt and a red sweater set.

"Serving 1956 Ruth Bader Ginsburg," Steph says when Sandy tries it on. "This might be my new kink. Preppy-law-student fantasy."

"Wait until I start talking about torts," Sandy says, trying to be coy.

"God, you're lame," Kaya snorts. "I'm a better lesbian than both of you combined and I'm straight."

Professor Mayer is a man of the same age and general appearance as Sandy's father. He has her dad's tall-man habit of slumping his shoulders and the same thinning, combed-back hair that is inexplicably greasy and dry at the same time. The familiarity makes Sandy feel both relaxed and triggered, and the next thing she knows she is telling Mayer her whole custody saga. He nods and groans in all the right places, as though he understands better than she does what she's been through.

"Who's your magistrate?" he interrupts at one point.

"I . . . don't know," Sandy says.

"Do you know what a magistrate is?" he follows up.

She doesn't. Professor Mayer nods calmly, making this all seem very normal, forgivable, understandable.

"The person you keep referring to as the 'judge' might not actually be a judge. It sounds to me like you've been assigned a magistrate. He looks like a judge, sits up there on that tall bench like a judge, but he is just a lawyer with some extra, though limited, powers. It's not insignificant to note they also make less money than judges. Magistrates tend to be insecure. They bring all that to the bench. You might have better luck with a real judge, and you have the right to ask for one. I can walk you through how to do that."

"Thank you. Yes. I don't know if she's a magistrate or a judge. All I know is that it feels like she hates me."

"They're supposed to be impartial, but everyone is human. Brooklyn family court is an awful place. I worked cases there for twenty years. When I got offered a teaching job, I sprinted away from that windowless box in hell and never looked back."

"You sit there for hours, and it feels like the granite is slowly pushing in on you."

"Try doing it day after day. There is no amount of money to get me back there." He takes off his glasses and cleans them on his shirt, which has a spray of crumbs on it. This also reminds Sandy of her dad. "What's the name of the guy presiding over your case?"

"Her name is Thorpe," Sandy says.

"Blond? Short hair? Looks like she used to be cute before she had kids?"

Sandy nods uneasily.

"I know her," Professor Mayer says. "She's a magistrate, and she's ultraconservative. A member of the Federalist Society. Which is not supposed to affect her decisions in court, but again, people are people. Who's your child-support magistrate?"

"Is it not Thorpe?"

"No. Separate case, separate magistrate, separate chamber in the same granite box. You can probably get some leverage there. I'm assuming your ex owes you back pay."

Another student knocks on the door for a scheduled meeting. Sandy stands up to let him in. Professor Mayer stands up, too. "Come back next week and I'll talk you through the procedure of dumping Thorpe and getting a real judge. Then we can strategize about how to get off on a better foot with the new guy."

"Does this mean I'm in your class this semester?"

"I'm sorry," he says, smiling. "There's no room for first-years. Though I am very much looking forward to having you next year. Regardless, we will be seeing a lot of each other this semester."

Sandy is so relieved. She extends her hand, and Professor Mayer takes it in a firm grasp. Inside the handshake, he strokes her palm with his index finger. Sandy has shaken a lot of hands in her life, and no one has ever tickled her palm this way before. It feels sinister and violating. But maybe it's a generational thing. Or a lawyer thing. Maybe lawyers of a certain age all do this. *What do I know? Maybe this is normal.* She smiles nervously, flashing too much teeth, and waits for him to drop her hand.

* * *

At home, she tells Steph what she's learned about magistrates versus judges and behind the scenes on Thorpe.

"That's awesome, babe! Sounds like you found a mentor!"

"Yeah," Sandy says, wishing away the lingering creepiness of her meeting. This man had given her his time, had been honest and helpful and generous. It was just a handshake.

At her next meeting with Professor Mayer, Sandy wears a huge sweatshirt and no makeup. Her hair is in a messy ponytail, and she doesn't brush her teeth after eating a falafel with extra pickles. Perhaps it is paranoia and a little overkill, but she wants to make sure she is giving the unsexiest impression, just in case. Professor Mayer welcomes her into the office and immediately launches into a lecture of some past cases he's had, peppered with details from historical cases she would study in his class next year. To her relief, he maintains a professorial tone the whole time. In fact, it's a little boring. She wants to talk about her case. She tries hard to see the possible connections between his lecture and her situation, but nothing Mayer says seems to have any similarities to her case.

Maybe he's senile. Maybe he forgot who I am and why I'm here.

Maybe. But there is a gratification in his voice she has heard too many times before: he is talking for the pleasure of hearing himself talk. Mayer references a divorce settlement with no children, no custody issues. He mentions more than once how much money he made on some clients, which doesn't seem relevant. Sandy dutifully keeps track of the unconnected details, hoping it is all part of something Socratic she hasn't learned about yet.

Maybe I'm wrong—maybe he's teaching me something with these other cases and I'm just missing the bigger picture?

As she sits across from him, she feels beads of sweat dripping down her chest. The weather that day is much too warm for a sweatshirt. She wants so badly to take off some layers but decides not to.

"You see that painting over there?" Professor Mayer says, pointing to a large abstract oil painting on his wall. "A client, a very famous artist, paid me with that during his divorce. It's worth way more than he owed me."

"It's beautiful," Sandy says, hoping he won't dwell on the painting. She never knows what to say about art, and it always makes her feel dumb.

Her plan to hide under a sweatshirt is backfiring. Sandy's armpits are swampy. She is starting to get a headache from the heat. When she can stand it no longer, she pulls off her sweatshirt, revealing a loose-fitting tank top that says *feminist* in black lowercase letters.

If he notices any of this, Professor Mayer does not show it. He keeps talking about himself and his past career as a litigator. At last he leans back in his chair and says, "But enough of all that. Tell me more about yourself. What are your passions?"

"My passions?"

Sandy hates the sound of her voice. She hates responding to a question by repeating the question. The lowercase letters of her tank top are humiliating, instructing this man not to take her seriously.

"I guess I don't know what my passions are yet. I'm interested in family law, but I can't tell if that's out of personal necessity or passion. I have a lot more to learn . . ."

Without making eye contact, Professor Mayer begins unbuckling his belt.

Okay, he's senile. He's out of it. I have to find a way to redirect him without embarrassing him, like a long-lost grandpa.

Then he unbuttons his pants, unzips his fly.

"That piece of shit!" Steph screams when Sandy comes home.

"What happened next?" Kaya asks.

"I pretended to get a text from Rosie's daycare and stood up and said I had to go. Then—oh god—I fucking *thanked him* for his time. . . ."

"You were scared," Steph assures her. "Don't judge yourself."

"I made sure he felt fine about it. What's wrong with me?"

"Fight or flight is a false binary," Steph says. "For women and femmes, it's more like fight, flight, or freeze and appease. It's okay, my love. You did what you had to do to get out."

"He didn't actually show me his dick. Maybe I'm overreacting?"

Kaya and Steph both shout, "No!"

Ash runs downstairs to join the discussion. Puberty is approaching like a rain cloud. New expressions of it appear every day. They demand to be allowed to dye their hair blue but then ask Steph to do it for them. That night they've been experimenting with yellow-star pimple patches on their perfect, devoid-of-acne skin.

"What happened? Why are you screaming 'no'?"

"Nothing, sweetheart," Steph says. "Go back to bed."

"Don't talk to me like a child, *Mother*," Ash snaps back. Another experiment Steph is indulging, a compromise after Ash tried to call Steph by her first name instead of the babyish *Mom*.

"It might be good for them to hear what's going on," Kaya pipes up. "Can you imagine if something like this happened to them?"

"She's right," Sandy agrees.

"Age-appropriate version." Steph waves her hand in front of her face, both grateful and exhausted by the consensus they are always making as mothers.

"My teacher at school did something inappropriate," Sandy tells Ash. "He tried to make me . . . kiss him. And I didn't want to. So I'm talking about it with my two best friends, Kaya and your mom, because that's what strong, smart people do. They ask for help."

"Hmmmm," Ash says. "Did you record it on your phone?"

"What?" Sandy says, taken aback. "No . . ."

"You should go back and make him do it again, but this time record it with your phone. Then let's sue the bastard," Ash says.

"Ash! Where the hell did you get that?"

Ash rolls their eyes so hard they could have gone blind. Not that they would have cared. Slaying their mother in a battle of words is the only thing that matters. "Mother. Please," is all they are willing to offer such a pathetic opponent.

"If I unlock the Wi-Fi, will you please go back to your room?" Steph begs. Ash sprints up the stairs. Kaya and Sandy try not to smirk. Steph has lost again, and she knows it.

"The kid has a point," Kaya says.

"I don't want to go back there," Sandy replies. She plops a bag of tea into a mug of hot water and stares at it.

"We could sue him. That's one way to make the money to buy this house," Steph says.

Sandy's head sinks into her hands. "Oh god," she groans, looking at her phone. "He just emailed me. Wanting to confirm the same time for next week's appointment. Not a word about what happened."

"He's gaslighting you!"

"I'm so sick of that word."

"Who cares? It's true."

"Mayer talked on and on about making a good first impression in court, how the judge makes up her mind about you on first sight, and the rest of the time you're either proving her wrong or proving her right. That would be me in law school—every professor, all the other students, anyone offering internships, would always know I was the woman who sued a professor I had met privately in office hours without ever taking his class. It might be the only thing anyone knows about me. And suing him sounds worse. I don't want to spend more time in court. Maybe I'm in the wrong field altogether."

"No, sweetheart. You're just discouraged. You're—"

"She's right," Kaya says. "You don't want to be the girl who sued the boss. That shit will follow you for your whole career. I've seen it a million times in the clubs. Sometimes sexual harassment is something you have to get over with. Every boss will try just to see what he can get. Most of them go back to being normal once you show them they can't fuck with you."

"But this is law school, not a strip club," Steph says. "I mean that with zero judgment."

"I've fucked enough boomers to write a users' manual," Kaya asserts. "Everything this guy does is deliberate, and you need to stay ready."

Both Kaya and Steph make very good points. That's the problem: Sandy wants singular, definitive instructions about what to do next. She wants a neon sign floating above their house that says, REPORT MAYER TO THE DEAN or DON'T REPORT HIM. DO THIS INSTEAD. She checks her email frantically, with the delusional wish that a message from the universe will appear in her inbox, laying out the precise steps of a plan. She consults her horoscope, Justin's horoscope, Steph's and Kaya's, even Rosie's horoscope, in a mainstream beauty magazine, a mainstream city paper, a woo-woo yoga journal, and a straight-up Wiccan website. The readings she gets are either too vague or too contradictory to make any sense. This leads her to an online tarot-card reader that does simple three-card spreads for free. She refreshes the page so many times she hits a paywall. She is pulling out her credit card when Steph walks into their room with a pile of fresh laundry to fold.

"What are you buying me?" she says sweetly.

"A look into our future."

Sandy is hunched over her phone, jaw clenched, shades drawn in a darkened room. Steph takes the phone out of Sandy's hands.

"Hey!"

"You need to take a walk."

* * *

It is a humid September day full of confusing omens. The sky is moody with clouds broken by patches of hot sun. A strong wind whips through the leaves and trash and detritus, swirling it all over the sidewalk like a toddler trying to make a mess. A hawk rests in the high branches of an elm tree and Sandy watches it for a while, half-expecting the bird to swoop down and tell her what to do. Instead, a construction crew starts jackhammering the sidewalk in front of her, startling her. In all her searching for signs, she missed the orange cones everywhere. When she looks back up at the elm tree, the hawk is gone.

There is a ditch in the street where the construction workers are repairing a gas line. For a brief, sickening moment, Sandy imagines falling into it accidentally, Professor Mayer finding out and feeling bad about what he did, and then, as a tacit apology, he would email her his action plan for court and leave her alone forever. The judge would put the case on hold because of her injury, and in that pause Justin would come to his senses. If only being a passive victim were less shameful and more effective, Sandy would hurl herself into that ditch.

She returns from her walk and packs her bag for class.

"You know, he's probably done this to other women before," Steph says. "And he'll likely do it again to someone else."

"I need more time," Sandy replies.

On the subway, she can't focus on her reading. She keeps picturing Ash or Rosie or Kayla or Mykayla going to college and a professor whipping out his dick to them during office hours. Then she imagines telling an administrator at school what Mayer did and them asking, *Do you have any proof?*

Sandy ghosts on her third appointment with Professor Mayer. No email to warn him or explain and definitely no apology. She goes to her Torts class and sinks low in her seat, praying not to be called on. She had hoped to be a star student, to be enthusiastic or at the very least prepared. The professor does not call on her that day, and she vows to redouble her efforts. No creepy predator is going to get in the way of her education.

After class, Sandy sees Mayer sitting on a bench in the hallway, talking to a male student. He glances at her. No nod of recognition, no angry sneer. It is like they've never met.

The next day Steph has court. Waiting in line to go through the metal detectors, she gets a text from Justin. "Good luck lezzing out with my sloppy seconds. Your fucking pathetic. All of this is gonna blow up in your face."

Steph is struck silent. It's shocking but also inevitable. Ash must have told Justin about her and Sandy. The one rule she has drilled into her child's head is *We don't keep secrets.* While Steph is proud to see her hard work paying off, the current application of this tenet is bittersweet.

At the hearing, Justin's lawyer tells the magistrate that in addition to living with a prostitute, his child is being exposed to sexual depravity through her mother's life choices.

"If the home is unfit," the magistrate says, "I have no choice but to order an investigation of the children's welfare."

"When do you think Child Services will be coming?" Sandy asks.

"Any day now," Steph says. "Do we have guards on all the upstairs windows?"

"I think so?" Kaya says. "Is there any way we can find out when they're coming? Like make an appointment? So we can clean the bathrooms and stuff."

"It doesn't work that way," Steph says. "The social worker just shows up. They don't have to give you any notice."

"My brothers and I have hired a realtor and she wants to start showing the house to potential buyers this week, which is maybe not the picture of stability we want to give our bad-parent parole officer."

That night, none of the mothers has the energy to cook, though cooking is only half the battle. Getting the food they cook into the kids' stomachs is another. Dinner becomes choose-your-own-adventure. Ash eats two bagels with butter, Kayla has a bag of cheddar popcorn, and the only thing Rosie will consume is cereal with chocolate milk. No one has a bath, everyone cries at bedtime, and they all go to sleep feeling miserable. *Never go to bed angry* is ridiculous advice. Sometimes the only thing you can do is wait for tomorrow with its dumb hope that things might get better, and the fastest route to tomorrow is a terrible night of sleep.

The social worker assigned by Child Protective Services arrives the next day. His name is Stanley, and he is very tall, with thick hair graying at the temples. He speaks with a heavy Brooklyn accent that he's trained over the years to sound gentle and disarming. Kaya is the only parent home when he knocks on the door. Steph is at a parent-teacher conference at Ash's school, and Sandy is in class in the city. Mykayla and Rosie are at the daycare down the street; as both Sandy and Kaya pay by the month, they figure they'll use the days there even when a mom is available. Ash and Kayla are home because of parent-teacher conferences, and Kaya is baking cookies with them.

"The whole house literally smelled like vanilla and butter when he walked in. If that's not wholesome enough for Child Services, I don't know what is."

"What did he say?"

Steph and Sandy are exploding with stress. They thought they had at least a week to prepare. What they would have done, they don't know. Move back into separate rooms? Pretend they aren't a couple? They could have at least picked up the dirty clothes from the floor.

"Don't worry." Kaya sucks her teeth. "I handled it."

"Okay, but what happened?!"

"Steph. Sandy. In a long, illustrious career of hairstyling, I can say with total confidence that I was having not the best hair day of *my* life but the best hair day of *anyone's life. In history*. In my humble opinion, I have never looked so effortlessly gorgeous. I was wearing this shirt, which as you can see gives a tasteful amount of titty—good but not too good, you know? All pants make my ass look incredible, but these jeans have sparkles on the back pocket, so I basically punched him in the face with my hotness. I didn't need to blow him for us to win this case. We won. I only blew him for the fun of it."

"What?!"

"Just kidding. He was really nice. He ate a cookie and thanked me and said he'd be coming back tomorrow between three-thirty and five P.M."

Most families are too busy living their lives to consider what that life would look like under scrutiny. That nail jutting out from the doorway that snags you if you're not careful, the expired penicillin in the fridge—every house is full of tiny dangers that become invisible, things you learn unconsciously to avoid or forget about completely. But how would a social worker view these things?

Would they assign points to each domestic offense, and if so, how many? If black mold is ten points, then the grimy corner of the shower, the one no known chemical can annihilate, should be only one, right? All the laundry detergent is out of the children's reach, on a shelf above the washing machine, but there's an open bottle of wine on the kitchen counter. Do those points cancel each other out? Sandy cleans a toilet that is already clean, trying to calculate what score she will receive as a mother.

"Chill, psycho," Kaya says as she plucks her eyebrows in the bathroom mirror. Sandy wipes a rag across the narrow strip of tile behind the toilet.

"Stanley looks like he's got that girth, you know?"

"Kaya, please . . ."

She blots her lipstick on a square of toilet paper, then reapplies.

"Seriously, he's super nice. You have to believe me."

"I'm going to dump that wine down the sink," Sandy says.

"She's losing it," Kaya yells to Steph.

Steph's approach to preparation is more clinical. She emails all the social workers she knows to get intel on Stanley as well as asks her professors and colleagues for any advice they have to offer.

"Window guards, bookcases bolted to the wall, and slip mats in the bathtub—these are the main things he'll look for, and we have all of them so we should be okay," she reports.

Sandy is not pacified. "We've never made an official fire-safety plan with the kids. What if he asks them about that?"

Kaya purses her lips in the mirror. "I worry this red lipstick is *dangerous*. Like, it will make all Stanley's blood rush to his dick and give him an erection so hard that he has a heart attack." She blots her lips some more.

"My adviser knows him. She doesn't remember if he was a homophobe or not, as it was ten years ago that he was in her class, but she said he was a hard worker and seemed to be a decent person," Steph adds. "I'll drop all the names I can."

Stanley arrives at their door a little after 5 P.M. It is at the end of his rounds of home visitations, and he looks very tired. He carries a heavy backpack that makes an audible thud when he drops it gently on the floor. Sandy offers him snacks and coffee and tea, and when he says he wants just water, she is sure she is already failing.

"I'll get it," Kaya says sweetly. "You want ice?" She has switched to a neutral matte lipstick that somehow looks sexier than the red.

"Ice would be great, thanks." Stanley smiles.

Steph is upstairs, trying to explain to Ash and Kayla what is going on and why it is important not to say any swear words today. Rosie has ripped out the cute bow Sandy put in her hair, and Mykayla fusses in her high chair, cranky from gas pains.

Stanley asks a few basic questions: how long they have all lived together, how Sandy and Steph came to know each other, how they came to know Kaya. Steph and Sandy give him the most sanitary version of their story, editing out all the social-media stalking, the bonding over what a shit Justin is. They try to keep the focus on their children, what is best for them, nurturing a bond among the siblings, making sure they grow up together.

"But honestly, the biggest draw for me was having two extra mothers around," Kaya says. Steph and Sandy freeze. Kaya is going off book. Kaya is going rogue. This is not the message they are selling today. "I totally get why the Mormons do it now."

No! Behind Stanley's back, Steph makes a motion like slicing her own throat. Sandy jumps up and refills his water, which he's barely sipped. Stanley doesn't convey any judgment, but it could also be his professional poker face.

"Ha ha ha," Steph pretends to laugh, "it's like my mentor, Dr. Connie Ramirez, always says—"

"Dr. Ramirez? She's at Columbia now, right? I had her at Hunter when I was getting my master's."

"Yeah, that's her. Wow, you know her? Small world!"

They swap stories about Dr. Ramirez, and Steph starts to relax. Stanley asks their permission to have a tour upstairs. "I have to check out the windows and bookcases and stuff," he says apologetically. "I promise I won't take long. You're obviously all wonderful mothers, and these kids are some of the luckiest I've ever seen in my career. I just have to check all the boxes for my paperwork."

"Totally understand!" Steph affects the voice of a surfer chick about to hit the waves. She sounds unhinged. Sandy and Kaya exchange looks.

Is she trying to be . . . cool? Sandy mouths. Kaya covers her mouth, shrinks her brow, eyes bulging with the desire to laugh and possibly scream. *I have no fucking idea what she is right now,* her shrug replies.

For all three women, even on a good day, this is the hardest hour for the family, in which everyone's blood sugar levels are plummeting, with a soundtrack of whining and crying as shrill as steam whistles. Kaya starts dinner—a very weird menu of foods that should never be on the same table, let alone plate, unless there are children. Technically she is not being investigated, as Justin is still denying that Mykayla is his daughter, so Steph and Sandy bring Stanley upstairs. He peeks in the doorway of each bedroom but does not go in.

He asks to use the bathroom, and they listen outside the door as he opens and shuts their medicine cabinet.

"It's good that he's being thorough," Steph tries to soothe Sandy. "Think of all the kids in this city who are in danger in their own homes. They need people like Stanley to check out the medicine cabinet."

They have all-natural toothpaste—how many points for that?

Ash darts upstairs to get a sweatshirt, breezing past the three grown-ups lingering in the hallway. "Sorry my room is still messy," they say to Stanley. "Mom still needs to move the last of her stuff into Sandy's room, then I'm going to redecorate."

"Why's that?" Stanley asks.

"Now that they're sleeping together, I get my own room. Rosie and Kayla fart too much in their sleep. I had to move out."

"Oh god," Sandy says.

"So yeah . . ." Steph begins.

They all walk back downstairs, where Rosie is painting the table with ketchup, using a chicken nugget as the brush. Kaya shrugs her shoulders. "At least she's eating," she says. Steph talks right over her, trying in her best clinical language to explain their relationship, blathering out of control about all the boundaries in place to keep the whole family intact and healthy.

"And we plan to get married after all this custody stuff is over. We're ready to get married now, but it's just too chaotic—"

"She means we're focusing on our academic and professional goals first," Sandy interjects. "We are setting the standard for our children that goals are more important than dating. I mean relationships. I mean *serious* romantic relationships, which we are in, but law school and PhD comes first and—"

"Oh my god, relax," Kaya says. She is spooning yogurt right out of the container into Mykayla's mouth. "Stanley is a real person. He's not a cop."

"She's right," Stanley says. "It's true what you all have here is not traditional, but I see nothing but love and safety everywhere I look. You don't have to defend yourselves."

He sits down at the table in the empty chair next to Kaya and, after asking permission, reaches over to touch Mykayla's soft black curls. Sandy refills his water glass again, then he drinks it.

Kaya asks Stanley a lot of questions about himself, and he is surprisingly forthcoming. He was a foster kid in Brooklyn, grew up in a broken system, had been lucky enough to have a few nice teachers in elementary and high school who gave him the self-confidence he needed to eventually go to college, where his path was clear: to make a difference in the lives of children like him.

Kaya gets up from the table, deliberately touching Stanley's shoulder as she does, and gets a napkin to wipe Mykayla's face. Once behind Stanley's back, she gets Steph and Sandy's attention by performing a pantomime of removing her panties and throwing them at his head.

"You must be starving by now," Kaya says to him. "Stay for dinner. I made lasagna."

"That sounds like heaven," Stanley says, "but I really can't." He explains that he will be returning a few more times before being allowed to close out their case and asks what would work with their schedules.

"I'm gonna get you to eat dinner with us before this case is closed," Kaya says.

Stanley laughs. "Do you have any of those cookies left over from yesterday?"

"I saved one for you."

Later that night, after Stanley is gone and the kids are in bed, Steph tells Kaya that when Stanley looked at her, "His eyes quite literally twinkled."

"Stop," Kaya says sadly. "Nice guys like that never fall for women like me."

"But he did seem to like us," Sandy says. "That's got to help in court. Maybe things are swinging back in our favor now."

Steph goes looking for the open bottle of wine, and learning that Sandy dumped it out in a paranoid fit, she slumps sadly onto the couch. "Sure. I mean, we're losing the house, we're being sued for custody, you were sexually harassed by a professor in your first week of law school, I'm two hundred thousand dollars in debt, you're about to be twice that broke in three years, but yeah, the caseworker investigating whether or not we're unfit mothers seemed to like us, so I guess we're winning."

The magistrate has given them a temporary custody order that sets the weekend pickup time at 4:30 P.M., which Justin is rarely able to make happen. Most Fridays he can meet up by 5 P.M., but he's kept them in limbo until 7 P.M. enough times for everyone to be skeptical. Ash likes to decompress after the school week by watching videos of people assembling large, intricate Lego sets in fast motion, but because of their dad's time blindness, they never know if they can watch one three-minute video or a full hour of toy architectural bliss.

"Come on, kiddo, time to go," Steph says to them after finally getting the text that their dad is on his way.

"No," Ash replies.

"I can give you five more minutes on your tablet, but then we have to put on your socks and go."

"*We* don't have do anything. *I'm* staying here."

"Sweetie," Steph says through gritted teeth, "we do not have time for this. Please get your socks on."

"No."

"Do you want to tell me why not?"

"Nope."

"You gotta work with me, kid."

"No." Ash doesn't bother to lift their gaze from the tablet. "My answer is no. Deal with it."

They tuck the tablet under their arm and stomp upstairs to their bedroom. The door slams with so much incipient rage. Rosie gets up from the couch and tucks a pillow under her arm. She reproduces her sibling's fury as she slams the bathroom door. Steph starts for the stairs, but Sandy stops her.

"Let me try."

Steph feels her stomach tightening in a hard knot. She's been dreading this day. While it would certainly be convenient to have a kid with strong people-pleasing impulses, Steph is proud that Ash has always followed their own compass. She wondered how much conformity her kid would be able to stomach at their dad's house; today is the day they've reached their limit.

Rosie slams the bathroom door again and again, practicing different expressions of feeling on her little face, checking occasionally to see if Steph is noticing. She slams the door one more time.

"Enough, baby girl!" Steph shouts, and Rosie falls into tears.

"Omfg help," Steph texts Kaya. "Total chaos right now. Ash is refusing to go to their dad's and refusing to talk to me about it. Sandy is trying to get through to them, but we all know you are the only one Ash will talk to when they're in their feelings. Can you please call?"

It's odd when three whole seconds pass with no response from Kaya, who is surgically attached to her phone, even when she's cutting hair. Her ability to dictate a text while doing six other things is both impressive and horrifying. Steph apologizes to Rosie, pacifies her with a freshly opened box of graham-cracker bunnies, then texts Kaya again. "Are you alive? I don't think I've ever waited this long for a response from you."

Sandy returns downstairs. According to Ash, things have gotten worse at the Murray house. Mara has doubled down on the gender binary, making a lot of obnoxious, unnecessary comments about how baby Kyle is a boy and Ash is a girl. "Ash said Mara will say this stuff out of the blue, for no reason. Like, no one is talking about gender when she brings it up. Justin doesn't say a word. Ash spends the whole weekend alone in their room watching YouTube videos because Mara put a ban on video games."

"Justin used to love playing video games with Ash."

"He's not allowed to anymore. No one is. Mara's the boss."

Steph begins texting Justin. "What the fuck—"

Sandy grabs her hand. "We're in court, babe," she says gently. "The only thing we can do right now to improve our miserable case is follow the rules and do it politely."

"No," Steph says. "I'm not doing that to my kid. I'm not sending them into that environment."

Sandy looks at Rosie, who is eating graham-cracker bunnies by the fistful. She inhales deeply. "Okay," she says. "If this is a risk we are willing to take, we're going to need a real lawyer. A good one. And I'm going to pay for it, not you."

"You can't do that. I'll just put it on my credit card."

"No. I'm going to ask my dad for money. I've never done that in my whole life, but this is worth it. Ash is my kid, too. I'm not putting them or any of us at risk anymore."

Steph reaches for the bunny grahams. Rosie pulls the box away, tries to hide it under her shirt. "Share!" Steph demands. Reluctantly, Rosie slips her hand under her shirt, reaches inside the box, and produces a single tiny bunny for Steph. She pops the measly offering in her mouth. "Didn't you say that creepy professor said we can get back child support?"

"Yeah. We have to open a case in a separate department for that."

"So let's do it. Justin owes me over a decade of child support. That's a lot of money. Certainly enough to pay for a real lawyer."

"And if all three of us get child support from him, then maybe we can afford a place big enough for the whole family when the house finally sells."

"Have you heard from Kaya? She's not responding to my texts."

"Mine, either." Sandy tries Kaya again. No response. They pick up Kayla from her dance class then get Mykayla at daycare, as they had planned to in the collective mom calendar of pickups and drop-offs. Not knowing what else to do, Steph lies to Justin, saying Ash and Rosie are both sick and need to stay put this weekend. Justin re-

sponds with a check mark, passive-aggressive but quiet, a small comfort.

Sometime after dinner, Kaya texts Steph and Sandy on the mothers' group chat:

"I have something to tell you. I don't know how to begin . . ."

A few weeks after Mara had her baby, Justin texted Kaya that he was in his truck, circling her house. It was eleven o'clock, and everyone was in bed for the night. "I need you," he said, and within minutes Kaya slipped out the door.

"I made a mistake. The biggest mistake of my life," he told her. He stared out the windshield of his truck at the sleepy, tree-lined street and held her hand. This was not the life he was meant to live. Mara was not who he thought she was. She was demanding and impossible to please. She didn't understand him. "And if I'm being honest," he said, his blue eyes shining into hers, "she's not you."

They had sex in his truck that night and several more nights afterward while their families were asleep. At first, Kaya was so heartsick with wanting Justin back that it felt good simply to be near him again. She liked the way sneaking around made him so hungry for her. They barely spoke. She would hop into his truck and he'd drive a block or two away from the house, neither of them able to wait any longer. The sex was so much hotter than when they were dating. Afterward, he would talk about how much he missed her, that he couldn't stop thinking about her, how much more beautiful she was than Mara. "I think you're the only one who really understands me," he said.

"I'm a stupid bitch. I know," Kaya pleads now. "Please just listen and don't rub it in."

The three mothers have convened in the backyard in the hope that the chill evening air will be enough to cool their tempers and the half moon will be enough to light the way. Kaya sits motionless on a metal patio chair, with her knees tucked inside her sweatshirt. Sandy is vibrating with anxiety. It courses through her legs and arms, rattling so hard she could break apart at the joints. She finds a rusty pair of hedge clippers and begins pruning Yiya Devine's rosebushes.

"And what the fuck did he say about Mykayla?" Steph fumes. She is full of rage, pacing the length of the backyard, her arms flying with every word of her interrogation.

"He just cried and said he fucked up, that he was a fuckup, that he didn't deserve us, me and the girls," Kaya tells her. "Which I loved hearing at first. He said he needed to get out of his marriage but he didn't know how. He said he was trying. I believed him. Then, I don't know, it just hit me. I was literally holding him in my arms while he cried about how Mara made him quit the music industry and sell his guitars. How she's pressuring him to buy an apartment in this new high-rise in Williamsburg, which he can't afford, and I realized, he's a child. He's a pathetic child."

"Did you talk about us?" Steph asks. "About Sandy and me?"

"No," Kaya says. "He only brought it up once, and I made him change the subject. He mostly talked about himself. I barely said a word. It's like I wasn't really there. I was just a body to warm him. I could have been anyone."

Sandy collects an armful of trimmed stems and leaves and wilted roses with brown, ruffled edges. Her hands are scratched and bleeding a little from the thorns. She lays them all on the table like an offering and sits down. She reaches out and grabs Steph, pulls her to the table, where she takes the third seat. The three women look at one another, the moon dangling above them like an amber pendant. Their breath collides with the cold air in little clouds that glow briefly in the moonlight, then disappear.

"I'm sorry," Kaya says after a long pause. "Do you hate me?"

"No," Steph answers, much quicker than she'd planned to, and more certain, as if her body answered first and her mind scrambled to follow. "I'm sick to my stomach and a little freaked out, but I still love you. I can't help it. You're extremely hot and funny, and my kid is obsessed with you."

"I don't hate you," Sandy says next. "I kind of get it, actually. I felt the same way—not with Justin but with my ex Alex. For a long, long time I would have done anything, put up with anything, for him to take me back."

"I'm done with him, I swear to god," Kaya says. "As a boyfriend, a father, a human being. I'm sorry it took me a long time to get here. I'm a moron."

"No," Sandy says. "As much as he served all three of us repetitive material, he was different with you. I think the very best part of him did fall in love with you. But the other part won out."

"I'm sorry I was so judgmental, Ky," Steph offers. "I still see him as a skinny twenty-year-old punk, but he hasn't been that person in a long time. In many ways, he's worse," she laughs, "but he's also grown. A little. It's easier for me to deny his humanity. That way I can be a bitch and never feel bad about it. But it hurts the kids and it hurts you."

They sit in silence, believing the words they have all just spoken, but doubting if those words will be enough. From a window somewhere, a neighbor practices their trumpet. Strong, clear notes rise and fall into the night.

"Today is Yom Kippur," Kaya says. "It started at sundown. I'm a bad Jew. Yiya would be mad at me. But she was a bad Jew, too, so maybe not."

"What do you do on Yom Kippur?" Sandy asks.

"Yiya would take my brothers and me to the East River, and she'd tell us to whisper all the things we were sorry for into a piece of bread; then we'd throw the bread into the water. I was never sorry for anything, so I would make a wish instead. Always the same one— that I could live here, in this house in Astoria, permanently. Which I guess came true, for a minute at least." She wipes her eyes and sees that Sandy and Steph are crying, too, looking at Kaya as if holding her in their gaze. "Afterward she'd take us to a diner for pancakes and bacon. You're supposed to fast. And definitely not eat bacon. It's a time to reflect on your life, the past year, what you've done wrong, and who you need to make amends to."

"I think this might count."

"Maybe."

They listen to the trumpet, their minds following the notes up and down like steps always returning to the same place.

Sandy petitions the court for back child support on behalf of herself and Steph and petitions for an order of paternity for Kaya, so that she can get child support later on. It's surprisingly easy, and she's mad that she thought she needed a professor to hold her hand through the process. While she waits on the awful wooden benches for her documents to be scanned and returned, she gets an invite to a private women-and-nonbinary-folks-only law-student group on WhatsApp. Sandy scrolls through the long history of messages. There are second- and third-year students in the group, exchanging stories and advice that she wouldn't even know to ask about. For the first time, she feels a part of the law school, like she might actually be in the right place.

She puzzles over how to introduce herself: Should she keep it professional or mention that she has a family? What is the best way to explain that she is a single mom, or used to be, as she now has a girlfriend? And a roommate, who is more like a sister. And that all of them have kids with the same father. "Sandy, 1L, she/her" feels so deficient compared to the amazing bios of the other students in the group. As she debates this some more, a second-year student asks the group, "Has anyone else had a gross experience with Prof. Mayer?"

Immediately, six other students hop in to say they had.

"Hi," Sandy finally says. "Sandy, 1L, she/her, and yeah, me, too."

"Fuck him," a third-year student posts. "Let's do something about it."

Two weeks later, she is finishing her Torts reading in the student-union lounge when Justin calls. Sandy braces herself. In the four years since meeting Justin, this is only the second time he has picked up his phone and actually called her. The first time was to chew her out for having Christmas with Steph and her family. It can only be bad news.

Sandy glances at the picture of Justin that announces his call on her phone, a shot she took in her old apartment. Justin looks ten years younger than he does now, fresh-faced and smiling, a fat infant Rosie on his lap.

Memories and feelings come rushing in—how lonely and alive early motherhood was, how complicated it all felt then, how simple it actually was compared to now. She answers the phone.

"You're the only one I can trust," he says.

"Should I be recording this?" Sandy jokes.

Justin sniffs. Maybe it is a laugh. Sandy can't tell.

"I don't care anymore," he says sadly. "I'm done fighting."

"He's dropping the custody case!" Sandy tells the mothers in the group chat.

"For real???"

"He can't afford it anymore. He's run out of money, or so he says."

"Mara's sucking him dry."

"He's willing to do whatever we want as long we drop our child-support claims and settle out of court."

"You know that means we'll never see a dime from him. Like ever."

"Do you really care?"

"No."

"I guess not."

"We've made it this far . . ."

* * *

It is Ash who decides the terms of their visitation. They write it out on a piece of paper in a turquoise gel pen that they present to their mother, Sandy, and Kaya with the seriousness of a lawyer. In their document, ripped out of a spiral notebook, they stipulate that Justin can take them to dinner once a week, to Tara's house, to a restaurant, or to his apartment *if* Mara is not there. Only Tara, Rosie, Kayla, Mykayla, and Kyle are allowed to join them. If he follows the rules for three months, they will bump it up to twice a week, with room to grow from there.

"But if he wants to take me on vacation or something, like to California or Hawaii or whatever, he can also do that," they tell the three mothers.

"That's very generous of you, kiddo," Steph says.

Rosie will continue to spend every other weekend at Justin's house. "But she's allowed to change her mind and do my plan if she wants." Ash points to the place in their document where it says this.

"You're a good sibling, honey," Sandy tells them.

"Okay," Ash says, dropping the paper in Steph's hands. "Send it to him."

Steph takes a picture of her kid's plan. Their handwriting is so crooked and earnest it breaks her heart. She texts the image to Justin with no comment. A few minutes later he replies with a thumbs-up.

The real estate agents selling Yiya Devine's house request that the family go elsewhere while they show the property to prospective buyers. It is a cold and sunny Saturday morning in November when they finally stage an open house. The mothers decide to go to the diner where Yiya Devine used to take Kaya when she was little. It's early enough that they could easily snag two adjacent booths for their party of seven.

The children whine the whole walk there. It's too far, too cold, hats and gloves make them too hot, so they peel them off, then it's too cold again. When they arrive at the diner, the best worst thing has happened to their community: the local greasy spoon had recently been featured on a TV show, and a celebrity chef had staged a makeover of the interior and menu. The line to get in now wraps around the block, full of hip, child-free people willing to wait.

"Go back to Brooklyn!" Kaya shouts uselessly.

The mothers settle for a bag of donuts and cheap coffee in paper cups. They walk through Astoria Park to the waterfront. Across the shimmering water, Manhattan stretches wide and jagged like a jaw full of broken teeth.

"I'm going to miss you whores when we all move. Promise we can still meet up like this on weekends?"

"We're going to keep living together. I don't know how, but we will work something out," Sandy says.

"You two aren't going to keep living with me after you get married. I'd rather have a nice clean break now, before we get too attached."

"Kaya, it's way too late for that," Steph says. "We are a Gordian knot of enmeshment."

"What the fuck does that mean?"

"We're in too deep."

"You needed us so much when Mykayla was first born," Sandy says. "Now she's thriving and you don't need us the same way anymore. We needed you so badly when we were in court. Now that's all settled. But I still want this. I want us, all of us."

"I don't know what she's talking about," Steph says. "I still very much need both of you."

"Any place where we'd all fit is a place we can't afford."

"It's not impossible. Even in Astoria there are still deals."

"And with the sale, you'll have money to buy a place. You can make the down payment, and we can pay the mortgage until it all evens out."

"Maybe a duplex that we could renovate?"

Kaya lets the two of them dream. They're in love, in the beginning of their new life, and everything feels possible to them. A westbound plane thunders overhead. The sky is as smooth as the water is shattered. Kaya can't see a way forward. Anything beyond the end of the school year is too stressful and opaque. But then again, only a few years ago she was living in a one-bedroom apartment in the Bronx, praying that Doug would move in with her since she was pregnant and that the baby she was having would be a boy that looked just like him, to make him stay.

When the first buyer pulls out at the last minute, the realtors get scared. They take it upon themselves to hang Christmas lights around the front bay window. At showings they diffuse essential oils of pine and bergamot around the interior to make it more attractive. On these days, Steph instructs Ash and Kayla not to flush the toilet. She leaves their dirty clothes in heaps everywhere, on the floor, in the hallway, down the staircase. If she can't stop the inevitable, she can stall it by flaunting her old, slobbish ways.

It doesn't work. The housing market in New York City is ravenous. Before the end of the year, a cash offer comes in over the asking price, and the little house in Astoria, Queens, which Kaya's grandparents bought with the salary of a postal worker and a makeup-counter lady, sells for one million dollars.

"So we're millionaires?" Kayla asks.

"Absolutely not," Kaya replies. She tries to explain the broker's fees, taxes, the even split with Uncle Paul and Uncle Adam, but it's too late. Kayla is clicking toys into a virtual basket on her tablet with wild abandon. "Don't worry," she says, "I'm putting stuff in there for the other kids, too." Kaya glances down and sees that thirty-four items have been added so far.

* * *

There is a snowstorm on the weekend they have to move. Sandy sits on the kitchen counter and pulls down the vintage green studded wineglasses Yiya Devine reserved for special occasions. Steph washes each one by hand, and Kaya dries them with a towel before wrapping them up in paper.

"I looked it up and your date with Stanley falls a day after the new moon, which is very magical," Sandy says. "Bring, like, ten condoms with you."

"Stop. We're meeting for coffee. On a weekday. That's not a date."

"He waited until the case was closed to ask you," Steph says. "I think that means legally, he considers it a date."

They've signed a one-year lease for a four-bedroom apartment in a new high-rise building they call the Ooh-La-La. Its real name is no less ridiculous. It's not a dream home for any of them, much smaller than Yiya Devine's house, "modern" in a way that will prove cheap and dated before long, but for now the rent is below market, as buildings like this struggle to attract the renters they'd hoped for. The new address keeps the kids anchored in the same school, and this consistency becomes the deciding factor. It's temporary, a step toward something else, something that might not exist yet, that the women may have to build themselves from the ground up.

After she's sure Yiya's wine goblets are safe, Kaya walks around the house, stress-eating a bag of crunchy plantains. When those are finished, she polishes off the leftover Goldfish crackers, followed by the half bag of corn chips.

"This is mostly crumbs at this point, but I cannot stop eating."

"You're not processing your feelings, that's why," Steph says. Her hair is shorter, chic-er, and sporting a pea-sized dab of texturizing pomade. It was a stipulation of their agreement to continue living together: Kaya would be in charge of Steph's hair.

"You're, like, actually hot now," Kaya says, twisting a healthy lock of Steph's hair. "That's how good I am at this."

"You can't distract me. Didn't you say this house was the only stable place in your childhood? Maybe you're eating to push down some unacknowledged grief."

"Bitch, please," Kaya says, her mouth full of chips.

Steph is 100 percent right, but Kaya won't give that to her, not yet. She licks the salt off every finger and looks out the front window. She remembers the day the old green canvas awning blew clean off in a hurricane, how Grandpa crisscrossed duct tape over the glass in large silver Xs, how he'd scraped every last bit of the glue off the panes with a small razor blade and some rubbing alcohol after the storm passed and they'd survived. She remembers the day her grandfather replaced the awning with an ugly clamshell-looking thing made of wavy, overlapping, fake terra-cotta tiles. This one also blew off in an another hurricane, then he died before anyone could replace it. There is still a tiny hole in the floor of the bathroom under the staircase, where she and her brothers would drop pennies to one another in the basement and try to catch them.

Steph appears at her side and looks out the window with her. She takes the empty bag and hands her a glass of water.

"This house is busted in a way I'd never be able to fix up. I've watched enough HGTV to know that." Kaya takes a huge gulp of water and feels the last mouthful of corn chips slide painfully down her throat. "It's just a house. You bitches are my home."

"I feel like there's a lot more you're not unpacking."

"Sandy, watch out," Kaya yells. "She's trying to therapize us instead of looking at her own shit." She calls the kids to meet her in the bathroom, to throw some pennies down one last time.

Steph is full of mad energy with nowhere good to land. After yelling at the kids, apologizing to the kids, then yelling at them once again, she goes searching for Sandy. She finds her in their room, stripping their bed of blankets and sheets and folding them into a box.

"I feel restless, angry, sad, a little horny, tired, and sweaty right now," she says, flopping onto the bare mattress. "Mostly I feel so unsettled about this. I kind of wish we were still in court."

"Are you insane?" Sandy replies.

"Justin tortured us for no reason and then he got away with it. I want a judge to lay into him for everything he's done. Don't you think he deserves some kind of punishment?"

Sandy thinks for a moment. "His life is his punishment," she says.

"Mara controls his every move, she's never satisfied, never happy, and because of his inability to stand up to her, the coolest kid in all of New York City won't spend a weekend with him. He lost his music career, which was never going to happen, but it was the one safe place for all his dark feelings to go. Now the only release he gets is having affairs with women who pretty quickly wise up and dump him." She tears a strip of translucent brown tape and seals the box shut. "I wouldn't switch places with him for all the money in the world."

The moving van is due to arrive any minute now. It's been snowing for hours, with no end in sight. The snow piles up outside and the wind sweeps it against the front of the house in a great, sloping drift. Kayla opens one of the bay windows and kicks out the screen to touch the snow, which reaches her fingertips.

"We could sled right out of the house all the way to the sidewalk," Ash observes. They flatten one of the many cardboard boxes and shoot it out the window to test how fast it slides.

"The front window is open for some reason," Steph reports to the mothers. "They're scheming."

Sandy winds the last roll of bubble wrap around Yiya Devine's hanging lamp and then goes to check on the kids herself. In the hallway, she stops and listens. Laughter, shrieking, a whoosh of cold air, and a clatter. She returns to the kitchen.

"Everything's okay?"

"I think so."

She's not going to stop them. No one is. They are their mothers' children, wild and brave. They're going to do whatever they want, because the future belongs to them.

ACKNOWLEDGMENTS

I would like to thank all the women and nonbinary people who cared for my kids, without whom not a word of this could have been written; my parents-in-law, who paid for my youngest's part-time daycare, a profoundly generous gift that enabled me to work; the talented and creative teachers at my oldest's public school; Jim Rutman, who read a hideous version of this book and would have been justified in dropping me immediately but instead offered wise and measured advice; Andrea Walker, who saw what others couldn't, not even me, and was the very best advocate and shepherd for this book; Kathy Lord, who attacked this manuscript like the Queen of Swords and whipped it into a better book and me into a better writer; Clio Seraphim, Naomi Goodheart, Christopher Combemale, and Kelly Chian, who worked to make this whole process look and feel seamless; Cindy Spiegel, whose brief notes were wise and generous as always; Katie Skau, my sensitivity reader extraordinaire, and Kathleen Cunningham, my brilliant beta reader; Melisse Gelula, an essential Capricorn champion, guide, and friend; my godsister who made my life so much better the moment she entered it; my two kids and my *afilhada,* who inspire, delight, terrify, and annoy me every day and because of whom every day is a gift; my oldest's dad, for all that he does and for being nothing like Justin; my brother, who has kept me sane for four decades now, and his partner, who has become a true sister to me; all my doctors and nurses, of whom there were many these past few medically fraught years, with a special shout-out to Dr. K and Nurse T; my incredible network of friends in and out of the rooms, an embarrassment of riches, thank you for being my village; and finally my partner, co-parent, best friend, love—thanks for carrying what I couldn't and being so damn good-looking.

ABOUT THE AUTHOR

DOMENICA RUTA is the *New York Times* bestselling author of the memoir *With or Without You* and the novel *Last Day*. She is a graduate of Oberlin College and holds an MFA from the Michener Center for Writers at the University of Texas at Austin. She currently teaches in the creative writing program at Sarah Lawrence College, and her writing has appeared in *The Iowa Review, The Cut, The American Scholar, Oprah* online, and many others. She lives in New York City with her family.

domenicaruta.com
Instagram: @domenicaruta
TikTok: @domenica.ruta

ABOUT THE TYPE

This book was set in Caslon, a typeface first designed in 1722 by William Caslon (1692–1766). Its widespread use by most English printers in the early eighteenth century soon supplanted the Dutch typefaces that had formerly prevailed. The roman is considered a "workhorse" typeface due to its pleasant, open appearance, while the italic is exceedingly decorative.